Empire of the Senses
General Editor: Mike Mitchell

Le Calvaire

D1617054

Octave Mirbeau

Le Calvaire

translated by Christine Donougher
and with an introduction by Adrian Murdoch

Dedalus/Hippocrene

Dedalus would like to thank the French Ministry of Foreign Affairs in Paris and The Eastern Arts Board in Cambridge for their assistance in producing this translation.

Published in the UK by Dedalus Ltd, Langford Lodge, St Judith's Lane, Sawtry, Cambs, PE17 5XE

UK ISBN 0 946626 99 5

Published in the US by Hippocrene Books Inc, 171, Madison Avenue, New York, NY 10016

Distributed in Australia & New Zealand by Peribo Pty Ltd, 58 Beaumont Road, Mount Kuring- gai N.S.W. 2080

Distributed in Canada by Marginal Distribution, Unit 102, 277, George Street North, Peterborough, Ontario, KJ9 3G9

First published in France in 1886 ·
First published by Dedalus in 1995
Translation copyright © Christine Donougher 1995
Introduction copyright © Adrian Murdoch 1995

Printed in Finland by Wsoy
Typeset by Datix International Limited, Bungay, Suffolk

A C.I.P. listing for this book is available on request.

THE TRANSLATOR

Christine Donougher was born in England in 1954. She read English and French at Cambridge and after a career in publishing is now a freelance translator and editor.

Her many translations from French and Italian include the Sylvie Germain novels: *The Book of Nights* and *Days of Anger*; Jan Potocki's *Tales from the Saragossa Manuscript* and Octave Mirbeau's *Le Calvaire*.

Her current projects include editing *The Dedalus Book of French Fantasy* and translating Sylvie Germain's *Nuit d'ambre*.

THE EDITOR

Adrian Murdoch was educated in Scotland and at The Queen's College, Oxford. After graduation he taught in Berlin for a year, working as well for the Ministry of Education as a translator and interpreter. He now works as a journalist in London. He collaborated with his father, Brian Murdoch, in translating material for Geoffrey Farrington's *The Dedalus Book of Roman Decadence* and has edited other works for Dedalus. He is currently editing Octave Mirbeau's *Abbé Jules*.

French Literature from Dedalus

French Language Literature in translation is an important part of Dedalus's list, with French being the language *par excellence* of literary fantasy.

French books from Dedalus include:

Séraphita – Balzac £6.99
The Quest of the Absolute – Balzac £6.99
Episodes of Vathek – Beckford £6.99
The Devil in Love – Jacques Cazotte £5.99
Les Diaboliques – Barbey D'Aurevilly £6.99
Angels of Perversity – Remy de Gourmont £6.99
The Book of Nights – Sylvie Germain £8.99
The Weeping Woman – Sylvie Germain £6.99
Days of Anger – Sylvie Germain £8.99
The Medusa Child – Sylvie Germain £8.99
La-Bas – J.K. Huysmans £7.99
The Cathedral – J.K. Huysmans £6.95
En Route – J.K. Huysmans £6.95
The Phantom of the Opera – Gaston Leroux £6.99
Monsieur de Phocas – Jean Lorrain £8.99
Le Calvaire – Octave Mirbeau £7.99
The Diary of a Chambermaid – Octave Mirbeau £7.99
Torture Garden – Octave Mirbeau £7.99
Smarra & Trilby – Charles Nodier £6.99
Tales from the Saragossa Manuscript – Jan Potocki £6.99
Monsieur Venus – Rachilde £6.99
The Marquise de Sade – Rachilde £8.99
The Mysteries of Paris – Eugene Sue £6.99
The Wandering Jew – Eugene Sue £9.99
Micromegas – Voltaire £5.99

'And when they were come to the place, which is called Calvary, there they crucified him, and the malefactors, one on the right hand, and the other on the left.'
Luke Chapter 23, verse 33

Le Calvaire is a young man's novel. With its themes of social injustice and a miserable love affair it marks Octave Mirbeau as a product of his time. Like his colleagues, contemporaries and friends Guy de Maupassant, Émile Zola, Claude Monet, Camille Pissarro, Paul Gauguin and Auguste Rodin, Mirbeau's novel is imbued with the ideals of Baudelaire, the pessimism of Schopenhauer and the pragmatism of Darwin.

Published in 1886 in serial form, *Le Calvaire* bears the mark of Mirbeau's recent seduction by the anarchist tracts of Peter Kropotkin (*Paroles d'un révolté*) and Leo Tolstoy (*Ma religion*).

What makes *Le Calvaire* stand out first of all is its vigorous stance against war. Jean Mintié, Mirbeau's hero, asks 'What was this patriotism, embodied for us by that stupid marauding general who persecuted old men and old trees, and by that surgeon who kicked the sick and bullied old mothers grieving for their sons [. . .] I wanted to learn the human rationale for religions that stupefy, governments that oppress, societies that kill.'

Mirbeau is clearly drawing on his own experiences as an officer during the Franco–Prussian war and when the novel was first serialised the passages on the war were edited out: they were deemed too unpatriotic. They show a dislike of a military system that was very soon to persecute Dreyfus, and although the novel predates the Dreyfus affair by eight years, it comes as no surprise that Mirbeau stood firmly behind Zola's *J'accuse* letter. Mintié was born out of the intellectual pacifist tradition that produced Erich Maria Remarque's Paul Bäumer in *All Quiet on the Western Front* in the First World War, and to some extent Jaroslav Hasek's soldier Schweik too and in a later war the still dumb insolence of Yossarian in Joseph Heller's *Catch-22*.

The caricatures of the buffoonery of the generals and the careless cruelty of the surgeons are set pieces that are completely timeless. When someone tells Mintié who is curious about what the Prussians are like – he and his colleagues are fighting in a war which they do not understand – he is told: 'They're Germans, old man, just as we're French'. The simplicity of the statement makes it all the more powerful.

Mirbeau's polemic against war – early on in the novel – is however merely a distraction to the book's main topic: the passion and downfall of Jean Mintié. Mirbeau bears the mark of the Jesuit upbringing that he fought so hard against all his life (speaking of his own education by Jesuits in Vannes, he referred to them as *éducastrateurs* and pilloried their 'sacerdotal pomposity'). It is a theme that is explored more fully in his second novel *L'Abbé Jules*. *Le Calvaire* tells of Mintié's own slow crucifixion – his seduction, betrayal, obsession, humiliation and finally his ultimate rejection not only by society and his friends, but by the beautiful Juliette Roux.

A frequent charge against Mirbeau is that his female characters are barely two-dimensional. Indeed his eroto-misogynism is viciously cruel at times, but it is a style that is worked to perfect effect in *Le Calvaire*. The three most important female characters – Mintié's mother, Mary Magdalene and Juliette, the sacred whore – are three sides of the same character. The mother, the maiden and the mistress.

At the beginning of the novel Mintié describes the incestual love of his mother in most erotic terms. 'She was frenzied in her demonstrations of love, which terrified me and terrify me still. As she clasped my head, gripped my neck let her lips wander over my forehead, cheeks and mouth, her lips grew fretful and became mingled with bites, like animal's kisses. She kissed me with the truly carnal passion of a lover.'

After her death, he transfers his erotic affections onto a statue of the Virgin at the chapel at home and speaks of his 'violent need to take her'. After this relationship, any human being can only be a disappointment. Here too there is an irony when the housekeeper suggests that his passion for the Madonna is such that he will surely become a priest. It is when Mintié moves to Paris to work – as Mirbeau himself did to become a journalist – that his decline and plummet really begin. His closest male companion, the painter Lirat – we never learn his full name – warns him off Juliette. But Lirat starts off as his Tiresias and as he betrays him, becomes his Judas on Mintié's march to Golgotha.

From the very first innocent invitation to tea, the reader is surprised by Mintié's violent dislike of Juliette's dog, Spy. A dislike that is carried out in an extreme form in the book's denouement as the only way Jean finds to affect his torturer.

Mintié is aware the whole time of what he is doing and what must be done. He himself says: 'This was not Love, as before, curly-haired, pomaded, and beribboned, swooning in the moonlight, with a rose between his teeth, strumming his guitar under balconies; this was Love smeared with blood, wallowing in the mire, Love in onanistic frenzy, accursed Love that leeches on to man and drains his veins, sucks outs his marrow, strips his bones of flesh.'

Embracing this love wholeheartedly, Mintié loses all his money, self respect and friends, selling even the Priory, his family home – as a drug addict might – for his love for Juliette. From the beginning their relationship is a prostitute/client one and even at the end of the novel when for Jean:

'Juliette became impersonalised: she was no longer a woman with her own individual existence, she was prostitution itself, sprawled vastly all over the world, the eternally sullied, unchaste idol that panting crowds rushed after, in hideous darkness lit by monstrous torches fashioned in the image of the androgynous demon Baphomet.'

He still gives her his last money in a desperate attempt to keep her.

Le Calvaire is very clearly a first novel. It does not show the exquisite cruelty of *Torture Garden*, the de Sade-like degeneracy of the *Diary of a Chambermaid* or even the sustained anti-clericical polemic of *L'Abbé Jules*, but no where else does Mirbeau capture the total and utter passion of love that has been perverted. *Le Calvaire* is the most accessible of Mirbeau's novels for the reader to identify with. Who cannot fail to be moved, when Mintié says in one of his bursts of clarity that become rarer and rarer throughout the book of his declining relationship:

'Alas! I must see through to the very end the painful ascent of this Calvary, even if my flesh is left in bleeding shreds, even if my bare bones shatter on the rocks and stones.'?

Octave Mirbeau

1848 Born February 16, in Trévières (Calvados)

1859 Sent for schooling by Jesuits in Vannes

1870 Joined the army

1885 Conversion to anarchism. Stopped writing for monarchist newspaper *Le Gaulois* and started writing for radical paper *La France*

1886 Published *Letters from My Cottage*

1888 Published *L'Abbé Jules*

1890 Published *Sebastien Roch*

1894 Dreyfus affair

1898 Published *Torture Garden*

1900 Published *Diary of a Chambermaid*

1917 Died February 16

I was born one October evening at St-Michel-les-Hêtres, a village in the département of Orne and I was immediately christened with the names Jean François Marie Mintié. In due celebration of this entry into the world my godfather, who was an uncle of mine, handed out sweets aplenty and threw lots of small coins to the local urchins gathered on the church steps. Fighting over them with his companions, one child fell so badly on the edge of a step that he fractured his skull and died the next day. As for my uncle, he went down with typhoid on his return home and passed away a few weeks later. My nurse, old Marie, often recounted these events to me with pride and admiration.

St Michel-les-Hêtres is situated on the edge of a big state-owned forest, the forest of Tourouvre. Despite a population of fifteen hundred inhabitants, the village creates no greater stir than the trees, grass and corn on a still day in the country-side. A brake of giant beech-trees that turn crimson in autumn shelters it from the north winds, and its tile-roofed houses come all the way down the hillside to the broad ever-green valley where herds of cattle are to be seen wandering freely. The river Huisne, glinting in the sunlight, capri-ciously loops and twists through meadows divided from each other by rows of tall poplars. Strung out along the river's course, humble tanneries and little windmills are clearly visi-ble among the alder-groves and over on the far side of the valley are fields with hedges that run in straight lines and straggling apple-trees. Little pink farm-houses and small vil-lages glimpsed here and there amid almost black foliage grace the horizon. Because of the forest near by, there is a to-ing and fro-ing in the sky, all year round, of crows and yellow-billed jackdaws.

My family lived on the outskirts of the village, opposite the very ancient, dilapidated church, in a strange old house called the Priory – the outbuilding of an abbey destroyed during the Revolution of which only two or three bits of crumbling ivy-covered wall remained standing. I distinctly recall, but not with any fondness, the most minor details of those scenes of my childhood. I recall the extremely warped gate that creaked open on to a big courtyard boasting a scraggy lawn, two stunted rowans that blackbirds dwelt in, some very old chestnut-trees so wide-boled that four men together – as my father proudly informed every visitor – could not have got their arms round them. I recall the house, with its grimly forbidding brick wall, its semi-circular flight of steps with some wilting geraniums, its irregular windows that looked like holes, its steeply pitched roof, topped with a weathervane that would hoot like an owl in the breeze. I recall the pond behind the house, where some muddy aurum lilies floated and thin white-scaled carp darted about. I recall the gloomy curtain of fir trees that concealed the outhouses, the back yard, the office my father had built by a road skirting the edge of the property, so that the coming and going of his clients and clerks should not disturb the silence of the house. I recall the park with its enormous bizarrely twisted trees, overgrown with polyps and mosses and bound to each other with tangled creepers; with its paths that were never raked and its weathered stone seats, like old tombstones, standing at intervals along them. And I recall myself, too, a puny child in a glazed-cotton smock, running round in all this cheerless neglect, scratching myself on brambles, persecuting the animals in the back yard, or else trailing around all day long in the vegetable garden after Felix who served us as gardener, valet and coachman.

Many years have passed. All that I loved is dead now; all that I knew has changed. The church has been rebuilt: it has a carved door, pointed arch windows and elaborate gargoyles representing the faces of demons roasting in hell; its bell-tower of new-cut stone grins cheerfully against the azure sky. On the site of the old house stands a pretentious chalet, built by the new owner, who has filled the forecourt with coloured glass balls, miniature waterfalls and plaster cupids besmirched by the rain. But everything remains so deeply etched in the hard agate of my memory that time has failed to erode it.

I want now to speak of my parents, not as I saw them as a child, but as they seem to me today, completed by memory, made more human by revelations and confidences, in the full glare of light, in the total truthfulness of aspect that life's uncompromising lessons confers on faces too briefly loved and known too closely.

My father was a notary. From time immemorial, this was the way it had always been in the Mintié family. It would have seemed unnatural and completely revolutionary had a Mintié dared to break with family tradition and renounce the gilt wooden plaques that, like some aristocratic title, were handed down religiously from generation to generation. At St-Michel-les-Hêtres, and in neighbouring parts, my father held a position that memories of his ancestors, his own rotund appearance of a country gentleman and above all his income of twenty thousand a year rendered solidly unassailable. Mayor of St-Michel, county councillor, deputy justice of the peace, vice-president of the agricultural association, member of numerous land economy and forestry societies, he disdained none of these small and coveted honours of provincial life that bestow prestige and bring influence. He was a very kind man, extremely courteous and mild, with a mania for killing. He could not lay eyes on a bird, cat, insect or any living thing whatsoever, without at once being seized with the strange desire to destroy it. He was merciless in going after blackbirds, goldfinches, chaffinches and bullfinches, waging a trapper's bitter war against them. Felix was detailed to alert him as soon as a bird appeared in the park and my father would drop everything – clients, business, meals – to slaughter the bird. Often he lay in ambush for hours at a time, motionless behind a tree where the gardener had told him there was a little blue-headed tit. When out for a stroll, every time he saw a bird on a branch, if he did not have his shot gun with him, he would aim his walking stick at it, never failing to say, 'Bang! Got it, by God!' Or else, 'Bang! I'd have missed it, for sure, it's too far away.' These were the only comments he was ever inspired to make about birds.

Cats, too, were one of his major preoccupations. Once he had detected a cat's footprint on the gravelled paths, he had no further rest until it was found and slain. Sometimes, on bright moonlit nights, he would get up and lie in wait until dawn. He was a sight to be seen, with his shotgun on his shoulder, holding up by the tail the cat's stiff, bleeding carcass. Never did I behold anything so heroic, and David after killing Goliath could not have looked more elated with triumph. With a gesture of majesty, he would throw the cat at Cook's feet. 'Oh, the filthy beast,' she would say, and immediately set about cutting it up, keeping the meat for beggars and drying the pelt on the end of a pole to sell to tanners. If I dwell so much on these apparently trivial details, it is because all my life I have been obsessed, haunted, by these cat incidents in my childhood. One of these made such an impression on me that even now, despite the intervening years and the sorrows I have suffered, not a day passes that I do not think of it with sadness.

One afternoon we were in the garden, my father and I. My father had in his hand a long stick with an iron spike on the end of it, that he used to impale lettuce-devouring slugs and snails. Suddenly we saw a little kitten drinking at the edge of the pond. We hid behind a seringa bush.

'Son,' my father said to me a very low voice, 'quickly, run and fetch my gun . . . go round the back . . . take care it doesn't see you.'

And crouching down, he carefully parted the seringa branches so as to follow the cat's every movement. Firmly planted on its front paws, with neck outstretched and quivering tail, it was lapping the water in the pond, and raised its head from time to time to lick its coat and scratch its neck.

'Go on,' said my father, 'get moving.'

I felt terribly sorry for that kitten. It was so pretty, with its tawny fur with silky black stripes, its neat supple movements and its tongue like a rose-petal, dipping into the water. I wanted to disobey my father, I even thought of making a noise, of coughing, of deliberately rustling the branches to warn the poor creature of its peril. But my father gave me such a stern look that I headed off towards the house. I was soon back with the gun. The kitten was still there, happy and unsuspecting. It had finished drinking. It sat with its ears pricked, bright-eyed, its body quivering, following the flight of a butterfly through the air. Oh! That was a moment of unspeakable agony. My heart was pounding so hard I thought I was going to faint.

'Papa! Papa!' I cried.

At the same time, a shot was fired, a sharp shot like the crack of a whip.

'Damn it!' my father cursed.

He took aim again. I saw his finger press the trigger. Quickly, I shut my eyes and covered my ears . . . Bang! And I heard a mewling, at first plaintive, then heart-rending – ah! so heart-rending! – it sounded like a child crying. And the kitten leapt, twisted, clawed at the grass and stirred no more.

Of utterly undistinguished intellect, warm-hearted although apparently indifferent to all but his parochial considerations and the interests of his practice, generous with advice, eager to be of service, conservative, healthy and cheerful, in all justice my father enjoyed universal respect. My mother, the daughter of a local aristocrat, brought as her dowry not wealth but more solid contacts, closer relations with the local gentry – which to him was just as useful as additional money or more land. Although his powers of observation were very limited, and he made no claim to being able to understand people the way he could understand the terms of a marriage contract or the details of a will, my father soon realised completely what a difference there was, in breeding, upbringing and sensibility, between him and his wife. Whether this upset him at all, I do not know. In any event he did not show it. He resigned himself. Between them – he, a bit dull-witted, philistine and easy-going; she, educated, sensitive and emotional – there was a gulf that he did not for one moment try to bridge, finding in himself neither the desire nor the strength to do so. This moral predicament, of two people bound to each for ever with no thoughts or aspirations in common to draw them together, did not at all bother my father, who spent a lot of time in his office and was satisfied if the house was well run, his meals well organised and his little routines and idiosyncrasies rigorously respected. On the other hand, it was very difficult for my mother and weighed very heavily on her.

My mother was not beautiful – still less, pretty – but there was so much simple nobility in her bearing, so much natural grace in her gestures, such great kindness on those rather pale lips and there was in her eyes, by turns as pale as an April sky and then dark as sapphire, a smile so caressing, so sad, so defeated, you forgot the brow that was too high and rounded below an irregular hairline, the nose that was too big and the grey metallic complexion that sometimes went slightly blotchy. One of her friends often said to me – and I have since very painfully become aware of this – that in her presence you felt penetrated, then gradually overcome, then irresistibly dominated by a strange sense of sympathy, a mixture of fond respect, vague desire, compassion and the need to devote yourself to her. Despite her physical imperfections, or rather on account of the very same, she had the bitter potent charm of certain creatures favoured by misfortune, over whom there hangs some aura of hopelessness. Hers had been a sickly childhood and adolescence, marked by several disturbing occurrences of nervous disorder. But it was hoped that marriage, with the change of circumstances in her life, would restore her health, which the doctors said was affected only by an extreme sensitivity. It did nothing of the sort. On the contrary, marriage only encouraged the morbid germs within her, and her sensitivity increased to the point that, among other alarming symptoms, my poor mother could not stand the slightest smell without suffering an attack that always ended in a loss of consciousness. So what was wrong with her? Why those fits of melancholy, those states of exhaustion that for days kept her sunk in an armchair, motionless and uncommunicative, like some paralytic old woman? Why the tears that all of a sudden would choke her, and for hours on end would fall from her eyes like scalding rain? Why those aversions to all and sundry that nothing – neither distractions, nor entreaties – could conquer? She could not have said, for she did not know. About her physical pains, her mental anguish, the hallucinations that inspired in her heart and mind a yearning for death, she was none the wiser. She did not know why one evening in front of the hearth, where a large fire was burning, she suddenly felt a dreadful temptation to roll in the blaze, to surrender her body to the caress of the flames that allured her, fascinated her, sang to her hymns of mysterious love. Nor did she know why, while out for a stroll another day, on catching sight of a man walking with a scythe on his shoulder in a half-mown field, she ran towards him with outstretched arms, crying, 'Death, o blessed Death, take me, take me away!' No, truly, she did not know. What she did know was that at these moments the image of her mother, her dead mother, was always there, before her; her mother, whom she herself had found, one Sunday morning, hanged, from the chandelier in the drawing room. And she recalled the body gently swinging in the air – that black face, those white, pupilless eyes, and even that ray of sunshine, filtering through the closed blinds, splashing with dramatic light the lolling tongue and swollen lips. These ailments and aberrations, this infatuation with death – it was probably her mother that had passed them on to her, from birth. It was from her mother's loins that she had absorbed the poison, from her mother's breast that she had imbibed it; the poison that now filled her veins, impregnated her flesh, addled her mind, sapped her soul. In the intervals of calmness – that became rarer with the passing days, months, years – she often thought about these things, and while analysing her existence, tracing her most distant memories through to the present, comparing the physical resemblances between the mother who had killed herself and the daughter who longed to die, she felt the burden of this grim heritage weigh even more heavily on her. She thrilled with self-abandonment to the idea that it was not possible for her to resist the fatality of her ancestry, which now seemed to her like a long line of suicides, going back to the darkest night of long ago, and progressing through the ages to end

19

up . . . where? At this question her eyes grew blurred, a cold sweat dampened her temples and her hands clutched at her throat as though to tear from it the imaginary rope whose knot she felt bruising her neck and choking her. Every object was in her sight an instrument of fateful death, all things reflected its convulsed and bleeding image. The branches of trees rose up, for her, like so many sinister gallows, and in the green waters of ponds, amid the reeds and water lilies, in the river with its long weeds, she discerned her own form floating, covered with mud.

Meanwhile, my father would be crouched behind a seringa bush, shot-gun in hand, watching a cat, or blasting at a warbler trilling away, in hiding, behind the branches. In the evening by way of sole comfort he would say kindly, 'Well, my dear, your health's still no better, then? Bitters, I say, take some bitters. A glass in the morning, a glass in the evening . . . There's nothing to beat it . . .' He did not grumble, he never lost his temper. He would sit at his desk, looking through the papers the mayor's secretary had brought over to him during the day, signing them rapidly with an air of disdain. 'Hah!' he would then cry, 'it's typical of this rotten government. They'd be better employed doing something for farmers instead of bothering us with all this nonsense!' Then he would retire to bed, repeating placidly, 'Bitters, take some bitters!'

His resignation upset her, as though it might have been a reproach. Although my father was indifferently educated, and she found in him none of the feelings of male tenderness nor the fabulous poetry she had dreamed of, she could not deny his physical activeness and a kind of moral well-being that she sometimes envied, while at the same time despising his dedication to things she deemed petty and vulgar. She felt guilty towards herself, and towards her life, so fruitlessly wasted in tears. Not only did she not involve herself any more in her husband's affairs, but she gradually ignored her own duties, abandoning the housekeeping to the vagaries of the staff, and neglected herself to the point that her maid, that good-hearted old woman Marie, who had seen her come into this world, was often obliged to take her in hand, with fond scolding, and to look after her and feed her like a babe-in-arms. In her need for solitude, she came to find it impossible to tolerate the presence of her family and friends any more; and embarrassed and discouraged by the increasingly morose face, the mouth that never uttered a word, the forced smile that was immediately contorted by an involuntary trembling of her lips, their visits became less frequent until in the end they completely forgot their way to the Priory. Religion, like everything else, became a weariness to her. She no longer set foot in church, nor prayed, and two Easters went by with no sight of her at the altar rail.

Then my mother confined herself to her bedroom, where she kept the shutters closed and curtains drawn, intensifying the gloom around her. It was here that she spent her days, sometimes stretched out on a chaise-longue, sometimes kneeling in a corner, with her head against the wall. And she would fret at the slightest sound from outside − of a door slamming, of slippers shuffling down the corridor, of a horse whinnying in the yard − which intruded on her novicehood in non-being. Alas, what was the solution to all this? For a long time she had fought against this mystery illness, and the illness, being stronger than she was, had overwhelmed her. Now her will was paralysed. She was no longer free to pick herself up again, or to act. A mysterious force ruled her, making her hands inert, her mind confused, and her heart unsteady, like some small smoking flame at the mercy of the winds. And far from resisting, she sought to plunge even deeper in distress, savouring with a kind of perverse relish the appalling thrills of her own annihilation.

Inconvenienced by the disruption to his domestic life, my father finally brought himself to show some concern for the progression of an illness that passed his understanding. He had the utmost difficulty in persuading my mother to accept the idea of a trip to Paris in order 'to consult the lords of science'. The trip was disheartening. Of the three renowned doctors to whom he took her, the first declared that my mother was anaemic, and prescribed a fortifying diet; the second, that she was suffering from neuro-rheumatism, and prescribed a debilitative diet. The third said there was 'nothing wrong with her', and advised peace and quiet.

No one had any understanding of her. Even to herself she remained a mystery. Haunted by that terrible memory with which she associated all her unhappiness, she could not distinguish clearly what stirred vaguely in the secret of her heart, nor what indeterminate passions, frustrated aspirations, and captive dreams had accumulated there since childhood. She was like a young bird that, without any comprehension of the obscure and nostalgic need impelling it towards open skies of which it has no memory, batters its head and breaks its wings against the bars of its cage. Like the bird that hungers for the unknown sky, her soul, instead of yearning for death, as she believed it did, hungered rather for life, a life radiant with tenderness and full of love; and, like the bird, she was dying of that unassuaged hunger. As a child, she had committed herself, with all the exuberance of her passionate nature, to the love of objects and animals; as a young girl, she had yielded recklessly to the love of dreams; but objects brought her no satisfaction and dreams failed to acquire any precise and comforting form. There was no one to guide her, no one to rescue that young mind already assailed by inner turmoil; no one to open to wholesome reality the gates of a heart already guarded by vacant-eyed chimerae; no one with whom she could share the thoughts and feelings of love and desire brimming inside her that, finding no outlet for their expression, were kept bottled up, seething, until ready to burst out of that fragile shell ill-protected by overstrung nerves. Her mother, who was always ill, entirely immersed in the melancholia that would soon kill her, was incapable of intelligent, firm guidance; her father, being virtually bankrupt, and reduced to expedients, was fighting a desperate battle to keep the house that had belonged to the family for centuries and was in danger of being lost; and of the young men that called by – inane gentlefolk, conceited burghers, greedy peasants – not one of them bore on his brow the magic star that would lead her to God. Everything she heard, everything she saw seemed to be at odds with her way of thinking and feeling. For her, the sun was not sufficiently red, the nights sufficiently pale, or the skies sufficiently infinite. Her vague and shifting conception of people and things inevitably condemned her to sensory distortions and mental aberrations, and left her with nothing but the torment of a dream never realised and desires never fulfilled. And then came her marriage – not just a sacrifice, but a bargain, a deal to save her father from financial embarrassment! – and her disgust, her outrage at the sense of being treated as a degraded parcel of flesh, the prey, the passive instrument of a man's pleasure! To have soared so high and to sink so low! To have dreamed of heavenly kisses, mystical embraces, ideal possession, and then ... to come to this! Instead of infinities of dazzling light, in which her imagination could revel amid flights of enraptured angels and frenzied doves, darkness fell, a sinister, oppressive darkness, inhabited only by her mother's spectre, stumbling over crosses and graves, with a rope around her neck.

Silence soon descended on the Priory. The screech of wheels, of gigs and traps bringing friends from the neighbourhood to the foot of the geranium-bedecked steps, was heard no more on the gravel drive. The main gate was barred, to oblige carriages to enter by the back yard. In the kitchen the servants spoke to each other in hushed voices and walked about on tiptoe, as people do in a house where someone has died. The gardener, acting on instructions from my mother, who could not bear the noise of wheelbarrows and of rakes scraping the ground, left the suckers to the sap the yellowing rose-bushes, and the weeds to choke the flowerbeds and grow over the paths. And the house, with that black curtain of fir-trees, like a catafalque, sheltering it from the west; with its windows that were always shut; and with the living corpse it kept entombed within those plain old-brick walls was like some vast burial vault. The local people, who on Sundays would go for a walk in the forest, did not pass by the Priory any more without a kind of superstitious terror, as though the house were under some curse and haunted by ghosts.

Before long, there was even a legend that grew up; a woodcutter related how, one night on his way home from work, he had seen Madame Mintié, all in white, with dishevelled hair, way up in the sky, moving across the heavens, beating her breast with a crucifix.

My father shut himself up in his office even more, avoiding, as much as possible, being in the house, where he hardly appeared except at meal-times. He also began regularly to travel to remote fairs, to attend more frequently the committees and associations he presided over; he contrived to create for himself new distractions, distant activities. The county council, the agricultural meeting, the assize-court jury were great resources to him. When anyone asked after his wife, he would reply by nodding his head, and saying: 'Well, I'm very worried, very anxious . . . Where's it all going to end? I tell you, I fear the poor woman's going mad . . .'

And he would counter any protest: 'No, no, I'm not joking . . . As you well know, they're a bit soft in the head in that family!'

Yet he never uttered a word of reproach, although every day he could see for himself the damage this state of affairs was causing to his business, and he could not understand at all my mother's exasperating refusal to attempt any cure.

It was in this bleak atmosphere that I grew up. I was born a sickly and puny child. What care and attention, what fierce love, what mortal anguish this gave rise to! Faced with the poor creature that I was, in whom the breath of life was so weak it seemed rather a death rattle, my mother forgot her own troubles. Motherhood restored her dispirited energies, wakened her conscience to the new responsibilities and sacred duties that now fell to her. What hectic nights, what feverish days she lived through, bent over the cradle in which something stirred that was born of her own flesh and blood! Ah, yes, her own flesh and blood! I was hers, and hers alone. It was not of conjugal submission that I was born; unlike other sons of men, I was free of original impurity. She had carried me in her womb from the very beginning, and, like Jesus, I issued from a long cry of love. She now understood

24

her earlier confusion, terror and distress; it was that a great mystery of creation had occurred within her.

She had much difficulty in raising me, and that I survived can be accounted a miracle of love. More than a dozen times my mother wrested me from the arms of death. So, what joy it was to her, and how rewarding, to see that little crumpled body thrive, and that puckered face acquire a pink glow, and those eyes open brightly at her smile, and those eager lips move searchingly, greedily sucking life from her nurturing breast! My mother enjoyed a few months' complete and salutary happiness. She rediscovered a need to act, to be good and useful, to keep her hands and heart and mind occupied, in short, to live, and she was able to take in even the most mundane aspects of housekeeping a new and absorbed interest that was underlaid with a profound sense of peace. She regained her cheerfulness, a gentle, natural cheerfulness, with no violent throes. She made plans, looked to the future with confidence, and often marvelled that she no longer thought of the past, that dissipated nightmare. I was developing: 'You can see him getting bigger every day,' the maid used to say. And my mother observed with delight the secret work of nature, which was refining this embryonic flesh, moulding it into shape, firmed its features, giving it better-controlled movements, and instilling in its unformed brain, that had scarcely come into being, the first glimmerings of instinct. Oh! how everything now seemed dressed in lovely bright colours! Anthems of welcome and love's blessings were all that existed, and even the trees, once so full of terror and menace, spread their leaves over her like so many protective hands. It was possible to hope that motherhood had saved her. Alas, this hope was short-lived.

One day she noticed that I was prone to nervous spasms, to abnormal muscular contractions, and she fretted. At about the age of one, I had convulsions that almost killed me. The fits were so violent that for a long time afterwards my mouth remained as if paralysed, twisted in an ugly grimace. My mother did not say to herself that most children have these attacks when they are growing rapidly. She saw it as something peculiar to her and to her people, the first symptoms of the terrible hereditary disease that was going to be perpetuated in her son. Yet she resisted the thoughts that came crowding back to her; she drew on her newfound energy and activeness to dispel them, taking refuge in me, as if I could provide inviolable asylum from spectres and demons. She clutched me to her breast, covering me with kisses, saying, 'My little Jean, isn't not true, is it? You'll live and be happy? . . . Answer me? . . .Alas, poor angel, you can't talk! . . . Oh! Jean, don't cry, never cry, my Jean, my dear little Jean!'

But for all that she questioned me, for all that she could feel my heart beating against hers, and my clumsy hands scrabbling at her breasts, and my little legs waving cheerfully, out of loosened diapers, her confidence had fled, and her misgivings triumphed. An incident occurred that has been related to me many times with a kind of religious horror, which threw my mother's soul into confusion once more.

She was in the bath. Marie was bent over me, supervising my first hesitant steps, across the black-and-white tiled bathroom floor. Suddenly, gazing at one of the black tiles, I seemed very frightened. I screamed, and trembling all over, as if I had seen something terrible, I hid my face in my nurse's apron.

'What on earth's the matter?' my mother asked sharply.

'I don't know,' replied old Marie. 'Monsieur Jean seemed to be scared of a tile.'

She led me back to the very spot where my face had so suddenly changed expression . . . But at the sight of the tile, I screamed again. My whole body shuddered.

'There's something there!' cried my mother. 'Quick, Marie, quick, pass me a towel . . . My God, what did he see?'

She got out of the bath, not waiting to be dried, and had no sooner put on her robe than she was bent over the floor, examining it.

'That's strange,' she murmured. 'And yet he saw something! But what? There's nothing there'

She took me in her arms and rocked me. By now I was

smiling, babbling incoherent syllables, playing with the ties of her robe . . . She set me down . . . Walking with my stiff, staggering gait, holding both arms out in front of me, I was purring like a kitten. None of the tiles I stopped in front of scared me in the slightest, but at the fatal tile my face once again expressed terror, and all upset and tearful, I abruptly turned back to my mother.

'I tell you, there's something there,' she cried. 'Call Felix . . . tell him to bring his tools, a hammer . . . quick, quick . . . And tell monsieur . . .'

'Well, it's very peculiar,' said Marie, staring open-mouthed and wide-eyed at the mysterious tile. 'He must be clairvoyant!'

Felix removed the tile, examined it from all angles, and dug out the plaster underneath.

'Take up the next one,' ordered my mother . . . 'Go on, and that one as well, and . . . all of them, all of them. I want whatever it is found . . . Will monsieur never come!'

So carried away was she in her movements that, forgetting the presence of a man, she left herself uncovered, revealing her naked body. Kneeling on the floor, Felix continued to remove tiles. He picked them up one by one in his big hands, shaking his head.

'If madame really wants to me to say . . . For a start, monsieur is at the bottom of the garden, stalking a woodpecker . . . And besides, there's nothing here . . . tiles are tiles, to all intents and purposes, and that's that!.. Madame may be assured . . . Only, it could well be it's Monsieur Jean's imagination . . . As Madame knows, children aren't like grown-ups, and they see things! . . . But as far as these tiles are concerned, they're just tiles, neither more nor less.'

My mother had grown pale and haggard.

'Be quiet,' she ordered, 'and get out of here, both of you.'

And without waiting for her orders to be acted upon, she carried me away. Her cries resounded on the stairs and down the corridors, punctuated by slamming doors.

It did not occur to the poor dear creature to provide some perfectly natural explanation for the incident in the bathroom. Had it been demonstrated to her that what had frightened me so much was perhaps the movement of a towel reflected on the damp surface of the tiling, perhaps the shadow cast by a leaf outside the casement window, she certainly would not have agreed that it could be anything of the sort. Her mind, reared on dreams, tormented by pessimistic exaggerations, instinctively drawn to the mysterious and the fantastic, accepted with dangerous credulity the most indeterminate reasons, and was susceptible to the most disturbing suggestions. She imagined that her caresses and kisses and cuddles were contaminating me with the germs of her illness, that the nervous fits which had almost caused my death, the delusions that had put a dark glint of madness in my eyes, were a kind of warning from heaven, and in that very instant the last hope died in her heart.

Marie found her mistress writhing, half-naked, on her bed.

'My God! My God!' she moaned, 'it's come to this. My poor little Jean! They'll take you away, too! My God, have pity on him! Can it be possible? So little, so weak!'

And, as Marie pulled up over her the fallen bedclothes and tried to calm her, she stammered, 'Listen, my dear Marie. Promise me, yes, promise me that you'll do what I ask . . . You saw just now, you saw, didn't you? Well, you take Jean and bring him up, because, you see, I can't do it any more . . . I'd be the death of him . . . Now, you're to come and live in this room, to be close to him . . . You'll take good care of him, and tell me what he's been doing . . . I'll know that he's here, I'll hear him . . . but he mustn't see me, you understand . . . I'm what's making him like that . . .'

Marie held me in her arms.

'Now, madame, that's not reasonable,' she said, 'and you'd well deserve a scolding for it! Just look at your little Jean . . . He's a picture of health . . . You're in fine fettle, aren't you, my little Jean? Look at him laughing, the little darling . . . Go on, give him a hug, madame.'

'No, no!' my mother blurted out. 'I mustn't . . . Later . . . Take him away . . .'

And she sobbed, terror-stricken, with her face buried in a pillow.

It was impossible to make her give up this idea. Marie could see very well that if her mistress had any chance of returning to normal life, of being cured of her 'black moods', it was not by separating herself from her child. In the sorry state that she was in, my mother had only one hope of salvation, and here she was, rejecting it, prompted by some new incomprehensible madness. All that an infant instils in its mother's heart in the way of joy, anxiety, busyness, excitement and self-forgetfulness − that was what she needed, and instead she said, 'No, no! I mustn't . . . Later . . . Take him away . . .'

With blunt-spoken familiarity, sanctioned by long devoted service, the old woman urged on her mistress all the good reasons and arguments dictated by her practical mind and simple peasant heart; she even reproached her for neglecting her duties; she spoke of selfishness, and declared that no good mother with any fear of God, not even a wild animal, would behave like her.

'Yes,' she concluded, 'it's wicked . . . you've already been less than kind towards your husband, poor man! And are you now to be the cause of your child's unhappiness!'

But my mother, still sobbing, could only keep repeating, 'No, no! I mustn't . . . Later . . . Take him away . . .'

What was my childhood like? A long-lasting lethargy. A poor orphan, kept away from my mother whom I saw only rarely, avoiding my father for whom I had no love, living almost exclusively in the company of Marie and Felix, in that big gloomy house and that big desolate garden whose silence and neglect oppressed me like darkest night − I was bored! Yes, I was that rare and accursed child, a child that is bored! Always grave and sad, almost never talking, I had none of the enthusiasm, curiosity and recklessness of my age. It was as though my intelligence were still slumbering in the limbo of maternal gestation. I search my memory, trying to recall any feelings I had as a child: I truly believe I had none. I trailed around, mooning about in a total stupor, not knowing what to do with my legs, arms, eyes, my poor little body that vexed me like some tiresome companion to be got rid of. Nowhere was I arrested by any sight or impression. Wherever I was, I always wished I were somewhere else, and toys, with a lovely smell of pinewood, accumulated around me without my ever thinking of touching them. I never dreamt of a knife, rocking-horse, or picture-book. Today, whenever I see toddlers, on garden lawns or sandy beaches, running and jumping about, chasing each other, I am at once painfully reminded of those dismal early years of my life, and listening to that clear ringing laughter, like the angelus marking the dawn of their lives, I tell myself that all my troubles derive from that deadly solitary childhood on which no brightness ever shone.

I was twelve when my mother died. On the day that it happened, dear Father Blanchetière, who was very fond of us, hugged me against his chest, then gazed at me for a long time and with tear-filled eyes murmured several times, 'Poor little devil!' I cried bitterly, principally at the sight of the good parish priest shedding tears, for I did not want to accept the idea that my mother was dead, never to return. During her illness I had been forbidden to enter her room, and she had passed away without my kissing her! How could she possibly have gone and left me like that? When I was about seven, seeing that I was in good health, she had allowed me back into her life a bit more. It was mostly from then onwards that I realised I had a mother and that I adored her. And to me, my mother – my sorrowful mother – meant just her eyes, two big, round, staring, red-rimmed eyes that wept constantly, without blinking, that wept like a raincloud, like a fountain. I had suddenly felt acute sorrow for my mother's sorrows, and it was through that sorrow that I had first become conscious of life. I did not know the cause of her suffering, but I knew she must be in terrible pain from the way she kissed me. She was frenzied in her demonstrations of love, which terrified me and terrify me still. As she clasped my head, gripped my neck, let her lips wander over my forehead, cheeks and mouth, her kisses grew fretful and became mingled with bites, like an animal's kisses. She kissed me with the truly carnal passion of a lover, as if I had been the adored chimerical being of her dreams, the being who had never materialised, whom her body and her soul desired. So how could she possibly be dead?

I fervently beseeched the lovely image of the Blessed Virgin that I used to address my prayer to every night before getting into bed: 'Holy Mary, grant my darling mother good health and a long life.' But my father was very pale and silent that morning, and when he accompanied the doctor to the gate, they both had such grave expressions it was easy to see that something irrevocable had happened. And besides, the servants were crying. And why would they have been crying, if not for the loss of their mistress? And had not the priest just said to me, in a hopelessly pitiful tone of voice, 'Poor little devil!' And why would he have pitied me like that, if not for the loss of my mother? I remember, as if it were yesterday, the smallest details of that dreadful day. From the bedroom, where I was confined with old Marie, I heard various comings and goings, and unaccustomed sounds, and with my forehead pressed against the window, through the slats of the closed shutters I watched the alms-women crouched on the lawn, holding candles and muttering prayers. I watched the people coming into the courtyard, the men in dark suits, the women with long black veils. 'Ah, that's Monsieur Bacoup! And there's Madame Provost.' I noticed they all had sad faces, while near the gate that stood wide open, some choirboys, embarrassed-looking cantors in their black copes, and Brothers of Charity in their red dalmatics, one of whom carried a banner and the other the heavy silver cross, were covertly laughing and amusing themselves by pummelling each other in the back. The verger drove some curious beggars back into the road, shaking his little bells at them, and a passing hay cart was obliged to stop and wait. I looked in vain for little Sorieul, a crippled child of my own age to whom I gave a loaf of bread every Saturday; I could not see him, and this upset me. And suddenly the bells in the church tower started to toll. Ding! Dang! Dong! The

31

sky was a deep blue, and the sun was blazing down. Slowly the procession moved off: first, the Brothers of Charity and the cantors, the gleaming cross, the waving banner, the priest in a white surplice, shading his head with his psalter, then something very long and heavy, a flowery mass of bouquets and wreaths, carried by men who staggered beneath it; then the crowd, a teeming crowd that filled the approach to the house and flowed out into the road, a crowd in which soon I was able to distinguish only my cousin Merel, wiping his head with a chequered handkerchief. Ding! Dang! Dong! The bells tolled for a long time, a very long time – ah, that mournful knell! Ding! Dang! Dong! And while the bells tolled and tolled, three white pigeons kept fluttering in pursuit of each other round the church that stood before me, with its warped roof and its slate tower leaning over a cluster of acacias and horse-chestnut trees.

After the ceremony my father came into my room. He paced up and down for a few minutes without speaking, with his hands clasped behind his back.

'Ah, poor sir,' wailed old Marie, 'what a tragedy!'

'Yes, yes,' replied my father, 'it is indeed a terrible tragedy.'

He sank into an armchair, heaving a sigh. I can see him now, with his swollen eyelids, his despondent gaze, his dangling arms. He had a handkerchief in his hand and from time to time he dabbed his eyes that were reddened with tears.

'Do you see, Marie, perhaps I didn't take enough care of her? She didn't like me to be with her . . . Yet I did what I could, everything I could . . . How frightful she looked, completely rigid on the bed! Oh God! I shall always see her like that! You know, she would have been thirty-one the day after tomorrow?'

My father drew me to him and took me on his lap.

'You love me, though, my little Jean,' he asked, cradling me, 'don't you? You love me? You're all I have left . . .'

Talking to himself, he said, 'Perhaps it's all for the best! What would have happened later! Yes, perhaps it's just as well . . . Ah! my poor child, look at me!'

And he hugged me tightly against his chest and burst into tears, as if at that very moment he had detected, in my eyes that resembled my mother's, a whole lifetime of suffering.

'My little Jean . . . ah, my poor little Jean!'

Overcome with emotion and the weariness of recent nights, he fell asleep, holding me in his arms. And with a sudden rush of immense pity, I listened to that stranger's heart, for the time beating against mine.

It had been decided a few months before that I would not be sent away to college, and that I would have a tutor. My father did not approve of this type of education, but he had come up against such hysterical opposition that he declined to put up any further resistance, and just as he had sacrificed marital rule over his wife, he sacrificed his paternal rights over me. Since my father wanted to remain faithful to my mother's wishes, even after her death, I had a tutor. And one fine morning I saw the arrival of a very serious, very fair-haired, very close-shaven gentleman who wore blue glasses.

Monsieur Jules Rigard had very fixed ideas about education, a pedantic rigidity and a sacerdotal pomposity that, far from encouraging me to learn, quickly put me off studying. He had probably been told I was mentally lazy and backward, and since I understood nothing of his first lessons he adhered to that original judgement and so treated me like an idiot child. It never occurred to him to probe my young mind, to question my heart; he never asked himself whether, behind the sad mask of a lonely child, there did not exist ardent aspirations that were precocious for my age, a totally passionate and apprehensive nature, thirsting for knowledge, that had developed inwardly, defectively, in the silence of repressed thoughts and unspoken enthusiasms. Monsieur Rigard stupefied me with Latin and Greek, and that was all. Ah, how many children, with understanding and guidance, might have become great men perhaps, had they not been ruined for ever by the terrible influence over their minds of a imbecile father or an ignorant teacher! Did it all end, then, with the bestial fathering of the child, one ruttish night? And was there not an obligation to continue the job of procreation, by giving the child the intellectual nourishment to sustain his life, by arming him to defend it? The truth is that my soul felt isolated, even more in the presence of my father than that of Monsieur Rigard. Yet he did everything he could to please me, persisting in loving me foolishly. But when I was with him, he could never find anything to say to me, other than fairy-tales, silly ghost-stories, terrifying legends of the 1848 revolution, which had left an indomitable terror in his mind, or an account of the subversive activities of someone called Lebecq, a great republican, who was scandalising the neighbourhood with his relentless opposition to the clergy, and his refusal on religious holidays to hang festive drapings over his walls. He often took me in his gig, when he had to go out on business, and if, troubled by the mysteries of nature that became greater to me every day, I asked him a question, he would not know how to answer, and extricated himself by saying, 'You're too young for me to explain that to you. When you're older.' And I would huddle in the back of the gig, all puny next to my father's large body that swayed with the bumps in the road, while he used the handle of his whip to kill the horse-flies that kept settling on our mare's rump. And every time he said, 'I've never seen so many of these nasty insects. There's a storm coming, that's for sure.'

On an altar decked with embroidered cloths and vases filled with paper flowers, at the back of a little chapel in the church of St-Michel, illuminated by the ruddy reflections of a glass window, stood a statue of the Virgin. She was rosy-complexioned, and wore a blue mantle spangled with silver stars and a lilac gown whose folds fell chastely over her golden sandals. In her arms she held a pink, naked infant with a golden halo round its head, and her eyes gazed, enraptured, at the child.

For several months this plaster Madonna was my only friend, and I spent all the time I was able to steal from my lessons in contemplation of this soft-coloured image. She looked so beautiful, so kind and gentle that no human creature could have rivalled in beauty, kindness and gentleness that lump of inert and painted matter, which spoke to me in a strange and charming language, and from which came a heady smell, as it were, of incense and myrrh. In her presence I really was a different child. I felt my cheeks grow pink, my blood pulsed more strongly in my veins, my thoughts cleared, becoming brighter and lighter. It was as though the black veil hanging over my mind gradually lifted, to reveal a new brilliance. Marie became an accomplice of my secret visits to the church. She often took me to the chapel, where I would spend hours conversing with the Virgin, while that good old woman devoutly recited her rosary, kneeling on the steps of the altar. She had to wrest me by force from my trance, for absorbed as I was in dreams that transported me to heaven, I am certain I would not have thought of going home. My passion for the Virgin became so strong that I was unhappy when I was away from her, and wished never to leave her. 'Monsieur Jean will become a priest for sure,' old Marie used to say. It was like a need to possess, a violent desire to take her, embrace her, and cover her with kisses. I had the idea of drawing her: you cannot imagine with what love! When she assumed some kind of rough form on my drawing paper, my joy was boundless. I brought to this task, which I considered wonderful and superhuman, every effort I was capable of. I started on the drawing at least a dozen times, getting annoyed with my pencil that did not capture the softness of line, and with my paper on which the image did not appear eloquent and lifelike, as I would have wished. I persisted, straining my will to this sole purpose. Finally, I managed to give a fairly good – and oh so naive! – impression of the plaster Madonna. And my thoughts abruptly turned away from her. An inner voice told me that nature was more beautiful, more compassionate, and more splendid, and I began to observe the sun caressing the trees, playing on roof-tiles, gilding plants, setting rivers alight, and I began to listen to all the palpitations of life that living creatures are full of and that make the earth pulse like a body of flesh and blood.

The years passed, boring and uneventful. I remained

solemn and retiring, always wrapped up in myself, with a fondness for running through the fields and plunging deep into the forest. It seemed to me that there at least, lulled by the great voice of things, I was less alone and I could better hear myself live. Without being endowed with the dreadful talent of some characters for self-analysis, for questioning themselves, for constantly seeking the reason for their actions, I often wondered who I was and what I wanted. Alas, I was nobody, and there was nothing I wanted. My childhood had passed in darkness, my adolescence passed in a blur: I was no more a young man than I had ever been a child. I lived as it were in a fog. A thousand ideas seethed inside me, but so vague were they, I could not pin them down. Not one emerged distinctly from this misty haze. I had aspirations and enthusiasms, but would have been incapable of expressing them, of explaining their cause and their object. I would have been incapable of saying into which world of dream or reality they propelled me. I felt infinite tenderness that melted my heart, but for what and for whom? I did not know. Sometimes, all of a sudden, I began weeping profusely: but the reason for these tears? Truly, I did not know. What is certain is that I cared for nothing, I could see no purpose in life, I felt incapable of any effort. Children say to themselves, 'I'm going to be a general, a bishop, a doctor, a hotelier.' I never said anything of the sort to myself. I never thought beyond the present moment, never ventured to look to the future. Man seemed to me like a tree that spreads its leaves and extends its branches in a stormy sky, without knowing what flowers will blossom at the foot of it, what birds will sing at the top of it, or what thunderbolt will strike it down. And yet the sense of moral solitude I felt oppressed and scared me. I could not open my heart to my father, my teacher, or anyone else: I had no playmate, not a living soul able to understand, guide, and love me. My father and my tutor lamented my 'limited aptitudes', and in the neighbourhood I was commonly thought to be cranky and feeble-minded, Nevertheless, I passed my exams, and although neither my father nor I had any idea what career I might follow, I went to study law in Paris. 'Law leads to everything,' my father was wont to say.

Paris amazed me. It seemed a great noise and pandemonium. Bizarre, disorderly and frantic, individuals and crowds hurried past, going about their business, which I imagined to be monstrous and terrible. Jolted by horses, jostled by people, deafened by the roar of the town, like some colossal and demonic factory in full swing, blinded by the glare of unaccustomed lights, I walked about in a lunatic dream that defied explanation. It was a great surprise to come upon trees. How could they have germinated there, in that paved ground? How could they have grown in that forest of stone buildings, amid that swarming mass of humanity, their branches blown by an ill wind? It took me a very long time to get used to this life that seemed to go against nature. And in the midst of this seething hell, my thoughts often returned to those peaceful fields back home, that filled my nostrils with the good smell of freshly turned and fertile earth; to those verdant woodland retreats where I heard only the gentle rustling of leaves, and from time to time, at a deeper level of sound, the dull thuds of an axe and the almost human groan of aged oak-trees. Yet a curiosity to learn drove me out of the small room where I lived in rue Oudinot, and I wandered the streets, boulevards and embankments, driven to walk on feverishly, my fingers twitching, my brain battered, as it were, by the titanic and nervous activity of Paris, all my senses in some way thrown out of kilter by these colours, smells and sounds, by the perversion and strangeness of this contact that was so new to me. The more I plunged into crowds, the more I revelled in the din, the more I saw these thousands of human lives going by, brushing past each other, with indifference, with no apparent connection between them; then others, coming into view, disappearing, and being replaced anew, all the time . . . and the more I felt the oppression of my relentless solitude. Although I had been lonely at St-Michel, at least there were people and things I knew there. Everywhere, I had landmarks to guide my mind: a peasant's back bowed over the soil, a wooden shack on the bend of a path, a dip in the ground, a dog, a marl pit, an attractive pollard – all was familiar, if not dear, to me. In Paris, everything was alien and hostile. In the dreadful haste with which these people, these phantoms, raced about, in their profound egoism and staggering oblivion of one another, in which they were immersed, how was I for one moment to capture their attention – I do not mean attention in the sense of any kindness or feeling of pity, but of a mere glance! One day I saw a man killing another: he was admired and his name was at once on everyone's lips. The next day I saw a woman lifting her skirts in an obscene gesture: the crowd followed her in procession.

Being awkward, unschooled in the ways of the world, and very shy, I had difficulty in making friends. I did not once set foot in the houses where I had an introduction, for fear of being thought ridiculous. I had an invitation to dinner from a wealthy cousin of my mother who lived in great style. The sight of the house, the footmen in the hall, the lights, the carpets, the scent of flowers in that airlessness – all scared me, and I fled, bumping into a woman in a red coat coming up the stairs who began to laugh at my terrified expression. I also disliked the noisy gaiety of young people – my fellow students – whom I encountered at lectures, at restaurants, in cafés. The vulgarity of their pleasures offended me, and the women, with their darkened eyes and overpainted lips, with their cynicism, and the indecency of their conversation and dress, did not tempt me in the least. Yet one evening, in a state of enervation and driven by a sudden carnal urge, I went into a brothel, and came out feeling ashamed, remorseful and annoyed with myself, with a sensation of defilement on my skin. So, it was from that mindless and unsavoury act that men were born! From that moment I paid more attention to women, but my gaze was no longer chaste, eyeing them, like dirty pictures, trying to discern the sexuality and nakedness beneath the clothes they wore. I then became acquainted with solitary pleasures that made me even more dejected, restless and vacant. A kind of dissolute torpor overcame me. I remained in bed for days on end, sinking into the brutishness of obscene slumbers, wakened from time to time by sudden nightmares, by violent pangs of anguish that made the sweat trickle down my skin. In my room, with the curtains drawn, I was like a corpse conscious of being dead, who, from the depths of his tomb, in the terrifying dark, hears the ruffle and rumble of a town's distant murmur, of the masses tramping overhead. Sometimes, wrenching myself from this prostration, I would go out. But what was I to do? Where was I to go? Everything was a matter of indifference to me, and I had no desire, no curiosity. With a fixed gaze, heavy-headed and sluggish-blooded, I would just keep on walking, aimlessly, and end up collapsing on a bench in the Luxembourg Gardens, where for interminable hours I sat motionless, huddled up like a senile old man, without seeing or hearing anything, without wondering why there children running around, and birds singing, and couples passing . . .

Of course I was doing no work or giving thought to anything . . .

The war came, then defeat . . . Despite my father's opposition and old Marie's entreaties, I enlisted.

CHAPTER TWO

Our regiment was what was then called a temporary regiment. It had been scraped together in Le Mans, from all that survived of various different units, from the odds and sods thronging the town. Zouaves, militiamen, irregulars, forest rangers, dismounted cavalrymen, even policemen, Spaniards and Vlachs – there were all kinds, and they were all commanded by an old stores captain, promoted in the emergency to lieutenant-colonel. In those days advancements of this kind were not unusual: the holes blasted in the French lines by the cannons of Wissemburg and Sedan had somehow to be plugged. Several companies were without a captain. Mine was headed by a poor militia lieutenant, a pale and delicate young man of twenty, who was so far from robust that after a few kilometres he was out of breath and limping, and he completed the day's march in an ambulance wagon. The poor young devil! You had only to look him in the face to make him blush, and he would never have dared give an order, for fear of making a mistake and exposing himself to ridicule. We made fun of him, because of his shyness and weakness, and probably, too, because he was kind-hearted and sometimes issued the men with cigars and extra meat rations. Led by example, and overexcited by the feverishness of my surroundings, I quickly adapted to this new life. Reading the harrowing accounts of our lost battles, I felt overtaken by a kind of fervour, without this fervour being imbued with any notion of the country's imperilment. We were in Le Mans for a month, equipping ourselves, training, haunting the bars and brothels. On 3 October, we finally left.

A bunch of errant soldiers, of leaderless detachments, of vagrant volunteers, ill-equipped, ill-fed – and more often, not fed at all – without cohesion or discipline, each man thinking only of himself, all driven by the same sense of unrelenting, fierce egoism, this one wearing a policeman's cap, that one with his head wrapped in a scarf, while others were dressed in gunners' britches and service corps jackets – we marched along, ragged, tired and fierce. In the twelve days after being drafted into a newly formed brigade, we roamed the countryside, crazed and, as it were, aimless. Heading right today, left tomorrow, making a forty-kilometre advance one day, and retreating as far the next, we were constantly going round in the same circle, like some stampeding herd of cattle that had lost its cowherd. Our excitement certainly dwindled. Three weeks' hardship sufficed to achieve that. Even before we heard the canon's roar and the whistle of bullets, our forward march resembled the rout of a defeated army, carved up by cavalry charges, plunged into the frenzy of ambushes, the confusion of headlong flight. The number of times I have seen soldiers getting rid of their ammunition, scattering cartridges alongside the road!

'What use is it to me?' said one of them. 'I only need one, to blow the captain's head off, the first time we fight.'

Crouched round the cooking-pot, in camp in the evening, or stretched out on the cold moorland, with their heads resting on their kit-bags, they thought of the homes they had been brutally torn from. All the strong-armed, young men had left the villages. Many were already lying on the ground, over there, disembowelled by shells. Others wandered the plains and forests, broken men, phantom soldiers, awaiting death. Only increasingly bowed old men and weeping women were left in the bereaved countryside. The threshing-floors were silent and the barn doors closed. In the deserted fields, where weeds thrived, the ploughman was no longer to be seen, with his tired horses, plodding back to the farm, silhouetted against the purple sunset. And men with big sabres came, taking the horses one day, and emptying the cowshed the next, in the name of the law. For the war was not satisfied with gorging itself on human flesh, it also had to devour livestock, land, everything that lived in tranquillity, in the peace of work and love . . . And as these wretched soldiers slumped around the camp fire, their emaciated faces caught in its lurid glow, at the bottom of all their hearts a single hope reigned, hope in the impending battle, meaning desertion, surrender, and German imprisonment.

Yet we were preparing the defence of the villages we passed through, which were not yet under threat. To this end, we conceived of felling trees and throwing them on the roads; we blew up bridges, we violated cemeteries on the edge of villages, on the pretext of throwing up barricades, and we forced the inhabitants at bayonet point to assist us in the destruction of their property. Then we set off again, leaving behind nothing but ruin and hatred. I remember that once we had to level an extremely fine park down to the very last sapling, so as to erect shelters that we did not occupy. Our behaviour did nothing to reassure people. So houses were barred at our approach, and the peasants would bury their food supplies: everywhere we were met with hostile faces, ill-tempered words, empty hands. There would be bloody brawls among us over a pot of rillettes found in a cupboard, and the general ordered the execution of a man who had hidden in his garden, under a pile of manure, a few kilos of salted lard.

On November 1, we had been marching all day, and at about three o'clock we reached the station at La Loupe. There was enormous chaos at first, an indescribable confusion. A great many men, breaking ranks, overran the town, about a kilometre away, and dispersed themselves among the bars near by. For more than an hour the bugles sounded the rally. Troopers went sent into the town to recover the fugitives and lingered there drinking. There was a rumour that a train made up at Nogent-le-Rotou was to pick us up and take us to Chartres, under threat from the Prussians, who had supposedly sacked Maintenon and were now encamped at Jouy. A railway employee, questioned by our sergeant, said that he did not know, he had not heard anything. The general, a gesticulating, short, fat, old boy who had trouble keeping his seat, went galloping off to left and right, wheeled round, rolling about on his mount like a barrel, and, purple-faced with irascible whiskers, kept saying over and over again, 'Oh, damn! Damn, damn, damn!'

He dismounted with the help of his orderly, got his legs tangled in the straps of his sabre that trailed along the ground, and having summoned the stationmaster, engaged the fellow, whose face expressed bewilderment, in the most animated discussion.

'And the mayor?' shouted the general. 'Where is the fellow? Bring him here! Am I being made a fool of here?'

He huffed, mumbled unintelligibly, stamped the ground with his feet, and hurled abuse at the stationmaster. Eventually, both of them, one with a very hang-dog look and the other making furious gestures, disappeared into the telegraph office, from which we soon heard a frantic, ear-splitting, relentless ringing, punctuated from time to time by outbursts of the general's voice. A decision was finally taken to have us line up on the platform, in companies, and we were left there, standing motionless, with our kit-bags on the ground, and our arms piled in front of us. Darkness had fallen, and it was raining – a cold steady rain that managed to seep through our greatcoats, already wet from previous downpours. Here and there, the track was illuminated by dim little lights, making the warehouses and the mass of the wagons that men were pushing into the engine shed, appear darker. And standing on its turntable platform was the hoist tackle, with its long neck, like that of a startled giraffe, profiled against the sky. Apart from a swiftly-drunk coffee that morning, we had eaten nothing all day, and to our dismay the word went round that, although our bodies were shattered with weariness, and our stomachs gnawed with hunger, we would have to go without supper as well. Our water-bottles were empty, our rations of biscuit and lard exhausted, and the service corps trucks, having lost their way the previous day, had not rejoined the column. Several of us complained, with openly threatening and rebellious words, but the officers, who, too, looked dejected as they paced in front of the row of piled arms, seemed not to pay any attention. I consoled myself with the thought that the general had perhaps requisitioned food supplies from the town. Vain hope! The minutes ticked by; the rain went on making our water-bottles resonate, and the general continued to heap insults on the stationmaster, who continued to take his revenge on the telegraph wire, whose ringing became increasingly vehement and frenzied . . .

From time to time trains stopped, crammed with troops. Militia and infantrymen – undisciplined, bare-headed, with their ties loosened, some of them drunk, with their caps awry – escaped from the carriages where they were cooped up, invaded the bar, or shamelessly relieved themselves in the open. Rising from this milling crowd of humanity, above the herd-like stamping of feet on the wagon floors, came oaths, snatches of singing of the Marseillaise, and obscene refrains, mingling with the cries of railmen, the jingling of the station bell, the steaming of the engines. I recognised a young boy from St-Michel, with puffed and rheumy eyes, who was coughing and spitting blood. I asked him where they were going. He had no idea. After leaving Le Mans, they had been stuck at Connerré for twelve hours because of congestion on the line, with nothing to eat, and too densely crowded to stretch out and sleep. That was all he knew. He hardly had the strength to speak. He went off to the station bar to bathe his eyes in a little warm water. I shook his hand, and he said that at the first engagement he sincerely hoped to be taken prisoner by the Prussians . . . Then the train moved off and disappeared into the darkness, taking all those gaunt faces and already defeated bodies to who knows what pointless and bloody carnage?

I was shivering. I was getting chilled to the bone under that freezing rain dripping on my skin, and my limbs felt numb. I took advantage of the confusion caused by the arrival of a train to escape through an open gate and run off down the road, looking for a house, a place to shelter, where I could get warm and find a piece of bread or something. The hotels and bars near the station were patrolled by guards under orders not to let anyone in . . . Three hundred metres away in the dark I saw the soft glimmer of light at some windows. Those lights gave me the impression of two kindly eyes filled with pity, beckoning, smiling, affectionate eyes . . .

It was a small isolated house set back a few paces from the road. I ran towards it . . . There, shouting and cursing, was a sergeant, accompanied by four men. I saw an old man sitting by the empty hearth on a very low straw-bottomed chair, with his elbows on his knees and his head in his hands. A candle burning in a metal holder lit half of his face that was deeply lined and furrowed with wrinkles.

'Will you give us some wood, damn it?' shouted the sergeant.

'I have no wood,' replied the old man. 'The army came by a week ago, I tell you . . . they took everything . . .'

He sat hunched on his chair and in a feeble voice he murmured, 'I've nothing . . . nothing . . . nothing!'

The sergeant shrugged his shoulders. 'Now, don't try to be clever, you old scoundrel . . . So, you're hiding your wood to warm the Prussians! Well, if it's Prussians you want . . . Just you wait!'

The old man shook his head. 'But I have no wood . . .'

With an angry gesture the sergeant ordered the men to search the house. They went through the place from top to bottom — there was nothing, nothing but traces of violence, broken furniture. In the cellar, which was dank with spilt cider, the barrels had been smashed, and the whole place reeked appallingly. This incensed the sergeant, who struck the floor with the butt of his rifle.

'Now, come on, you senile bastard,' he shouted, 'tell us where your wood is!'

And he roughly shook the old man, who fell back and almost hit his head against the andiron in the fireplace.

'I've no wood,' the poor fellow simply replied.

'So you're going to be stubborn, are you? So you've no wood! Well, you've got some chairs, a sideboard, a table, a bed . . . if you don't tell me where your wood is, I'll burn the lot!'

The old man made no protest. Shaking his old white head, he repeated once more, 'I've no wood.'

I tried to intervene, and stammered out a few words, but the sergeant did not let me finish. He eyed me from head to foot with a scornful gaze.

'And what are you doing here, sonny?' he asked. 'Who gave you permission to break ranks, you miserable whipper-snapper. Go on, about turn, quick march! Up, two, three, four, up, two, three . . .'

Then he gave an order. Within a few minutes, chairs, table, sideboard and bed were reduced to fragments. The old man struggled to his feet, and went and huddled at the back of the room, and while the fire burned and the sergeant, with his overcoat and trousers steaming, warmed himself, laughing, in front of the crackling blaze, the old fellow watched his last few sticks of furniture go up in flames and kept obstinately repeating, 'I've no wood.'

I went back to the station.

The general had emerged from the telegraph office, more agitated, redder-faced, and angrier than ever. He mumbled something, and a great deal of activity at once ensued. There was a rattling of sabres; voices called out to each other, back and forth; officers went running off in all directions. And the bugle sounded. At a complete loss to understand this counter-order, we had to put our kit-bags on our backs again and our rifles on our shoulders.

'Forward! March!'

Crashing into each other, with our limbs stiff from standing still and our heads buzzing, we set off again on our breathless progress through the rain, mud and darkness . . . To left and right lay fields lost in shadow, out of which rose clumps of apple-trees that seemed to writhe against the sky. Occasionally a dog barked, a long way off . . . Then came deep forests, with dark trees rearing up like walls on either side of the road; then, sleeping villages where our footsteps echoed more ominously, and where the vague glimpse of a terrified white figure appeared at windows that were quickly opened and quickly shut . . . and more fields, more forests, more villages. There was no singing, and not a word spoken, only a great silence marked by the dull trampling of feet.

The straps of my kit-bag dug into my shoulders, and the rifle was like a red-hot iron on my shoulder. For a while I felt as though I was harnessed to a big bogged-down wagon loaded with quarried stones, and that the carters were lashing me with their whips. Straddle-legged, bent double, with my neck outstretched, choked by the halter, and a wheezing chest, I pulled and pulled . . .

It soon reached the point where I was no longer conscious of anything. I marched on, automatically, numbed, in a dream . . . Strange hallucinations passed before my eyes . . . I saw a path of light running into the distance, bordered by palaces and brightly coloured whirligigs . . . The blooms of big scarlet flowers stood poised in space on pliant stems, and a joyous crowd sang before tables covered with cool drinks and delicious fruit . . . On illuminated lawns women in gossamer skirts that flared out danced to the sound of multitudinous orchestras hidden in groves of hanging leaves spangled with jasmine and cooled by fountains.

'Halt!' the sergeant ordered.

I stopped, and had to cling to the arm of a companion so as not to fall on the ground. I came to . . . Everything was in darkness. We had arrived at the edge of a forest near a little town where the general and most of the officers went to take lodgings. Once the tent was up, I tended my raw and bleeding feet, treating them with a candle that I kept in reserve in my haversack, and like some poor tired dog, I stretched out on the damp earth and fell into a deep sleep. All through the night fellow soldiers who had collapsed with exhaustion on the way continued to rejoin the camp. There were five of whom nothing was ever heard again. It was always the same, with every strenuous march: a few that were weak or sick would fall into ditches and die there; others deserted . . .

The next day reveille was sounded at first light. It had been a very cold night; the rain was incessant, and we had not been able to obtain the least bedding of straw or hay. I had great difficulty in getting out of the tent. At one point I had to drag myself on my knees, on all fours, because my legs refused to support me. My limbs were frozen, as stiff as iron rods. It was impossible to move my head since my neck was paralysed; and my eyes, which felt as though pricked by multiple little needles, wept continuously. At the same time I had an unbearable acute stabbing pain in my shoulders and back. I noticed that my companions were no better off. They moved with ashen faces and drawn features, some limping terribly, others bent and staggering, stumbling over clumps of heather at every step: all of them lame, pitiful and muddy. I saw several gripped with violent attacks of colic, writhing and grimacing, clutching their bellies with both hands. A few, convulsed with fever, had chattering teeth. All around, you could hear chest-wrenching, dry coughs, laboured breathing, groans and wheezing. A hare scampered from its form and fled in terror with its ears laid flat, but no one thought of chasing it as we once used to . . . When roll-call was over, there was a distribution of rations, for our supplies had finally caught up with the brigade . . . We had a meal, which we ate as ravenously as starving dogs.

I was still unwell. After the meal I suffered a spell of dizziness, soon followed by vomiting, and I was shivering with fever. Everything around me was spinning . . . the tents, the forest, the plain, the little town over there, with its smoking chimneys in the mist, and the sky, in which huge, low-lying, dark clouds rolled. I asked the sergeant for permission to go and see a doctor.

The tents were lined up in two rows, backing on to the forest, on either side of the Senoches road, which emerges through a magnificent gap in the oak-trees into open countryside, and three hundred metres further on crosses the road to Chartres, then leads through the town of Bellomer, before continuing on to La Loupe. At the junction of these two roads stood a wretched little shack, a kind of derelict barn, covered with thatch that served as a shelter from the rain for roadmenders. It was there that the surgeon had set up an improvised treatment unit, identifiable by the Geneva Cross that graced it, which was stuck in a crack in the wall. There were lots of men waiting in front of the house – a long line of worn-out, deathly-pale individuals, some standing there with big staring eyes, others seated on the ground in dejection, their shoulder-blades hunched and angular, holding their head in their hands. Death had already left its horrible mark on these gaunt faces, scraggy backs and dangling limbs, drained of blood and marrow. And forgetting my own troubles, I was saddened by this sorry sight. So, it had taken only three months to crush these vigorous bodies, though they were no strangers to hard work and tiredness. Three months! And now it was all over for these young men, with their love of life, these children of the soil who had grown up in the freedom of the fields as dreamers trusting in the bounteous provision of nature! A sailor who dies is given the sea for a tomb. He is lowered into eternal darkness, lulled by the music of the waves . . . But these men! Another few days perhaps, and all of a sudden these vagabonds would fall flat on their faces into some muddy ditch, their carcasses left to the fangs of scavenging dogs, to the beaks of night-birds. I felt a sense of such brotherly and sorrowful commiseration that I wished I could hug all these poor wretches to my chest, in a single embrace, and I wished – oh, how fervently I wished! – that, like Isis, I had a hundred female breasts, swollen with milk, to offer to all these bloodless lips . . . They went into the house one by one and came out again straightaway, with grumbles and curses at their backs . . . In fact, the surgeon was not attending to them. He was raging at a nurse, demanding his field pharmacy-case, which had not been found among the baggage.

'My pharmacy case, for God's sake!' he shouted. 'Where's my pharmacy case? And what about my instrument kit? What have I done with my instrument kit? God damn it!'

A young militiaman, suffering from an abscess on his knee, came hobbling out again, weeping, tearing his hair in despair. No one would see him. When it was my turn to go in, I was shivering violently. In the murky depths of the room, four men on their death-bed lay curled up on the straw; a fifth was waving his arms about in a delirium, uttering incoherent words; yet another, half sat up, with his head drooping over chest, moaned, asking for a drink in a weak

49

childish voice. A nurse crouched in front of the fireplace held a stick up to the flames with a piece of sizzling sausage on the end of it that made the room stink with the smell of burnt fat. The assistant medical officer did not even look at me.

'What's the matter with him?' he shouted. 'Bunch of malingers! Ten miles' footslog, slacker, that'll sort you out . . . Go on, beat it! About turn.'

I passed a peasant woman at the door, who asked me, "Ees 'ere, is 'ee, the surgin?'

'Now it's women!' growled the assistant medical officer. 'What do you want?'

'Sorry, 'scuse me, doctor,' said the peasant woman, who came forward, very intimidated. 'I come for my son who's a soldier.'

'Listen, woman, is it my job to look after your son?'

Very timorous, with her hands crossed on the handle of her umbrella, she gazed round the room.

'They say 'ees very poorly, my son, very, very poorly . . . So I come to see if you didn't have 'im 'ere with you, doctor.'

'What's your name?'

'The name's Riboulleau.'

'Riboulleau . . . Riboulleau! It's possible . . . Have a look among that lot over there.'

The nurse, grilling his sausage, turned his head.

'Riboulleau?' he said. 'But he died three days ago . . .'

'What do you mean?' cried the woman, whose weather-beaten face suddenly paled. "Ow can 'ee be dead? Why's my little boy dead? . . .'

The assistant medical officer cut in, giving the old woman a rough shove towards the door.

'Now, now,' he shouted, 'don't make a scene here! He's dead, I tell you, and that's that . . .'

'My little boy! My little boy!' the woman moaned, heart-rendingly.

I went off, saddened to the core, and so despondent that I wondered if it would not be better to put an end to it all there and then, by hanging myself from the branch of a tree, or blowing my brains out. As I staggered back to the tent, turning over in my mind the darkest plans, I barely paid any attention to the young militiaman who, having stopped at the foot of a pine-tree, had himself lanced his abscess with his knife, and, white as a sheet, with sweat dripping from his brow, was bandaging the bleeding wound.

The morning turned out better than I thought. I was lucky enough not to be detailed for fatigue duty, and after polishing my gun, rusted by the rain, I enjoyed a few hours' rest. As I lay stretched out on my blanket, my body suspended in a pleasant half-sleep in which I could clearly distinguish the sounds of the camp – the bugle calls, the whinnying of a horse in the distance – I thought of the people and the things I had left behind. Countless faces and landscapes swiftly passed before my eyes . . . I saw the Priory, my dead mother, and my father with his big straw hat, and the little tow-haired beggar-boy, and Felix crouched among the lettuces in the vegetable patch, watching for a mole. I saw my student digs, my college companions, and dominating the turmoil of Bullier was Nini, slightly drunk and vexed, with her red-haired chignon, and pink stockings that showed, like carnal flowers, when her skirts lifted as she danced. Then the image came back to me – sweet, enduring vision! – of a woman in a purple dress, a stranger I had glimpsed at the theatre one evening in the shadows of a box.

Meanwhile, the most able-bodied among us had been roaming round the farms in the countryside. They came back, cheerfully loaded with bundles of straw, chickens, turkeys and ducks. One used a stick to drive a fat grunting pig in front of him, another carried a sheep on his shoulders, whilst yet another dragged along, on the end of a withe twisted into a rope, a calf that put up comic resistance, shaking its muzzle and bellowing. Peasants came running to the camp to complain of being robbed; they were jeered at and chased away.

The general, accompanied by our lieutenant-colonel who stood on his right, very stiff and pop-eyed, came and inspected us in the afternoon. His glistening gaze, heightened colour and thick voice revealed that he had enjoyed a hearty lunch. He chewed the end of an extinguished cigar, spat, snorted, railed against who knows what or whom, for he did not address anyone directly. Faced with our company, he gave the lieutenant-colonel a dour look, and I heard him muttering, 'Nasty-looking customers, your men, by Jove!'

Then he walked off, carrying all the weight of his belly on those short legs shod in yellow boots, with his red breeches above them as full and pleated as a skirt. The rest of the day was dedicated to plying the bars of Bellomer. There was such a crush everywhere, such a din – besides, I was all too familiar with those assaults on bars, those violent scrambles for liquor that often degenerated into a general brawl – that I preferred to wander off down the road, away from all the scuffles, with a few quiet friends. In fact the weather had improved, with a pale sun now shining in a cloudless sky. We sat on an embankment, our backs yielding to those warming rays the way a cat responds to a hand that strokes it. Vehicles kept passing – heavy wagons, drays, carioles covered with tilts, tumbrils drawn by mules. These were the peasants from the Chartres plain fleeing the Prussians.

Panic-stricken by reports that spread from village to village, of fire, rape and massacre, of the various atrocities inflicted by the Germans on occupied territories, they had gathered up their most valued possessions, abandoned their fields and their homes, and gone on the move, in total terror, without knowing where they were going. At night they would stop somewhere along the way, near a town, or sometimes in open countryside. The horses would be left unharnessed and fettered to graze at the roadside, and the people ate and slept by the grace of God, guarded by their dogs, in the wind and the rain and the cold of misty nights. Then the next day they would set off again. An endless succession of men and beasts herded past, and the dark, doleful line of those fleeing could be seen stretching back along the yellow highway, up to the higher ground closing the horizon. It was like the exodus of a nation. I questioned an old man leading a ass-drawn cart, in the bottom of which, among the bundles knotted with handkerchiefs, among the carrots and cabbages, on the straw, were crowded a snub-nosed peasant girl, two pink porkers, and some braces of poultry bound by their feet.

'So you've got Prussians in your parts?'

'Those brigands!' said the old man. 'Don't mention 'em. They came one morning, a band of 'em, with feathers in their 'ats . . . They made such a rumpus! Sweet Jesus! And then they took everything . . . At first I thought they was Prussians . . . I found out afterwards they was irregulars.'

'What about the Prussians?'

'Prussians! Prussians! I don't think I seen any Prussians . . . They must have got to our place by now, though! Our Jacqueline thinks she saw one the other day behind a hedge. He was tall, very tall, and red, she said, red like the devil . . . They're extremists, then, are they, or savages, or ghouls? Tell me, what are they exactly?

'They're Germans, old man, just as we're French.'

'Germins? I see . . . But what do these blessed Germins want with us, do you think, sir? Well, I did manage to save our two pigs, and our daughter, and some poultry as well . . . by God!'

And the peasant went on his way, repeating to himself, 'Germins! Germins! What do they want with us, these blessed Germins?'

That evening, fires were lit all along the camp-line, and big cooking-pots, full of fresh meat, bubbled cheerfully over improvised stoves made of earth and stones. It was for us a spell of exquisite relaxation and delightful oblivion. A calm seemed to descend from a sky all blue with moonlight and twinkling with stars. The fields that stretched away like gently rolling waves had some quality of compassionate tenderness about them that penetrated our spirits and instilled our aching limbs with less acrid blood and renewed strength. The memory of our afflictions, our suffering and despair, though so immediate, gradually faded, and once again we felt the need to be active, at the same time as a sense of duty awakened in us. An unusual liveliness reigned over the camp. Everyone was busy with some voluntary task. Some came rushing, poker in hand, to rekindle fires that had died, others blew on the embers to revive them, or else peeled vegetables and chopped up pieces of meat. A few comrades that were gathered round some smoking wood-chips chanted mockingly: 'Have you seen Bismarck?' Rebellion, the daughter of hunger, melted amid the simmering of cooking-pots, the clattering of mess-tins.

The next day, when the last of us had answered 'Present' to his name being called, the young lieutenant gave the order, 'Form a circle!'

And in a droning voice, stumbling over his words and missing out phrases, the quartermaster sergeant read out a pompous 'order of the day' from the general. What this piece of military literature said was that, after having occupied Chartres, a hungry, ill-clad Prussian army corps, was advancing on us by forced march. They had to be stopped in their tracks and forced all the way back to the walls of Paris, where the valiant Ducrot was only awaiting our arrival to sally forth and drive out the invaders once and for all. The general recalled the victories of the Revolution, the Egyptian campaign, Austerlitz and Borodino. He said that we would know how to prove ourselves worthy of our glorious ancestors of Sambre-et-Meuse. Accordingly, he gave detailed instructions for the strategic defence of our territory: we were to set up an impassable roadblock at the eastern approach to the town, and another even more impassable block before the crossroads on the route to Chartres; to notch the walls of the cemetery; to cut down as many trees as we could, so as to make it impossible for enemy cavalry, and indeed infantry, to outflank us on the Senonches sides by scattering through the forest; to beware of spies; and finally, to remain vigilant . . . The country was counting on us . . . Long live the Republic!

This cry went unechoed. The young lieutenant, who was pacing round with his hands clasped behind his back and his gaze resolutely fixed on his toe-caps, did not look up. We stared at each other, appalled, our hearts sinking to learn that the Prussians were so close, that the war was to begin for us tomorrow, perhaps even today, and I had a sudden vision of ruddy Death standing on a chariot drawn by two rearing horses, and bearing down us brandishing a scythe. As long as the battle remained distant, we had yearned for it, at first out of patriotic enthusiasm, then bluster, and later out of enervation and lassitude, as the solution to our troubles. Now that it was close, we felt scared, we shuddered at the mere mention of it. Instinctively, my eyes travelled to the horizon, in the direction of Chartres. And the countryside seemed to contain a sense of mystery and dread, of terrible uncertainty that lent a new aspect of inevitability to things. Over there, above the line of trees fading into blueness, I expected to see helmets appearing all of a sudden, and bayonets glinting, and the thundering mouths of cannons blazing. A ploughed field, all red in the sunlight, gave me the impression of a pool of blood; and the hedges seemed to be engaged in manoeuvres, spreading out, coming together and criss-crossing, like regiments, bristling with arms and flags, about to enter into combat. The apple-trees had the startled look of horsemen put to flight.

'Men . . . fall out!' shouted the lieutenant.

We hung about for a long time, like complete cretins, with our arms dangling, in the grip of a vague unease, trying mentally to travel beyond that terrible skyline, where the secret of our fate was evolving. In the disturbing silence, the ominous stillness, carts in ever greater number passed with increasing haste on the ever more densely thronged road. A flight of crows coming from that direction, like a black vanguard, appeared as a blot on the horizon, grew larger, broadened and lengthened, wheeled and hung above us like a funeral pall, then disappeared into the oak trees.

'So, we're finally going to see these famous Prussians,' said a wavering voice belonging to a very pale-looking big fellow who, in order to give himself the jaunty air of a seasoned soldier, wore his cap pulled down over one ear.

No one replied and several men moved away, but our

corporal shrugged. He was a cynical little chap with a pock-marked, spotty face.

'Well, as far as I'm concerned . . .' he said, and making a contemptuous gesture to show what he thought, he sat down on the heather, slowly filled his pipe and lit it. 'What the hell!' he concluded, exhaling a puff of smoke that melted into the air.

While a company of light infantry headed off towards the crossroads to set up those 'impassable roadblocks', my regiment went into the forest, to cut down 'as many trees as we could'. Every axe, bill hook and hatchet in the area had been immediately requisitioned – anything served as a tool. All day long the blows rang out and trees fell. To get us even more fired up, the general insisted on taking part in the massacre.

'Ah, by Jove!' he would shout at every turn, clapping his hands. 'Ah, hah! Go to it, boys! Let's have that one down!'

He himself picked out the tallest of the trees, with trunks that had grown as straight and smooth as the columns of a temple. What a frenzy of criminal, mindless destruction! What brutish glee every time the trees came crashing down on each other. The forest thinned; it looked as though it had been attacked with a huge supernatural scythe. Two men were killed by a falling oak.

'Go to it, boys!'

And the few trees left standing, untamed among the smashed trunks lying on the ground and the twisted branches that reached up towards them, like arms in supplication, displayed large wounds, deep red entrails, weeping sap.

Alerted by a warden, the keeper of the forests came rushing over from Senonches and was appalled by this pointless devastation. I was close by when he respectfully approached the general, cap in hand.

'Excuse me, general,' he said, 'I can understand your cutting down the trees at the sides of the road, and fortifying the lines . . . But laying waste to the heart of the forest seems to me a little . . .'

But the general cut him short.

'Eh? What? Seems to you? What the blazes are you doing here? I do what I please . . . Who's in command here, you or me?'

'But . . .' stammered the forester.

'I tell you, there are no buts, sir . . . And you're annoying me, is that clear? Now, you get back to Senonches, quick, or I'll have you put in the guard-house . . . Go to it, boys!'

The general turned his back on the aghast official and went off, clearing his path of dead leaves and twigs with the end of his cane.

While we desecrated the forest, the infantry for their part did not remain idle, and the roadblock rose up, high and imposing, barring the way before the crossroads. It had not been achieved without difficulty and above all without some hilarity. Suddenly halted by a trench impeding their flight, the peasants protested. As their carts and livestock massed in the road, which was very narrow at that point, there was at first an indescribable uproar. They complained, their woman-folk moaned, their cattle bellowed, the soldiers laughed at all the terrified-looking men and beasts, and the captain in command of the detachment did not know what action to take. Several times, the soldiers made a pretence of using their bayonets to drive back the peasants, but the latter stood their ground and insisted on passing, invoking their rights as Frenchmen.

Having completed his tour of the forest, the general came to inspect work on the barricade. He asked who these 'lousy civvies' were, and what they wanted. He was given the facts of the matter.

'That's fine!' he shouted. 'Seize all these carts and throw the whole lot on to the barricade. Be quick about it! Come on, go at it, lads!'

The soldiers were only too happy to hear this, and fell on the first carts, which were abandoned with what they contained, and smashed to pieces with a few pick-axe blows . . . Then panic seized the peasants. The congestion became such that it was impossible to advance or retreat. Furiously whipping their horses as they tried to free their jammed carts,

they shouted, jostled, and swore at each other without suc-
ceeding in moving one step backwards. The last to arrive
had turned tail and fled, their horses spurred to a gallop by
all the commotion; the others, despairing of saving their
carts and provisions, settled for scrambling up the bank and
walking off across the fields, uttering cries of indignation,
with soldiers hurling clods of earth after them. The smashed-
up carts were piled on top of each other, and the gaps
plugged with sacks of oats, mattresses, bundles of clothes,
and stones. At the highest point of the barricade, on the end
of a pole rising straight up like a flagstaff, a young infantry-
man stuck a wedding bouquet found among the chattels.

Towards evening, groups of militiamen arriving from Chartres in great disorder came streaming into Bellomer and into
the camp. What they had to say was terrifying. The Prussians
were over a hundred thousand, a whole army. They, who
scarcely numbered two thousand, without cavalry and without cannons, had been forced to fall back. Chartres was burning, the villages around were smoking ruins, the farms were
destroyed. The main body of the French detachment covering the retreat could not be far behind. The fugitives were
questioned; they were asked if they had seen any Prussians,
and what they looked like, their interrogators insisting on
details of their uniforms. Every fifteen minutes more militiamen would turn up, in bands of three or four, looking pale
and exhausted. Most of them had no knapsack, and a few
had not even a rifle, and they told stories each more terrible
than the next. It must be said that none of them was
wounded.

It was decided to billet them in the church, to the great
indignation of the priest, who threw up his hands and cried,
'Holy Virgin! In my church! Oh! oh! oh! Soldiers, in my
church!'

Solely occupied with capricious destruction, the general
so far had not had time to give any thought to protecting the
camp, other than by a small outpost established one kilometre from Bellomer, on the road to Chartres, in a tavern used
by carters. This post, commanded by a sergeant, had received

no precise instructions and the men had nothing to do except laze around, drinking and sleeping, although the sentry sauntering in front of the inn with his rifle on his shoulder did arrest a local doctor as a German spy, on account of his beard being fair and glasses being blue. As for the sergeant, a former poacher by profession, who 'didn't give a damn about anybody or anything', he spent his time snaring rabbits in the nearby hedgerows.

The arrival of the militia and the threat of the Prussians had sown panic among us. Horsemen arrived one after the other, minute by minute, bearing sealed missives, orders and counterorders. Officers bustled about, without knowing why, getting all het up. Three times we were ordered to strike camp, and three times we were ordered to pitch camp again. All night long, trumpets and bugles sounded and great fires burned, around which strangely agitated shadows and demonic silhouettes passed to and fro amid an ever increasing confusion of sound. Patrols searched the countryside in every direction, scouring byways, probing the edge of the forest. The artillery that had been parked on the far side of town had to move forward, on to the hill top, but came up against the roadblock. This had to be dismantled piece by piece, to allow the cannons to pass, and the trench had to be filled in.

At daybreak my company set off to man an outpost. We met dispersed militiamen and irregulars, pathetically limping along. Further on, the general with his escort were observing the manoeuvres of the artillery. He held an ordinance survey map spread out on his horse's neck, and was vainly searching for the Saussaie windmill. Poring over the map, which the movements of the horse's head kept shifting, he shouted, 'Where's the blessed windmill? Pongoin ... Courville ... Courville ... Do they think I'm familiar with all their blessed windmills?'

The general ordered us to halt, and asked, 'Is any one of you from this area? Does any one of you know where the Saussaie windmill is?'

No one replied.

'No? Well, the hell with it, then!'

And he hurled the map at his aide-de-camp, who began carefully to refold it. We continued on our way.

The company was installed on a farm and I was put on sentry duty, right by the road, on the edge of a spinney, from where I could see the plain, lying vast and flat as the sea. Here and there, little copses emerged from the land ocean, like islands; village bell-towers and farms blurred by the haze appeared like distant sails. There was a great silence, a great solitude, in that enormous expanse, where the least sound or the least object moving against the sky contained some indefinable mystery that instilled the soul with anxiety. Dark blots up above in the sky were crows; dark blots over there, coming this way at ground level, that grew larger, and passed by, were fleeing militiamen; and from time to time the distant barking of dogs, responding to each other from east to west and north to south, sounded like the empty fields' lament.

Guards were supposed to be relieved every four hours, but hours and hours went by, slow, interminable hours, and no one came to replace me. No doubt they had forgotten about me. With my heart in my mouth, I searched the horizon on the Prussian side, and on the French side; I could see nothing – nothing but that hard, unforgiving line girding the huge grey sky around me. The crows had stopped flying and the militia had stopped fleeing past a long time ago. At one point I saw a cart coming towards the wood where I was, but it turned down a side-road and was soon lost in the greyness of the landscape . . . Why had I been left like this? I was cold and hungry; my fingers were numb and my stomach was rumbling . . . I ventured a few paces down the road. I called out several times . . . Not a soul replied, and nothing stirred. I was alone, completely and utterly alone on that empty, deserted plain . . . A shudder ran through my veins, and tears welled up in my eyes . . . I called again . . . Nothing . . . Then I returned to the wood and sat at the foot of an oak with my rifle across my thighs, ears pricked, waiting . . . Alas, the light gradually faded. The sky turned yellow, grew slightly purple, then darkened in deathly silence. And a starless, moonless night descended over the fields, and a chilly mist rose out of the gloom.

Shattered with tiredness, always busy doing something, and never alone, I had not had time to think since we first set out. Yet at the strange cruel sights I was always seeing, I felt awakening within me a notion of human life that until now had lain dormant in the torpor of my childhood and adolescence. Yes, this had been a confused awakening, as though at the end of a long and painful nightmare. And reality seemed to me even more terrifying than my dream. Transposing to the rest of society the instincts, appetites, and passions affecting the small group of lost souls that we were, and recalling the purely external, rapid glimpses I had in Paris of unruly crowds, of jostling individuals, I realised that the world was governed by the law of strife; an inexorable, homicidal law that was not content with arming nations against one another, but caused strife between children born of the same race, the same family, the same womb. I found none of the sublime abstractions of honour, justice, charity and patriotism that so larded the classical texts on which we are raised, that serve to beguile and hypnotise us – the better to delude the good and the young, the better to subdue and slaughter them. So, what was this patriotism in whose name so many acts of madness and so many heinous crimes were committed, that had torn us, replete with love, from motherly nature, to cast us, filled with hatred, starving and naked, into this hostile world? What was this patriotism, embodied for us by that stupid, marauding general who persecuted old men and old trees, and by that surgeon who kicked the sick and bullied poor old mothers grieving for their sons? What was this patriotism whose every step on the ground was marked by a grave, that had only to look on the quiet waters of rivers to turn them to blood, and that wherever it went left ever deeper burial pits for the best of men's children to rot in? And I felt sorely amazed as it occurred to me for the first time that only people who were celebrated and acclaimed were those who had the most pillaged, massacred and burned down. The modest murderer who knifes a passer-by at the corner of a dark street is condemned to death and his decapitated trunk hurled into an ignominious burial pit. But for the conqueror who has set fire to towns and decimated populations, all human folly and baseness conspire monstrously to extol him: triumphal arches and dizzingly high bronze columns are erected in his honour, and crowds kneel piously in cathedrals, around his consecrated marble tomb, which is guarded by angels and saints under the well-pleased eye of God!

With what remorse did I repent of having passed deaf and blind until now through this life so fraught with unexplained riddles! Never once had I opened a book, never once had I paused for a moment before those question marks that people and things constitute . . . I knew nothing. And now, all of a sudden, I was tormented by a curiosity to know, a need to wrest from life a few of its mysteries. I wanted to learn the human rationale for religions that stupefy, governments that oppress, societies that kill. I was eager to have done with this war, so as to devote myself to urgent tasks, to magnificent and absurd missions. My thoughts were drawn to impossible philosophies of love, fantasies of undying brotherhood. I saw all men bowed beneath crushing burdens, like the young soldier from St-Michel whose eyes were rheumy, who coughed and spat blood. And with no understanding of the necessity of the overriding laws of nature, I felt waves of tenderness mounting in my throat in suppressed sobs. I have noticed that we only really sympathise with others when we ourselves are unhappy. Was it not for myself alone that I felt so sorry? And if I so loved humanity, in that cold darkness, so close to the enemy who might perhaps appear in the morning mist, was it not myself alone that I loved, myself alone that I wished I could save from suffering? These regrets for the past, these plans for the future, this sudden passion for study, the obsessiveness with which I imagined myself in the future in my room on rue Oudinot, surrounded by books and papers, with eyes reddened by the fever of working – was not all this simply designed to set aside the dangers of the immediate present, to blot out other terrible images, livid images of death that kept emerging from the horror of the shadows?

The night dragged on, impenetrable. Beneath a mean and nasty brooding sky, the fields stretched out like a vast sea of darkness. Distantly spaced white blurs, long trails of mist floated above it, skimming the invisible ground in which clumps of trees appeared here and there, ever blacker against the blackness. I had not moved from the place where I had sat down, and the cold numbed my limbs and chapped my lips. Painfully I got to my feet and skirted the wood. My own footsteps on the ground frightened me; I had the constant feeling that someone was walking behind me. I advanced cautiously, on tiptoe, as if afraid of waking the sleeping earth, and I listened, trying to fathom the darkness, for despite everything I had not yet lost hope of someone coming to relieve me. There was not a quiver, nor a breath, nor a glimmer, nor any definite shape in that eyeless and voiceless gloom. Yet twice I distinctly heard footsteps, and my heart pounded . . . But the sound moved away, gradually faded, and ceased, and the silence returned, yet heavier, more dreadful and more hopeless . . . A branch brushed my face; I recoiled, seized with terror. Some way ahead, a bump in the ground gave me the impression of a man, with his back hunched, creeping towards me. I loaded my gun . . . At the sight of an abandoned cart, with its two shafts raised in the sky, like some monster's menacing horns, my heart failed, and I almost fell backwards . . . I was afraid of the dark, the silence, the least object that projected above the line of the horizon and to which my crazed imagination attributed some stirring of sinister life . . . Despite the cold, great drops of sweat trickled down my skin. I conceived the idea of leaving my post and returning to camp, convincing myself, with canny and cowardly arguments, that my comrades had forgotten me and would be very happy to see me again . . . Of course, since I had not been relieved of my post, since I had not seen any sign of an officer, they must have left! But what if I happened to be wrong? What excuse would I give? And what reception would I get? Should I go to the farm, where my company had stopped that morning, and ask for information there? I considered it . . . But in my state of agitation I had lost my sense of direction, and I would surely have gone astray in this vast plain in pitch darkness . . . Then a terrible thought crossed my mind . . . Yes, why not shoot myself in the arm, and run away, bleeding and wounded, and say that I had been attacked by Prussians? I made a desperate effort to regain control of myself, to collect my wandering wits together. I gathered all the moral strength left in me to resist this despicable and odious suggestion, this accursed narcosis of fear, and I tried desperately to retrieve memories of the past, to conjure up gentle, smiling images, of sweet fragrance, with white wings . . . Images and memories came to me, as in some horrible dream – deformed, mutilated, hallucinated – and were immediately put to flight by terror . . . I thought of the Virgin of St-Michel, with her lovely pink complexion, and her blue mantle spangled with silver, and I saw her as a whore, on a bed in a brothel, prostituting herself to drunken soldiers. My favourite parts of the forest of Tourouvre, those quiet spots where I so loved to spend whole days lying on the moss, grew tangled and chaotic, with their giant trees bearing down on me. Then, there were shells flying through the air, with familiar, jeering faces; one of these projectiles suddenly spread huge, flame-coloured wings, circled, and enveloped me . . . I gave a shout . . . My God! Was I now going mad? I felt for my throat, my chest, my back, and legs . . . I must have been deathly pale, and I sensed a little chill, like a steel bore, travelling from heart to my brain . . . 'Come, come, now!' I said to myself out loud, to reassure myself that I was not asleep, that I existed . . . 'Come, come, now!' I downed the rest of the brandy in my flask in two swigs, and I started to walk very fast, trampling the clods of earth beneath my feet with a fury, whistling the tune of a soldiers' song that we would all sing together to relieve the tedium of our long marches. A little calmer, I returned to my oak tree and delivered a few hasty kicks against the trunk. I needed the noise and the movement . . . And then I thought of my father, all alone in the Priory. It was more than three weeks since I had received a letter from him. Ah, how sad and upsetting that last one had been! He made no complaints, but you could sense in it a deep dejection, a jadedness from being in that big empty house, and a dread at the knowledge that I was wandering about, with a knapsack on my back, exposed to the perils of battle . . .

Poor father! He had not been happy with my ailing and always irritable mother, who did not love him and could not bear to have him near her . . . And never, even under the worst rebuffs and unkindnesses, never a word of reproach! He submitted to it all, like a good dog, and went away! Oh, how I repented of not having loved him enough! Maybe he had not brought me up the way he should. But what did it matter? He did the best he could. He was shy and fearful in his goodness, with no experience of life and no power against evil. And as my father's features came back to me in the most minute detail, my mother's face grew hazy and dim, and I could no longer recall those beloved lineaments.

At that moment, all the love and affection I had given to my mother, I transferred to my father. I remembered, with a melting heart, when he took me on his lap the day my mother died and said to me, 'Perhaps it's for the best.' And now I understood all the past sorrows and dread of the future that were summed up in this phase. It was not for himself that he was speaking – poor man, he was resigned to enduring everything – but for her, and also for me, who was so like my mother . . . He had aged considerably in the last three years; his tall frame was getting stooped, his face, so ruddy with health, was turning yellow and wrinkled, and his hair was becoming almost white. He no longer lay in wait for the birds in the park, and he left the cats to roam among the creepers and lap at the water in the pond. He barely took any interest in his office, trusting in his chief clerk – who was robbing him – to run it for him. And he no longer bothered with his little tasks of local importance. He would not have gone out, nor stirred from his wing chair – which he had had brought down to the kitchen, not wanting to be left on his own – but for Marie, who brought him his cane and his hat.

'Come on, sir, you must shift yourself a bit. You're for ever stuck there in your corner . . .'

'Very well, Marie, I'll shift myself . . . I'll go down to the riverbank, if you like.'

'No, sir, you should go into the forest . . . The air there's better for you . . .'

'Very well, Marie, I'll go to the forest.'

Sometimes, seeing him dull and sleepy, she would tap him on the shoulder. 'Why don't you take your gun, sir? There are an awful lot of finches in the park.'

And my father, looking at her with air of reproach, would murmur, 'Finches! Poor creatures!'

Why did my father not write any more? Were my letters even reaching him? I reproached myself for having expressed such coldness in them until now, and I vowed to write the next day, as soon as I could, a long affectionate letter, in which I would give vent to all that I felt in my heart.

The sky was getting a bit brighter on the horizon, whose line, over there, was more clearly marked against the bluer light. It was still night, the fields remained in darkness, but you could sense that dawn was approaching. The cold became even more biting, the earth even firmer as it crunched underfoot, and the moisture crystallised on the branches of the trees. And gradually the sky was illumined with an intensifying, pale golden light. Slowly, shapes emerged, still vague and blurred, from the shadows. The opaque darkness of the plain turned to a dull purple, touched here and there with brightness . . . Suddenly, I heard a noise, faint at first, like the very distant roll of a drum . . . I listened, with my heart pounding . . . At one moment the noise stopped and some cocks crowed . . . After maybe ten minutes it started again, louder, clearer, and getting closer . . . Rub-a-dub! Rub-a-dub! It was a galloping horse, on the road from Chartres . . . Instinctively, I fastened my knapsack on my back, and checked that my gun was loaded . . . I was very nervous; the veins in my temples bulged . . .

66

Rub-a-dub! Rub-a-dub! Hardly did I have time to crouch down behind the oak, when a tall dark figure, suddenly coming to a halt twenty paces away from me, appeared standing in the road, like a bronze equestrian statue. And this enormous dark figure, almost all of it looming up against the background of the light in the east, was fearsome to behold! The man looked superhuman to me, hugely magnified against the sky!

He wore the flat cap of the Prussians, and a long black overcoat over a very barrelled chest. Was he an officer or an ordinary soldier? I do not know, for I could not see any badge of rank on his dark uniform . . . His features, indeterminate at first, became more defined. He had clear, very transparent eyes, a light beard, and a vigorously youthful bearing. His face exuded strength and goodness, and there was something noble, bold and sad about it that impressed me. With his hand laid flat on his thigh, he scanned the countryside around him, and from to time the horse pawed the ground with its hoof, and blew long jets of steam into the air through its quivering nostrils . . . Evidently the Prussian was there as a scout – he had come to check out our positions and the lie of the land. No doubt a whole army was massed behind this man, only awaiting a signal from him to hurl themselves into the plain! Well concealed in my thicket, motionless, with my gun at the ready, I examined him . . . He was truly handsome. The utmost vitality coursed through that robust body. What a pity! He was still viewing the countryside, and I could tell, I thought, that he viewed it more like a poet than a soldier . . . I caught a look of emotion in his eyes . . . Perhaps he had forgotten why he was there, and was allowing himself to be seduced by the beauty of that young, virginal and triumphant morning. The sky had turned very red. It blazed gloriously. The wakened fields stretched themselves, and emerged one after the other from their veils of pink and blue mist that drifted like long scarves gently shaken by invisible hands. All this pink and blue emanated from the slender trees and the tiny thatched cottages. The dovecote of a big farm, whose newly tiled roofs began to glisten, raised its whitish cone into the crimson conflagration of the east ... Yes, having started out with thoughts of massacre, this Prussian had stopped, dazzled and piously moved, before the splendour of the dawning day, and his soul was for a few moments vanquished by Love.

'Perhaps he's a poet,' I thought to myself, 'or an artist. He must be good; he shows feeling.'

And on his face I traced all of a decent fellow's feelings with which he was imbued, all the quivers, all the delicate, shifting reflections of his charmed, affected heart ... He no longer terrified me. On the contrary, I felt almost lightheadedly drawn to him, and I had to cling to my tree to stop myself from approaching the man. I wished I could speak to him and tell him it was good to contemplate the sky like that, and that I liked him for his enrapturement. But his face darkened, a mournfulness clouded his eyes ... Ah! the horizon they embraced was so distant, so distant! And beyond that horizon lay another, and beyond that, yet another! And all this was to be conquered! When would there ever be an end to urging his horse on and on across this emotive land, to continuously battling his way through the ruination of things and the deaths of men, to this ceaseless killing, to being always detested! And no doubt he thought, too, of what he had left behind: his house filled with the laughter of his children; his wife waiting for him, praying to God ... Would he ever see them again? I am convinced that at that very moment he was recalling the most ephemeral details, the most delightfully innocent rituals of his life back home ... a rose picked one evening after supper, with which he had adorned his wife's hair; the dress she was wearing when he left; a blue ribbon in his little girl's hat; a rocking horse; a tree; a stretch of river; a paper-knife ... Each blessed joy came back to mind, and with an exile's strength of vision, he embraced in a single despondent glance everything that had previously made him happy ... And the sun rose, further broadening the plain, further distancing the distant horizon ... I felt sorry for this man, and I loved him. Yes, I swear, I loved him! So, how did it happen? A shot rang out, and I glimpsed, through a puff of smoke, a boot in the air, the twisted flap of an overcoat, a streaming mane flying down the road, then nothing . . . and simultaneously I heard the clink of a sword, the thud of a body falling, the furious sound of galloping, then nothing . . . My weapon was hot, and there was smoke issuing from it . . . I dropped it . . . Was I the victim of an hallucination? No! Of the tall dark figure that had stood in the middle of the road like a bronze equestrian statue, there remained only a little black corpse, lying face down in the road with outspread arms . . . I remembered the poor cat that my father had killed, while it followed the flight of a butterfly through the air with an entranced gaze . . . Stupidly, thoughtlessly, I had killed a man – a man I loved, a man with whom my soul had just identified, a man who, in wonder at the rising sun, was entertaining the purest dreams of his life! I had perhaps killed this man at the precise moment when he was saying to himself, 'And when shall I ever return home again?' How? Why? After all, I loved him. After all, had soldiers threatened him, I would have defended him – the man that I had murdered! I rushed to his side . . . I called out to him. He did not stir . . . My bullet had gone through his neck, below his ear, and the blood was bubbling from a severed vein, spreading to form a red pool, already coating his beard . . . With trembling hands I gently lifted him. His head rolled, then fell back, inert and heavy. I felt his chest, where his heart was . . . his heart was no longer beating . . . Then I lifted him higher, with his head on my lap, and suddenly I saw his two eyes, two clear eyes, gazing at me sadly, without hatred, without reproach; two eyes that looked as if they were alive! I thought I was going to faint, but making a supreme effort to gather my strength I clasped the Prussian's body in my arms, stood it upright against me, and planting my lips on that bleeding face, streaming with crimson gore,

I kissed it, with desperation.

I do not have a very clear memory after that . . . I recall smoke, snow-covered plains, and burning ruins; constant, dismal routs, nightmarish marches in the dark; crushes in narrow cuttings clogged with munitions wagons, where dragoons, with their cavalry swords raised in the air, would urge their horses into our midst, trying to force their way past the wagons; and I recall death carts, full of young men's corpses that we buried at dawn in the frozen earth, telling ourselves that it would be our turn the next day. I recall big horse carcasses, lying stiffened and battered near the shell-shattered cannon mountings, on which we would fall in the evening, taking back into our tents red hunks that we devoured, grunting and baring our fangs, like wolves . . . ! And I recall the surgeon, operating on a farm table, by the light of a smoking lamp, with his tunic sleeves rolled up, and a pipe between his teeth, amputating the foot of a young soldier who still had his boots on! But most of all I recall the Priory, when one bright sunny day I arrived back there, very tired and weary, completely traumatised by these sufferings and bruised by the tribulations of defeat. The windows of the big house were closed and shuttered . . . A yet more stooped Felix was raking the drive, and Marie sat by the kitchen door, knitting a pair of socks, wagging her head.

'Well! Well!' I called out. 'What kind of a welcome is this?'

As soon as they saw me, Felix disappeared in seeming dismay, and Marie, very white-faced, gave a cry.

'What's wrong?' I asked with a heavy heart. 'Where's my father?'

The old woman kept staring at me. 'You mean to say, you don't know? You haven't received word? Ah, my poor Monsieur Jean . . . my poor Monsieur Jean!'

And with tear-filled eyes she lifted her arm in the direction of the cemetery.

'Yes, yes, that's where he is now, with madame,' she said in a dull voice.

CHAPTER THREE

Knock, knock, knock.

And simultaneously, a little seal-skin hat appeared in the half-open doorway, then two smiling eyes behind a veil, then a long fur coat hugging the slender body of a young woman.

'I'm not disturbing you, am I? Is it all right to come in?'

The artist Lirat looked up.

'Ah! It's you, madame!' he said in a curt, almost irritated voice, shaking his pastel-stained hands . . . 'But yes, of course . . . Do come in!'

He left his stool, offering her a seat.

'Charles is well?' he asked.

'Very well, thank you.'

She sat down, still smiling, and she really had a charming, sad smile. Despite the thin veil over them, her very big, clear, pink-blue eyes that lit up her whole being seemed to me infinitely gentle. She was very elegantly dressed, without straining for effect, although a little too heavily perfumed . . . There was a moment's silence.

Lirat's studio, in Faubourg St-Honoré, on a quiet estate called the Rodrigues estate, was an enormous bare room, with grey walls, bare beams, and no furniture. Lirat nicknamed it his barn – a barn indeed, with the north wind blowing through it, and rain coming in through little chinks in the roof. On two long white-wood tables lay boxes of pastels, notebooks, drawing-pads, fan-handles, Japanese picture-books, casts, a jumble of useless and outlandish objects. By a book cabinet covered with old newspapers, in one corner, were lots of boards, canvases, and pictures stacked face to the wall. A very broken-down sofa that made noises like an out-of-tune piano as soon as anyone attempted to sit on it, two rickety armchairs and a frameless mirror were the only luxury in that very bright studio. In winter, when he had a model, Lirat would light his little cast-iron stove with

71

rust-covered, wire-suspended piping that zigzagged across the room, cutting sharp angles, before disappearing through an oversized hole in the roof. Those days apart, without the heat from the stove even in the coldest weather, he relied instead on a filthy old astrakhan coat, a worn and shabby garment that he was always very ostentatious about wearing. Lirat took pride – a childish pride – in this spartan studio, and he paraded its bareness as other painters paraded their embroidered velvets and invariably antique wall-hangings. Indeed, he would have preferred it even more wretched; it vexed him that floor was boarded and not of beaten earth.

'It's here in my studio that I can tell who my real friends are,' he would often say. 'It's easy: they're the ones that come back; the others don't.'

Very few came back.

The young woman was prettily seated on her chair, slightly leaning forward, with her hands hidden in her muff. Now and again she pulled out an embroidered handkerchief that she slowly raised to her mouth, which I could not see because the more opaque border of her veil obscured it, but I could tell that it was very lovely, very red, exquisitely curved. All I could clearly distinguish of this elegant and delicate creature – who, despite the smile that made her so seductive, emanated a great air of propriety and even aloofness – were those wonderful eyes that rested on objects in the way of star-beams, and I followed her radiantly bright and caressing gaze as it travelled from floor to ceiling. The continued silence was unnerving. I thought I was the only reason for this constraint, and I was preparing to leave when Lirat cried out, 'Ah, forgive me! I'd forgotten ... Dear lady, allow me to introduce my friend Monsieur Jean Mintié.'

She acknowledged me with a gracious and winsome nod, and in a very soft voice that gave me a delicious thrill, she said, 'Delighted, sir ... but I'm already well acquainted with you.'

Very red-faced, I was stammering out a few embarrassed and foolish words, when Lirat cut in caustically.

'You're not by any chance suggesting that you've read his book?'

'I beg your pardon, Monsieur Lirat . . . I have read it . . . It's very good.'

'Yes, like my studio and my painting, you mean?'

'Oh no, not at all!'

She said this unhesitatingly, with a laugh that trilled through the room like the full-throated song of a bird.

It was a laugh I did not like. Although it had a bold and resounding quality, it rang false. I did not find it in keeping with the delicately sad expression on her face, and besides, it offended me, like an insult, in my admiration for Lirat's genius. I do not know why, but it would have pleased me if she had appreciated this neglected artist, if she had at that very moment displayed superior judgement, loftier sentiments than those of other women.

On the other hand, I was deeply shocked by the painter's scornful manner, his tone of bitter hostility. I resented this affected rudeness, this wilful, childish vulgarity that seemed to diminish him in my eyes. I was annoyed and very embarrassed. I tried to find something innocuous to talk about; I could not think of a single topic of conversation.

The young woman stood up. She strolled around the studio, stopped in front of a pile of pictures, examined two or three with an air of distaste.

'My God, Monsieur Lirat!' she said. 'Why do you insist on painting such ugly, peculiar-shaped women?'

'If I told you,' replied Lirat, 'you wouldn't understand.'

'Thank you! And when are you going to do my portrait?'

'You'll have to ask Monsieur Jacquet or a photographer to do that.'

'Monsieur Lirat?'

'Madame!'

'Do you know why I came here?'

'To flirt with me, I suppose.'

'In the first place! And besides that?'

'So, we're playing innocent little games, are we? That's very refined.'

'To ask you to come to dinner at my house on Friday. Will you?'

'You're very kind, dear lady, but Friday, as it happens, is totally impossible for me . . . It's my day at the Institute!'

'My, what a wit you are! Charles will be very disappointed by your refusal.'

'You'll convey my apologies, won't you?'

'So, goodbye, then, Monsieur Lirat . . . your place is freezing.'

As she passed in front of me, she held out her hand.

'Monsieur Mintié, I'm at home every day from five to seven . . . I should be delighted to see you . . . delighted.'

I bowed in thanks. And she was gone, leaving a little of the music of her voice in my ears; a little of the sweetness of her gaze in my eyes; and the strong scent of her hair, coat, muff and small handkerchief in the studio.

Lirat returned to his work without a word. I leafed through a book, without reading it, and the image of the young visitor kept flicking past on the pages as they turned. I certainly was not considering what impression she had made on me, nor whether she had made any impression at all; but although she was gone, she had not entirely departed. I was left with some vague remnant of that brief apparition, like a mist that had taken her form, in which I recognised the shape of her head, the line of her neck, the movement of her shoulders, the curve of her waist, and this remnant haunted me . . . I could see her where she had been sitting, indefinable and yet more attractive, with that tender luminous smile that radiated from her and gave her a halo of love.

'Who is that woman?' I said all of a sudden, trying to sound indifferent.

'Which woman?' said Lirat.

'The one who just left, for heaven's sake!'

'Ah, yes! Oh, God, she's a woman like any other.'

'I imagine so . . . That doesn't tell me what her name is or who she is . . .'

Lirat was searching through his box of pastels . . . He replied carelessly, 'So it interests you, does it, to know what

74

woman's name is? Strange thing to be curious about! Her name is Juliette Roux . . . As for any biographical information, I imagine the vice squad will provide you with as much as you like . . . I presume that Mademoiselle Juliette Roux gets up late, has a fortune-teller read her cards, is unfaithful, and is doing her best to ruin that poor blighter Charles Malterre, a decent young fellow that you've met here several times – she's his mistress, at the moment . . .In short, she's just like the rest of them, with the added nuisance of being prettier than most, and therefore sillier and more harmful . . . Take that sofa you're sitting on – it was Charles who destroyed it, by lying there, weeping, for days on end, sharing his woes with me, do you understand?

One day he caught her with a croupier from the club; another day, with a bit player from the Italian opera . . . There was also some story about a wrestler from Neuilly, to whom she gave twenty-five francs and an old pair of Charles' trousers. You see how romantic it is . . . I'm very fond of Malterre, because he's a good sort, and I'm touched by his foolishness . . . I felt truly sorry for him . . . But what can you say to people like that, for whom love is the big event of their lives, and who are incapable of seeing a woman's back without attaching imaginary wings to it, and sending it soaring among the stars? Nothing, don't you agree? Especially as the poor wretch, in the midst of his anger and tears, would take pride in the fact that Juliette had received a good education . . . He congratulated himself, as he twisted his arms in anguish, that it was no caretaker who had fathered her, but a doctor . . . And he would show you her letters, harping on about her correct spelling and elegant turn of phase . . . It was as if he were saying: 'Ah, I'm in such anguish, but it's so well written!' It's pitiful!'

'You just don't like women!' I cried, when he ended his tirade.

And foolishly I added, 'They must have made you very unhappy.'

Lirat shrugged his shoulders and smiled.

'You talk like Monsieur Delaunay of the Comédie

Française. No, my good friend, they haven't made me unhappy; I've seen others suffer, and that was enough for me . . . do you understand?'

Suddenly his voice rose and there was an almost savage gleam in his eyes. He went on: 'People like that, poor devils like Charles Malterre, get downtrodden, they disappear in the blood and mire, that terrible mire kneaded by a woman's hands – it's doubtless sad . . . Yet humanity doesn't protest – it's not been robbed of anything . . . They disappear and that's all there is to be said . . . But that artists, men of our kind, great souls and great minds should be ruined, crushed, drained, killed! Do you understand?'

His hand was trembling; he ground his crayon into the canvas.

'I've known three such men, three worthies, three divines . . . two hanged themselves, and the other, my master, is in a lunatic asylum, at Bicêtre! All that remains of that pure genius is a bundle of pale flesh, a kind of grotesque animal that grimaces and screams, and foams at the mouth! And among the legions of abortive talents, how many young hopes have died in the beast of prey's claws? Just count the number of pitiful, frightened cripples, who had once wings and now drag themselves along on their stumps; who now scratch the earth and eat their own filth! Only a moment ago you yourself were gazing ecstatically at that Juliette . . . you were prepared to do anything for a kiss from her . . . Don't deny it, I saw you . . . Oh, come on, let's go out . . . it's no good, I can't work any more.'

He got up and paced restlessly about the studio. Angrily waving his arms about, he overturned chairs and boxes, kicked his sketches to shreds. I thought he was going mad. His rolling eyes were bloodshot. He was completely pale and the words that came out of his twitching mouth sounded grating and jerky.

'What madness that men should be born of women! That men should be fashioned in those unchaste wombs! That men should gorge themselves on woman's depravity, on her idiotic hysteria, her ferocious appetites; that they should suck

76

the sap of life from her abominable breasts! The mother! Ah, yes, the mother! The mother-goddess, is she not? It's she who creates this race of sick and exhausted creatures that we are, who smothers the man in the child, and casts us, without tooth or nail, brutish and tamed, on to the mistress' divan and the wife's bed . . .

Lirat paused for a moment; he was choking. Then, bringing his hands together in the air and locking his clenched fingers round an imaginary neck, frantically, appallingly, he shouted, 'That's what we should do to every single one of them, every single one . . . do you understand? Eh? Tell me! Every single one of them!'

And he began pacing up and down again, swearing and stomping. But this last cry of anger had evidently given him relief.

'Come now, my dear Lirat,' I said to him, 'calm down. It's silly to get yourself so worked up – and for what, I ask you? After all, you're no woman . . .'

'It's true, actually, that you annoyed me with that Juliette . . . What business of yours was it, who she was?'

'Wasn't it natural that I should want to know the name of a person you introduced me to? And anyway, to be honest, until someone invents an alternative to a woman for producing children . . .'

'And anyway, I'm a bear,' said Lirat, interrupting me as he sat down, somewhat ashamed, at his easel, and in a completely pacified voice he asked, 'My dear Mintié, would help me with this sketch by posing for me? You don't mind? Just for ten minutes.'

Joseph Lirat was forty-two years old. I met him one evening by chance, I don't remember where. And although he was not usually forthcoming, and had the reputation of being misanthropic, unsociable and disagreeable, he immediately took a liking to me. Is it not disturbing to think that our best friendships, which ought to result from long deliberation, and the most important events in our lives, which only a logical chain of circumstances ought to give rise to, are mostly just the instant result of chance. You are at home in your study, sitting quietly in front of a book. Outside, the sky is grey, the air cold. It's raining, the wind is blowing, the street is dreary and muddy. Consequently, you have every good reason in the world not to stir from your armchair . . . Yet you go out, driven by boredom, the want of something to do, you know not what reason, nothing at all . . . and a hundred paces on, you've encountered the man, woman, carriage, stone, orange peel, puddle of water that is going to turn your existence upside down. In my most agonising distress, I have often thought of these things, and often I have said to myself with bitter regret, 'Yet if I had stayed at home, working, dreaming, or sleeping on the evening when I met Lirat in that forgotten place where I surely had no business to be, I might perhaps be the happiest man on earth today, and none of what has happened to me would ever have occurred.'

And in that moment of banal indecision, the moment when I must have wondered, indifferently, 'Now, shall I go out, or shan't I?' – was contained the most important act of my life; my entire destiny was decided in that brief moment, which has left no more trace in my memory than the gust of wind that blows down a house or uproots an oak leaves in the sky! I remember the most insignificant details of my life . . . For instance, I remember a blue velvet suit that laced up at the front, which I used to wear on Sundays when I was small; I could, yes, I swear, I could count the grease stains on Father Blanchetière's cassock, or the specks of snuff that he dropped on it when taking his pinch. Crazy and disconcerting though it is, by one of those hateful twists of irony underlying our ideals, our dreams and our sufferings, very often, even when I'm weeping, or gazing at the sea, or watching the sun set on the enchanted plain, I remember the ludicrous, big knobbly wart that old Lejars, who used to be our watchman, had on his nose, with four hairs sticking out of it that flies used to settle on . . . Well, try as I might to recapture that moment which determined my life, which cost me my peace of mind, my honour, and turned me into the likes of a mangy dog, try as I might to recover it, with the aid of physical pointers and mental impressions, I cannot retrieve it. So, there has occurred in my life a single – because all others follow from it – momentous event, and it completely escapes me! I don't know when it happened, where, in what circumstances, or for what reason . . . Therefore, what do I know of myself? What can men know of themselves if they are actually incapable of tracing the source of their actions? Nothing, nothing, nothing! And are those enigmas that are the workings of our brain and the manifestations of our so-called will to be accounted for by the operation of that blind and mysterious force known as human fate? But that is not at all the case.

I said that I met Lirat one evening by chance, I don't remember where, and that he immediately took a liking to me . . . He was the most singular of men . . . With his stern manner, his automaton-like and authoritative stiffness, that something official about his demeanour, at first approach he gave the impression of one of those marionettes – of an Orleanist, or a state official – of the kind made in debating societies for puppet-theatre courtrooms and academies. From a distance he really looked like one who dispensed medals, tobacconist licences, and awards for distinguished conduct. This impression quickly faded: you only had to listen, even for five minutes, to his conversation, which was outspoken, colourful, and abounding with unusual ideas, and above all to be subjected to his extraordinary, domineering gaze, which was elated and cold at the same time, a gaze to which everything was familiar, that drilled deep into you, against your will. I liked him a great deal, but there was no softness, no tenderness in my friendship towards him; I liked him with apprehension, unease, with the painful feeling that I was very small beside him, and, as it were, crushed by the greatness of his genius . . . I liked him the way one likes the sea, or a storm, the way one likes a huge force of nature. Lirat intimidated me. His presence paralysed the few intellectual resources within me, so fearful was I of letting slip some inanity that he would have mocked at. He was so hard, so ruthless with everyone. He was so well able to detect the ridiculous in artists and writers I judged infinitely superior to myself, and to fix on it with a shrewd, unforgettable and savage quip, that I found myself in a state of perpetual wariness, constant anxiety, towards him. I was always wondering, 'What does he think of me? What sarcastic gibes must I inspire in him?'

I had that feminine curiosity, which was obsessing me, to know his opinion of me. I tried, with remote hints, with absurdly coy remarks, with hypocritical circumlocutions, to surprise or provoke it out of him, and I suffered even more if he tossed me a curt compliment, as you would toss a coin to a beggar you want to get rid of – at least, that was how I imagined it. In short, I liked him dearly, I assure you, I was totally devoted to him, but there was an uncertainty in this affection and devotion that destroyed their charm. There was also a resentment that made them almost painful – resentment of my inferiority. Never, even in the heyday of our friendship, was I able to overcome this feeling of mean and timid pride. Never was I able to enjoy with peace of mind a relationship on which I set the very highest value. Yet Lirat was natural with me, often affectionate, sometimes paternal, and of his very few friends I was the only one whose company he would seek out.

Like all despisers of tradition, like all those who rebel against the prejudices of a hide-bound education, against the debilitating dictums of the Schools, Lirat was very much discussed – no, that's not the word – very much derided. It also has to be admitted that his free and lofty conception of art offended all established conventions, all prevailing ideas, and that his works, by their powerful execution, of remarkable skill whose virtuosity was not apparent, baffled lovers of the picturesque, of elegance, admittedly, of the cold correctness of Academy compositions.

The return of modern painting to the great Gothic art, that is what they could not forgive him. He had portrayed modern man, in his eager pursuit of enjoyment, as one damned to perdition, his body sapped by neuroses and his flesh racked by lust, ceaselessly panting in the grip of passion, which sinks its claws into his skin. In these figures, cast in vengeful postures, with monstrous protuberances discernible under their clothes, there was something so human, a plaint for infernal pleasure so heartrending, a self-abandonment so tragic that you felt shaken with terror before them.

This was not Love, as before, curly-haired, pomaded, and beribboned, swooning in the moonlight, with a rose between his teeth, strumming his guitar under balconies; this was Love smeared with blood, wallowing in the mire, Love in onanistic frenzy, accursed Love that leeches on to man and drains his veins, sucks outs his marrow, strips his bones of flesh.

And to intensify the horror of these characters, to increase the hopelessness of their impending doom, he put them in calm and pleasant surroundings of supreme brightness, pink and blue landscapes with softened distances, glories of sunlight, troughs of dazzling sea. Around them, Nature was resplendent in all the magic of her delicate and changing colours . . .

The first time he agreed to exhibit with a group of friends in an independent show, the critics, and the public that gives the critics their lead, howled with indignation. But their anger was of short duration – for there is a kind of nobility and generosity in anger – and they merely laughed. Before long, raised fists gave way to mockery, always the expression of the man in the street's opinion, in a stream of foul spittle. Then, they creased up in front of Lirat's superb works, clutching their sides with both hands. Some waggish wits left coins on the edge of the frames, as in the wooden bowl of some legless cripple, and this game – for it turned into a game for men of the best taste and best circles – was considered delightful. In the newspapers, in studios, drawing rooms, clubs and cafes, Lirat's name served as a term of comparison, as the obligatory yardstick whenever it came to describing something crazy, or a piece of trash. It even seemed that women – and young girls – could not mention this outcast's name without blushing. The end-of-year revues dragged it through the spew of their couplets; it was lampooned in cafe performances of vaudeville songs. Then, from these 'seats of Parisian intellectual life', it even descended on to the streets, where it was seen to blossom, like a common weed, on the mucky lips of coachmen, in the puckered mouths of gutter-snipes. 'Hey, Lirat, attaboy!' Poor Lirat really was riotously well known for a few years . . .

People tire of everything, even scandal. Paris is as quick to forsake the jumping jacks that it chooses to lionise, as the martyrs it vilifies. In its capricious desire for new toys, it does not long persevere in acclaiming its heroes or baying for its victims' blood. Now silence had befallen Lirat.

Only very rarely would an echo of the past turn up in the odd newspaper, in the form of some offensive anecdote. He decided, moreover, not to exhibit any more, saying, 'Just leave me alone! Is painting done to be seen? Eh? Tell me! Do you understand? It's work you do for yourself, for two or three friends, who are alive, and for a few other people you haven't met, who are dead . . . Poe, Baudelaire, Dostoevksy, Shakespeare . . . Shakespeare! Do you understand? The rest! Well, what about the rest? The rest is crap!'

Having had to restrict his needs to the bare minimum, he lived on little with admirable and touching dignity. As long as he earned enough to buy his brushes, paints and canvases, to pay his models and his landlord, and to go on a study trip every year, he did not ask for more. Money did not tempt him, and I am convinced that he did not seek success. But if success had come to him, I am also convinced that Lirat could not have resisted the very human joy of savouring its pernicious delights. Although he would not admit it, al-though he pretended gaily to thumb his nose at the injustice, he felt it more than another man might, and deep down it pained him bitterly. Just as the abuse had pained him, so too did the silence. Just once, some young critic published an enthusiastic and bombastic article about him in a widely read journal. Though very well meaning, the article was full of banalities and errors. You could tell that its author was not very familiar with matters of art and had no understanding of the great artist's talent.

'Have you read this?' cried Lirat. 'Have you read it, eh, tell me? What morons these critics are! If they go on talking about me, you'll see, I'll end up having to paint in a cellar, do you understand? Do they take me for some hack? And what business is it of this fellow's whether I paint, or make boots, or knit socks? That's my private life!'

Yet he carefully put away the article in a drawer, and several times I caught him rereading it . . . It was no use his saying with supreme detachment, when we raged against the stupidity of the public, 'Well, what can you expect? You think there should be a revolution because I use a light palette?' This scorn of fame, this apparent resignation masked a secret rancour. In the depths of this very affectionate and generous soul, tremendous hatreds had accumulated, leading to outbursts of terrible and malicious vehemence against everybody. If his talent had thereby gained in strength and asperity, his character had lost a little of its original nobility and his critical genius some of its acumen and lucidity. He was apt to indulge in outrageous disparagement that was in danger of making him unbearable; sometimes it was childishness nonsense, which made him slightly ridiculous. Great minds nearly always have some small weaknesses – it's a mysterious law of nature, and Lirat did not escape this law. Above all else he valued his well-established reputation for being a spiteful man. That his talent should be denied, he could very well live with, but any questioning of his capacity for making humanity tremble, with a tongue-lashing, was something he would never have tolerated. To take their revenge for the scathing words that Lirat branded them with, his enemies accused him of vices against nature; others simply said he was epileptic. And these gross and despicable slanders, bolstered every day by clever commentaries and kept alive with 'irrefutable' stories that went round the studios, found willing souls inclined to be wonderfully receptive to them, and to spread them abroad.

'You know Lirat? He had another attack yesterday, in the street this time.'

And the names of important people were cited, members

of the Institute who had witnessed the event and seen him with foam all over his face, rolling in the mud, barking.

I have to confess that when we first became acquainted I myself was very disturbed by all these accounts. I could not look at Lirat without immediately picturing the dreadful fits he was said to thrash about in. Falling victim to the illusion that obsession with an idea gives rise to, I often thought I detected in him symptoms of that horrible illness; I thought he turned ghastly pale all of a sudden, that his lips were fixed in a grimace, that his body was convulsed with an unholy spasm, that his eyes, wild-looking, rolled back and bloodshot, were shunning the light and seeking the darkness of deep holes, like the eyes of hunted beasts that are going to die. And I was sorry not to see him fall on the ground, yelling and writhing, there, in that studio full of his genius; there, before my avid gaze, as I watched him, hoping! Poor Lirat! And yet I was his friend!

The day was drawing to a close . . . All across Rodrigues, you could hear doors slamming, footsteps quickly hurrying away down the road; and in the studios, the sound of voices celebrating a good job finished. Since he had returned to his drawing, Lirat had only spoken to me to correct the pose I did not keep well enough to please him.

'Your leg further this way . . . Come on, a bit more! Don't hide your chest! I'm sorry, my dear Mintié, but you're useless as a model!'

He worked a little feverishly, a little breathlessly, incessantly chewing his moustache, occasionally swearing. His crayon worked on the canvas with a kind of anxious haste, an angry nervousness.

'Oh, blast!' he cried, kicking away his easel. 'I'm botching everything today! Damn me, you'd think I was competing for a medal of honour!'

Pushing back his chair, he examined his drawing with a look of irritation and grumbled, 'Whenever women come here, it's always the same old story . . . I think that when they go, women leave you with Boulanger's soul, in

Henner's pretty paw . . . Henner, do you understand? Let's go.'

As we were leaving the estate, I said, 'Come and have dinner with me, Lirat?'

'No,' he replied curtly, offering me his hand.

And he went off, stiff, formal, and solemn, with the business-like air of a MP who has just been discussing the budget.

That evening I did not go out and stayed at home, on my own, letting my thoughts roam. Lying on a divan, with my eyes half closed, my body made languid by the warmth, almost dozing, I liked to return to the past, to revive things that were dead, to drum up fugitive memories. Five years had passed since the war, the war in which I had begun to learn something of life through the dreadful trade of killing men . . . Five years already! Yet it seemed like only yesterday – the smoke, the plains covered with reddened snow and ruins, those plains on which, like ghosts of soldiers, we strayed pathetically, on our last legs . . . Only five years! And when I got back to the Priory, the house was empty, my father was dead!

My letters came only rarely, at long intervals, and they were always short, dry letters, hastily written on the corner of my rucksack. Just once, after that night of terrible anxiety, I had been tender, affectionate; just once, I had unburdened my heart, and that letter, which would have brought him some pleasure, hope and comfort, he had not received! Every morning, Marie had told me, he would go to the gate, one hour before the postman arrived, and wait, in a state of mortal apprehension, watching the bend in the road. Some old woodcutters would go by, on their way to the forest. My father called out to them, 'Hey, Ribot, old man, you haven't by any chance passed the postman?'

'By gum, no, M'sieur Mintié . . . It be still early yet . . .'

'Not at all, Ribot . . . He's late . . .'

'Very likely, M'sieur Mintié, very likely.'

When he caught sight of the postman's red cap and collar, he turned pale, his terror of bad news giving him a turn. As the postman drew nearer, my father's heart would be pounding fit to burst.

'Just the newspapers today, M'sieur Mintié!'

'What? Still no letters? You must be mistaken, my boy. Have a look . . . have a good look . . .'

He would make the postman search through his box, untie parcels, turn them over . . .

'Nothing! But it's incomprehensible!'

And he would return to the kitchen and sink into his armchair with a sigh.

'Imagine,' he would say to Marie, who would then offer him a bowl of milk, 'imagine, Marie, if his poor mother had been alive!'

During the day, he would visit people in town who had sons away at the war. Their conversations were always the same.

'Well, now? Have you had news of the lad?'

'No, M'sieur Mintié . . . And have you heard from Jean?'

'No, I've not heard anything either.'

'That's very strange indeed . . . Now, why is that? Do you understand?'

That they should get no letters, they only half wondered at, but that Monsieur Mintié, the mayor, should not receive any either greatly surprised them. They aired the most extraordinary speculations, and made astounding commentaries on the information provided in the newspaper; they consulted old soldiers, who described their campaigns in remarkable, fanciful detail. After a couple of hours they would part, their minds set at rest.

'Don't worry, sir . . . Your son's bound to come back a colonel.'

'A colonel! A colonel!' my father would say, shaking his head. 'That's more than I ask. If he would just come back . . .'

One day – no one ever knew how it came about – St-Michel found itself full of Prussian soldiers. The Priory was invaded; there were great big sabres trailing round our old home. After that, my father became even more poorly; he was stricken with a fever and confined to bed, and in his delirium he kept repeating, 'Harness the horses, Felix, harness the horses, because I'm going to go Alençon, to try to get news of Jean.' He imagined he was setting out, that he was on his way. 'Gee-up, Bichette, gee-up there! We'll have news of Jean this evening . . . Gee-up!' And my poor father quietly expired in the arms of Father Blanchetière, with Felix and Marie sobbing at his bedside!

After six months at the Priory, more now cheerless than it ever was, I was bored to death. Despite her devotedness, I found old Marie, used to the running the house to suit herself, insufferable. Her little quirks irritated me, and there were arguments every minute of the day, in which I did not always have the last word. For sole company, there was the good priest, who considered nothing so fine as the legal profession, and whose rambling sermons got on my nerves. From morning till night he would go on at me in the following manner:

'Your grandfather was a notary, and your father, and your uncles, and cousins, in fact your whole family . . . You owe it to yourself, my dear child, not to desert this post . . . You will be mayor of St-Michel, you can even hope to replace your poor father on the county council in few years' time . . . Good heavens, that's something, isn't it? And, I tell you, times are going to get fiendishly difficult for any decent folk that love the good Lord . . . You see that ruffian Lebecq is now on the town council . . . The scoundrel! He dreams only of pillage and murder . . . We need a right-thinking man, who supports religion and defends good principles, to lead this area . . . Paris! Paris! Oh, these hare-brained young people! But tell me, in heaven's name, what good did Paris do you? The air there is unhealthy! Look at the eldest Maugé boy . . . and he's from a good family . . . That didn't prevent him from coming home wearing a red beret . . . Now, that's a pretty state of affairs, isn't it?'

And so he went on, for hours on end, taking his snuff, waving the spectre of Maugé's red beret that seemed to him more to be feared than the devil's horns.

What could I do in St-Michel? There was no one with whom I could share my ideas, my dreams; no sanctum for ardent souls where I could give vent to this intellectual fervour, this urgent desire to know and to create, which the war had awakened in me while developing my muscles and strengthening my body, and which my passion for reading whipped up even more, every day. I realised that only Paris, which had so scared me in the past, could provide sustenance for the still ill-defined ambitions that tormented me, and once the estate was settled and the legal practice sold, I was suddenly off, leaving the Priory in the care of Felix and Marie . . . And then I was back in Paris!

In five years, what good has it done me, to use Father Blanchetière's expression? Swept along by vague enthusiasms and confused excitement mingling who knows what illusory art with who knows what impossible ministry, how have I fared? I am no longer the timid child scared away by footmen in a light-filled hallway. Though I may not have acquired much self-assurance, at least I know how to behave in society without appearing too ridiculous. I pass almost unnoticed, which is the best that a man like me, with none of the outward charms and qualities needed in order to shine, could hope for. Very often, I wonder what I am doing in this world that is not mine, where all that anyone respects are success, no matter how bogus, and money however nefariously come by; where every word spoken wounds me in what I hold most dear, in what I most admire. After all, is not man the same everywhere, with differences of upbringing evident only in his gestures, style of greeting, in a greater or lesser ease of manner! So, this is what they were – those proud artists, those wonderful writers, whose praises were sung, whose genius was celebrated – these appallingly ill mannered, petty, vulgar creatures, of ludicrous vanity, of ferocious jealousy, aping the worldly habits they deride; they, too, prostrating themselves before money; kneeling in the dust in adoration of acclaim, that old whore they so idolise . . . Oh, how I prefer cowherds and their cattle, swineherds and their swine – yes those plump, pink swine that go snuffling at the earth with their snouts, and whose fat, smooth backs reflect the passing clouds! I have read a huge amount, indiscriminately, unsystematically, and what is left in mind from this haphazard reading is nothing but a confusion of mangled facts and incomplete ideas that I am at a loss to make any sense of . . . I have tried to educate myself in every possible way, and I realise I am as ignorant today as I ever was . . . I have had mistresses I have loved for a week – sentimental and romantic blondes, fierce brunettes impatient of lovemaking – and all that love has shown me is the frightful void man's heart is, the deceitfulness of caresses, the illusoriness of the ideal, the emptiness of pleasure . . . Believing I had come upon art's definitive formula by which I was going to achieve my aspirations, to pin down alive, in words, my quivering dreams, I published a book which was highly praised and that sold well. Of course, I was flattered by this small success; I, too, flaunted it proudly, as though it were something rare; I, too, put on airs, the better to delude others. And wanting to delude myself, I have often looked at myself in the mirror at home, with an actor's complacency, to detect sure signs of genius in my eyes, on my forehead, in the majestic carriage of my head. Alas! success has rendered even more painful my deep-seated awareness of my own incapacity. My book is worthless, the style is tortured, the conception childish: in place of thought, it resorts to violent haranguing, absurd phraseology. Sometimes I reread passages that were applauded by the critics, and I find it all there – Herbert Spenser and Scribe, Jean-Jacques Rousseau and Commerson, Victor Hugo, Poe and Eugène Chavette. Of myself, whose name is displayed on the front of the book, on the yellow cover, I find nothing. Depending on the vagaries of my recollection, on the memories that have remained with me, I think someone else's thoughts, I write what someone else has written; I have no thought or style of my own. And important people whose taste is sound, whose judgement is law, have commended my personality, my originality, the unpredictability and sophistication of my feelings! How sad this is! What shall I do? Today, as yesterday, I do not know. I have this conviction that I cannot be a writer, for all the effort of which I was capable, I have put into this worthless, scrappy book . . . If only I had a very vulgar, very base ambition, ignoble desires, the only ones that leave no remorse: the love of money, of official honours, of debauchery! But no. Only one thing tempts me, which I shall never attain: talent. If I could say to myself, ah, if I could only say to myself, 'This book, this sonnet, this phrase are yours . . . you wrested them from your brain, imbued with your passion. It is entirely your thinking that quickens them, casting upon these heartrending pages pieces of your flesh, drops of your blood. Your nerves vibrate in them, like the strings of a violin under the bow of a divine musician. What you have written is great and beautiful!'

For that moment of supreme joy I would sacrifice my fortune, my health, my life . . . I would kill for it! And I shall never be able to say this to myself, never! Oh, the unperturbed serenity of mediocrities! Oh, their eternal self-satisfaction! How I have envied them! Now, I have these desperate urges to return to St-Michel. I would like to drive the plough through the brown furrow, to roll in the young alfalfa, to inhale the good smells of the cowsheds, and then, above all, to get lost − ah, to get lost − deep in the woods, far, far away, and ever further!

The fire had died and my lamp was smoking. A chill, as light as a caress, crept up my legs and raced across my back in delicious little shivers. I could hear no more noise from outside; the street had fallen silent. Not for a long time now had I heard any heavy omnibuses rumbling by. And the clock struck two.

But idleness kept me pinned to my divan. Stretched out like that, I enjoyed a sense of great physical well-being, amid great spiritual despondency. I had to make strenuous efforts to rouse myself from this lassitude and drag myself off to the bedroom. I could not sleep. I no sooner closed my eyes than I felt as if I were falling down a very deep black hole, and suddenly I woke, panting, with sweat on my brow. I lit my lamp again and tried to read . . . I could not fix my attention on the lines of the book, which kept slipping away, criss-crossing, performing a fantastic dance before my eyes.

'What a stupid life mine is!' I thought . . . 'Young people of my age laugh and sing, they're happy and carefree . . . So why am I like this, tormented by odious dreams? Who has placed in my heart this mortal affliction of boredom and dejection? Before them, lies a vast sunlit horizon, while I walk into darkness, constantly brought to standstill by a wall barring my way, against which I vainly bang my forehead and knees . . . Perhaps it's because they have love . . . Love, ah yes, if I only knew how to love!'

And I saw the beautiful virgin of St-Michel, the lustrous plaster virgin with her silver-spangled mantle and golden halo. All around her, stars, like celestial flowers, turned and dipped, and doves, made jubilant with prayers, flew about, brushing her with their wings . . . I remembered the ecstasies, the transports of mystical adoration by which she used to enrapture me, and all the sweet joy I felt in mere contemplation of her. Did she not also speak to me there, in the chapel? And was not that unuttered language – a language that instilled my childish heart with ineffable tenderness, a language more harmonious than the voice of angels and the song of golden harps, more fragrant than the scent of roses – the divine language of love? As I listened, with all my senses, to this language that was music, I was translated into a wonderful unknown world; an enchanting new life sprang up, burgeoned, and flourished around me. The horizon retreated to the infinite bounds of mystery; the heavens were as brilliant as the heart of a sun, and I myself felt so big and strong I gathered to my breast in a single embrace all the creatures, flowers and skies of this paradise born of a loving gaze that had passed between a plaster virgin and a small child.

'Dear Virgin,' I cried, 'speak to me, speak to me again as you once spoke to me in the chapel. And restore love to me, since love is life, and not being able to love any more is killing me.'

But the Virgin no longer heard me. She came creeping into my bedroom, curtseying, climbed on the chairs and rummaged in the cupboards and drawers, singing strange melodies. A seal-skin hat now replaced her golden halo, and her eyes were those of Juliette Roux, very lovely, soft eyes, in a plaster face behind a thin veil, that smiled at me. From time to time she came up to my bed and dangled her strongly scented, embroidered handkerchief over me.

'Monsieur Mintié,' she said, 'I am at home every day from five to seven . . . And I should be delighted to see you . . . delighted!'

'Dear Virgin,' I implored again, 'speak to me, I beg of you, speak to me as you used to in the chapel.'

'Tee, tee, tee, tee,' hummed the Virgin, who began slowly to spin round as though dancing a waltz, with her head tipped back on her shoulders, holding out her silver-spangled mantle with the tips of her slender beringed fingers, and causing her lilac gown to flare out.

'Blessed Virgin,' I repeated, with some annoyance in my voice, 'speak to me, will you?'

She stopped, planted herself in front of me, and one by one let fall her plaster garments. Completely naked, shameless and magnificent, with a rapid, clear, deep laugh purling in her throat, she said, 'Monsieur Mintié, I am at home every day from five to seven . . . And I shall give you Charles' old pair of trousers.'

And she threw her seal-skin hat in my face.

I sat bolt upright in bed . . . With staring eyes and a wheezing chest, I looked around. But the room was quiet, the lamp continued to burn melancholically, and my book was lying on the carpet with its pages open.

I woke late the next day, having slept badly, pursued in my nightmare-broken sleep by the thought of Juliette. During this troubled and feverish latter part of the night, she had not left me for a moment, taking on the most outrageous forms, yielding to the most disgraceful caprices, and in the morning there she was again, this time just as she was when I met her the day before at Lirat's studio, with her air of decorum, her discreet and charming manners. I even felt a sense of sadness – no, not sadness, regret, the regret you feel at the sight of a rose-bush with all its roses faded and its petals strewn on the muddy ground – for I could not think of Juliette without at the same time thinking of Lirat's poisonous remarks:

'There was also some story of a wrestler from Neuilly, to whom she gave twenty francs . . . '

What a pity! When she came into the studio, I would have sworn she was the most virtuous of women . . . Even her manner of walking, greeting, smiling, and sitting spoke of a good upbringing, a quiet and happy life, free of any nasty impatience, unsullied by remorse. Her hat, coat, dress – all of her attire was of a quiet subtle elegance calculated to make one man happy, to bring joy to a house firmly locked and barred against those in pursuit of unchaste quarry . . . And those eyes, so filled with sanctioned tenderness, shining with such candour and ingenuousness, seemingly ignorant of deceit – those eyes, lovelier than moon-reflecting lakes!

'Charles is well?' Lirat had asked . . .

Charles? Her husband, for heaven's sake! And naively, I pictured to myself a respectable domestic scene, with pretty children playing on the carpets, a familial lamp and good honest souls gathered round its soft light, a modest bed under the protection of a crucifix and a blessed palm-leaf! All of a sudden this tranquillity was invaded by the bit player from the Italian opera, the club croupier and Charles Malterre, who had destroyed Lirat's divan by thrashing about on it, weeping with rage! I imagined the actor's appearance, a pale, lined, clean-shaven face, red-rimmed, impudent eyes, lubricious lips, a very open collar, a pink tie, a sordidly creased short jacket . . . I was edgy, irritable . . . What did I care, after all? Was this woman's life any concern of mine, or anything to do with me? Was I in the habit of getting emotionally involved in the fate of young women that chanced to cross my path? Let Mademoiselle Juliette Roux be whatever she pleased! She was not my sister, or fiancée, or friend; she was in no way connected with me . . . After my brief glimpse of her yesterday, as of some passer-by in the street, one of the countless obscure individuals we brush past every day, who are gone, and forgotten, she had already returned to the great vortex of oblivion . . .and I would never see her again . . . 'What if Lirat were mistaken?' I said to myself during lunch. I was familiar with his exaggerations, his need to be spiteful, his horror and scorn of women. What he said about Juliette, he said of all the others. Yes, perhaps the actor, the croupier, all the details of that debauched life, which had gratified his bitter zest, existed only in his imagination. And Charles Malterre?

Of course, I would have preferred that she had been married. It would have pleased me if she had been able to take the arm of a man freely, respected and envied by the most righteous! But she loved this fellow Malterre; she lived with him, decently; she was devoted to him. 'Charles will be very disappointed by your refusal.' The almost suppliant tone in which she had uttered these words lingered in my ears. So she worried about what might please or displease Malterre . . . And at the thought that Lirat, with his misrepresention of the situation, was slandering her shamefully, I felt sad at heart, a great sense of pity came over me, I caught myself saying out loud, 'Poor girl!'

Yet Malterre had thrashed about on the divan, he had wept and confided in Lirat, and shown him her letters . . . So what? Was I acquainted with this woman? What did it matter whether she had had every singer, croupier and wrestler in town . . . To hell with it! And I went out, humming a cheerful tune, with the relaxed air of a fellow without a care on his mind. And why not, I ask you?

I sauntered along the boulevards, stopping in front of shops. Despite the sun, a still mist-imbued December's pale niggardly smile, there was a keen chill in the air. Women walked by, on the pavement, wrapped up against the cold in long seal-skin coats, some wearing little fur hats like Juliette's, and every time I took an interest in the coat and hat. I looked at them with genuine pleasure, I liked to follow them with my gaze until they had disappeared into the crowd. At the corner of rue Taitbout, I recall, I passed an attractive, tall, slender woman who looked like Juliette, so much so that I raised my hand to my hat, about to greet her. I felt a stir of emotion – oh, it wasn't a violent heart-wrench of the kind that stops your breath, bursts your veins and makes your head swim. It was a flicker, a caress, something very gentle, to bring a smile to your lips, a brightness to your eyes . . . But that woman was not Juliette . . . I felt a kind of resentment, and I took my revenge by deeming her extremely ugly . . .

Two o'clock already! How about going to see Lirat? What was the point? To get him to talk about Juliette, to make him confess he had lied to me, and have him tell me some poignant and sublime things about her, touching stories of devotion and self-sacrifice . . . I was tempted by that . . . On reflection, I thought that Lirat would get annoyed, that he would laugh at me, and at her, and I dreaded his sarcasm; I could already hear the lurid comments, the beastly remarks hissed from the twisted corner of his mouth . . .

In the Champs-Elysées I hailed a cab to take me to the Bois de Boulogne . . . Why should I hide it? I hoped to run into Juliette there . . . That is indeed what I hoped, and at the same time feared. I felt it would be a disappointment not to see her; but I also felt that I would be upset if she regularly flaunted herself, like other young ladies, in this lovers' market-place, and I did not know which got the better of me – the hope of seeing her, or fear of meeting her . . .

There were not many people at the Bois. In the broad allée du Lac, the carriages moved at a walk, at quite some distance from each other, with their coachmen high on their boxes. Sometimes a brougham would leave the strung-out procession, turn round and disappear, as its horses trotted off, carrying away, the devil knows where, a woman's profile, faces that were all white and pale, snatches of shockingly bright fabric, all rapidly glimpsed through the window in the carriage-door. The pulse of my chest and temples quickened, my fingertips tingled with impatience. From looking in the same direction all the time, peering into the darkness of the carriages, my neck was strained and aching. I anxiously chewed on a cigar that I was reluctant to light for fear of letting a carriage go by that she might have been in . . . At one point I thought I had seen her in the back of a brougham travelling in the opposite direction to that of my cab.

'Turn round, turn round,' I shouted to the cabman, 'and follow that brougham.'

It did not occur to me that this was very inconsiderate behaviour towards a woman I happened to have been introduced to the day before, and whose name I desperately wanted to clear.

Half hanging out of the door over the lowered window, I did not lose sight of the vehicle. And I said to myself, 'She may have recognised me . . . she may stop, climb out, make an appearance.' Yes, I said this to myself without crediting myself with the slightest thought of making a libertine conquest. I said this to myself as if it had been something quite simple and natural . . . The brougham sped on, brisk and light, bouncing on its springs, and the cab was having difficulty in following it.

'Faster!' I commanded. 'Go faster and overtake it!'

The cabman whipped his horse, and it broke into a gallop, and in a few seconds the two vehicles were wheel to wheel, touching each other. Then a woman's head appeared at the window, her hair dishevelled beneath a very large hat, with a quaintly turned-up nose, and her lips, smeared with rouge, bleeding like an open wound. With a scornful glance she took stock of the coachman, the cab, the horse and myself, stuck out her tongue, and settled back into a corner of her carriage. It was not Juliette! I did not get home until nightfall, very disappointed and yet delighted with my fruitless outing!

I had no plans for the evening. However, I spent longer than usual getting dressed. I took extreme care over my turnout, and for the first time ever the knot in my tie seemed a serious matter. I willingly became engrossed in getting it right. This surprise revelation led to others of even greater importance. So it was that I noticed my shirts were badly cut; that my shirt-front bagged awkwardly in the neck-opening of my jacket; that the style of my suit had taken on an old-fashioned, strangely outdated look. In short, I found myself quite ridiculous, and vowed to do something about this in future. Without turning elegance into a tyrannical obligation that ruled my life, I think I was entitled to be like everyone else. Just because a fellow was well dressed did not necessarily mean he was a fool.

These reflections brought me to dinner time. Usually I ate at home, but that evening I found my apartment too small, too dismal; it was oppressive, and I needed space, noise, gaiety.

At the restaurant I took an interest in everything, in the to-and-fro of people, the gilt mouldings on the ceiling, the large mirrors reflecting to infinity the rooms, waiters, globes of light, flowered hats, the buffet with dressed meats laid out on it, and red and golden pyramids of fruit standing among the decorative foliage and sparkling crystal. I observed the women especially: I studied their somewhat ethereal way of eating, their flirtatious glances, the movement of their un-gloved arms that heavy bracelets encircled with gold and bright sparkles, the fine delicate flesh at the neck disappearing into their bodices, beneath a pale-pink covering of lace. All this delighted me, fascinated me, like some completely new thing, like the suddenly glimpsed landscape of a distant country. I felt the kind of wonder that a very young man experiences. Although of a melancholy turn of mind, which led me to place greater importance on a human being's inward, spiritual life, thereby branding him or her with ugliness or suffering, at that moment, on the contrary, I yielded to the pleasure of unreserved enjoyment of pure physical attractions: I feasted my gaze on the charms a beautiful woman expresses. Even in the ugliest of women I discovered something about the angle of her neck, a languishing look, a softness of the hands, no matter what, that satisfied me, and I reproached myself for having so badly organised my life till then, for having kept myself confined in unsociable isolation, in a dreary and gloomy apartment – in short, for not having lived, when Paris offered me at every step pleasures so easy to take and so sweet to savour.

'Monsieur is perhaps waiting for someone?' asked the waiter.

Waiting? No, I wasn't waiting for anyone. The restaurant door opened and I quickly looked round. I then realised why the waiter had asked me that question. Every time the door opened, I had been hastily turning round like that, and anxiously scanning the faces of the people that came in, as if indeed I knew that someone was supposed to arrive, and I was waiting for that person ... Someone! And just whom would I have been waiting for?

I very rarely went to the theatre; there had to be some occasion for it, some obligation, or impelling reason to go. I do believe that, left to myself, it would not have occurred to me to set foot there ... I even affected a lofty disdain for literature that hawks itself in these bazaars of mediocrity.

Since I regarded the theatre not as a futile distraction but a serious art, it offended me to see there, in plots that were always alike, human passion squawking out the same old sentimental romance, and mirth, plastered with make-up, descending into the same old vulgar buffoonery. I thought of a playwright, however celebrated, as one who had gone astray; he was to the poet what the unfrocked is to the priest, the deserter to the soldier. And I often bore in mind something that Lirat had said, of remarkable conciseness, of profound discrimination. We had been to the funeral of the great painter M; the famous dramatist, D, was chief mourner, and at the cemetery he delivered a speech. This surprised no one. Were M and D not equally renowned? When the ceremony was over, Lirat took my arm and we walked back through Paris, feeling very sad. Seemingly lost in sorrowful thought, Lirat remained silent. Suddenly he stopped, crossed his arms, and swinging his head in that comically serious way that he has, he exclaimed, 'But what the devil was D doing there, eh?' And he was right. What indeed? Were they of the same breed, and were they destined for the same glory – the proud artist with his grand ideas, his immortal works, and the other fellow, whose sole aspiration was to amuse an audience of bloated bourgeois upstarts for an evening with his insipid nonsense. Yes, indeed, what was he doing there?

How far from my mind were such peevish sentiments when, having sauntered down the boulevards after dinner, rejoicing in a sense of physical well-being that put a special lightness and spring in my step, I took my seat in the auditorium of the Théâtre des Variétés, where a musical opera that was enjoying great success was playing. With my face deliciously atingle from the cold air outside, and my heart entirely won over to universal indulgence, I felt genuinely gratified. By what? I did not know, and I didn't much care, not being in the mood to indulge in psychological investigations of myself.

As it happened, I had arrived during an interval, and the lobbies were thronged with a very elegant crowd. I gave my coat to the cloakroom attendant, and then made a tour of the ground-floor boxes, with the same sweet impatience, the same thrilling anxiety I had already experienced at the Bois; and I went upstairs to continue my thorough search of the boxes.

'Why wouldn't she be here?' I thought.

Every time I was unable to get a clear view of a woman's face, either because she was leaning forward, or because she was lost in shadow, or hidden behind a fan, I said to myself, 'It's Juliette!'

And every time, it was not Juliette.

The play amused me. I laughed aloud at the inept jokes that constituted the spirit of the piece: all this dull piffle, all this crass vulgarity enchanted me, and in all seriousness I detected in it an irony that was not devoid of literary merit. I was moved by the love scenes. During the last interval I met a young man I hardly knew. Pleased to have someone on whom I could unburden myself of the infectious banalities building up inside me, I latched on to him.

'Terrific play!' he said. 'Staggeringly good, old boy.'

'Yes, it's not bad.'

'Not bad! Not bad! But it's a masterpiece, old boy, a

terrific masterpiece. What I like best is the second act . . . There's a scene there . . . no, really . . . a tremendous scene! It's high comedy, you know! And the costumes! And that Judie! Ah, that Judie!'

And he slapped his thigh and clicked his tongue.

'I don't half fancy her, old boy! It's terrific!'

And so we discussed the merits of the various acts, scenes, and players . . . Just as we were about to part company, 'Tell me,' I asked him, 'you wouldn't know a certain Juliette Roux?'

'Now, wait a minute! Absolutely! A little brunette, very chic? No, I'm confusing her with someone else . . . Now, wait a minute . . . Juliette Roux! Don't know her!'

An hour later I was sitting over a soda-water at the Café de la Paix, where the finest specimens of fashionable society were wont to gather after leaving the theatre. Many women came in and out, brassy, showy creatures, plastered with a layer of rice powder, their lips freshly daubed with rouge. At the table next to mine a prematurely aged little blonde was very animatedly recounting heaven knows what in a voice husky with dissipation; another brunette further off was simpering with comically foolish grandeur, wielding her fan with the same hand that had once shovelled dung in the farmyard, while the man with her sat slumped in his chair, with his hat slightly tipped back and his legs spread apart, doggedly sucking on the handle of his cane. An unconquerable wave of nausea rose to my lips. I was ashamed to be there, and I drew comparison between the ridiculous, loud appearance of these women and sweet Juliette's very restrained manner, back there in Lirat's studio. These piercing or raucous voices made even more soothing the freshnesss of hers, of the voice I could still hear, saying, 'Delighted, sir . . . But I'm already well acquainted with you.'

I stood up . . .

'What a bastard, though, that Lirat is!' I cried to myself as I climbed into bed, furious that he should have spoken the way he did of a woman I had failed to encounter in the street, at the Bois, the restaurant, the theatre, or late-night bar.

CHAPTER FOUR

'Madame Juliette Roux?'

'Would you like to come in, sir?' said the maid.

Without asking my name, without waiting for a response, she led me through a small, very dark hall into a room where all I could make out at first was a lamp under its large pink shade, burning with a soft glow in one corner. The maid turned up the lamp, and carried off a seal-skin coat that lay tossed on a divan.

'I'll let madame know you're here,' she said.

And she disappeared, leaving me on my own.

So, I was at her house! For the past week, the thought of this visit had been tormenting me ... I had no plan, no scheme, I wanted to see Juliette, that was all. Something in the nature of a very keen curiosity, which I did not analyse, attracted me to her ... I had come to rue St-Petersburg several times with the firm intention of calling on her, but at the last minute my courage failed me and I had left without bringing myself to cross the threshold of her building ... Now I was the most embarrassed man in the world and deeply regretted my foolishness, for foolishness it was, obviously ... How would she receive me? What would I say to her? She had certainly invited me to come ... Would she remember me? What worried me most was that, no matter how much I racked my brains, I could not think of a single phrase or word to open the conversation when Juliette appeared! How ridiculous, if I was going to remain open-mouthed, at a loss for something to say! I examined the room where Juliette was soon going to appear. It was a dressing room that also served as a sitting room. The impression I had of it was unpleasant. The wash-stand, nakedly displayed, with its two bowls of cracked pink glass, shocked me. The walls and ceiling, hung with garish red satin, the embroidered plush furniture, the elaborate door-curtains, the very expensive and very ugly knick-knacks set out here and there on the furniture, odd tables that served no purpose, consoles laden with heavy ornaments – all this revealed a vulgarity of taste. I noticed a terracotta Cupid, occupying the middle of the mantelpiece, between two massive onyx vases; with its chest thrown out, and a humorously pouting smile, it held out a flower with the tips of its outspread fingers. Every detail revealed, here, a love of expensive and gross luxury and, there, a regrettable inclination towards romance and infantile mawkishness. It was both deplorable and sentimental. Yet – and this pleased me – there was not the jumble, ephemerality, and mismatchment to be found in the apartments of young women of easy virtue, those apartments where you sense a wild lifestyle, where from the number of accumulated knick-knacks you can count the number of lovers who have passed through there, lovers for a hour, a night, a year; where every chair cries out to you of shamelessness and betrayal; where you can see on a windowpane the anguish of a love affair, on a piece of marble the still-warm traces of a tear, on a chandelier the still-warm traces of blood . . .

The door opened and Juliette appeared, all in white, in a long floating gown. I was trembling . . . my face flushed . . . but she recognised me, and smiling the smile I was at last seeing again, she held out her hand.

'Ah, Monsieur Mintié, how kind of you not to have forgotten me. Is it long since you last saw that strange fellow Lirat?'

'Yes, madame, I've not seen him since the day I had the honour of meeting you at his studio . . .'

'My God! I thought you two were inseparable . . .'

'It's true,' I replied, 'that I see a lot of him, but I've been working every day.'

Thinking that I had detected a note of irony in her tone of voice, I added defiantly, 'A great artist, don't you agree?'

Juliette let this comment pass.

'So, are you still working?' she went on. 'Actually, I've been told that you live a truly monkish existence . . . The fact is that we don't see you anywhere, Monsieur Mintié.'

The conversation took a extremely trite turn; it was

mostly about the theatre. She was amazed, slightly outraged, at something I said.

'What, you don't like the theatre? Is that possible, and you an artist? I adore it . . . it's such fun! Imagine, we're going to the Variétés this evening, for the third time . . .'

There was a faint yapping sound at the door.

'Oh, my God!' cried Juliette, hastily jumping up. 'I left Spy in the bedroom! I must introduce you to Spy, Monsieur Mintié . . . you don't know my little Spy?'

She opened the door, and flung aside the door-curtain.

'Come on, Spy!' she said in a cooing voice. 'Where are you, Spy? Poor Spy, come in . . .'

And I saw a tiny animal with a pointed muzzle and long ears enter the room, dancing on fragile legs, like spider's legs, its entire body, thin and pigeon-chested, shivering, as if with a fever. Tied round its neck was a red silk ribbon carefully knotted in a bow on the side.

'Come on, now, Spy, say hello to Monsieur Mintié!'

Spy turned his stupid, cruel and bulging round eyes towards me, and barked viciously.

'Well done, Spy . . . Now give your paw . . . will you please give your paw, Spy . . . will you please?

Juliette had bent down and was wagging her finger sternly at him. Spy eventually put his paw in his mistress' hand and she picked him up, stroked and kissed him.

'Oh, what a darling! Good dog! Oh, sweet darling little Spy!'

She sat down again, still holding the dog in her arms like a child, rubbing her cheek against the ghastly creature's muzzle, whispering sweet endearments in its ears.

'Now, show that you're happy, Spy . . . show your little mama . . .'

Spy barked again, then he came and licked Juliette's lips, and she succumbed with delight to these odious caresses.

'Ah, how sweet you are, Spy! Yes, you're very, very sweet!'

And turning to me, who felt completely forgotten since Spy's tiresome arrival, she suddenly asked me, 'Do you like dogs, Monsieur Mintié?'

'Very much, madame,' I replied.

Then she told me, in extravagant, childish detail, the story of Spy, of his habits, demands, and comic behaviour, of the rows he had caused with the concierge, who could not stand him.

'But it's when he goes to sleep that you should see him,' she said. 'Do you know, he has a bed, with sheets and an eiderdown, like a real person ... I tuck him up every evening ... And his little black head looks so funny lying there ... You're very, very cute, aren't you, Monsieur Spy?'

Spy chose a more comfortable spot on Juliette's gown, and having turned round and round, he curled up in a ball, disappearing almost entirely in the silky folds of the fabric.

'That's right ... Beddy-byes, Spy, beddy-byes, my little darling!'

During this long conversation with Spy, I had been free to study Juliette at my leisure ... She was really very beautiful, even more beautiful than I had imagined her under that veil. Her face was truly radiant. It had such freshness, such dawn-like brightness that the air around was all illuminated by it. When she turned away or bent down, I saw her very black and heavy hair hanging down over her robe in one enormous plait that somehow made her youthfulness even more virginal and girlish. There seemed to be a wilful crease across the middle of her forehead, at the roots of her hair, but it was only visible in a certain light, and its harshness was tempered by the sparkling sweetness of her eyes, the exceptional kindness of her mouth. You could sense, under that loose garment, the arching of a body that was lithe and supple, a body of passionate sinuousness, of powerful embraces. What especially enchanted me were her hands, thin deft hands of surprising nimbleness, whose every movement, whether in anger or indifference, was a caress. I would have been hard pressed to give a clear opinion of her. There was in this woman a mixture of innocence and sensuality, of astuteness and folly, of kindness and spite that disconcerted me. Strangely enough, at one point, I saw the horrible image of the Italian opera singer take shape beside her. And this image formed, as it were, Juliette's shadow. Far from vanishing, as I watched it the image assumed a kind of corporal substance. It grimaced, and twirled, and leapt about in disgusting contortions. Its vile and obscene lips pursed themselves at Juliette, who drew it towards her, and her hand buried itself in the image's hair and ran, trembling, down the length of its body, happy to defile itself with this foul touching. And the unspeakable wretch undressed Juliette, and displayed her to me enraptured in the execrable magnificence of sin . . . I had to close my eyes, to make strenuous efforts to dispel this horrible vision, and once the image had faded, Juliette immediately recovered her enigmatic and guile expression of tenderness.

'And you must come back and see me often, very often,' she said, showing me out, while Spy, who had followed her into the hall, barked and danced on his fragile spider legs.

As soon as I was outside, I felt a sudden return of violent affection for Lirat, and reproaching myself for my coolness towards him, I resolved to go and ask him to dine with me that very evening. On the way from rue St-Petersburg to boulevard de Courcelles, where Lirat lived, my reflections were galling. My visit had disillusioned me, I was no longer under the spell of a dream, and I was rapidly returning to dreary reality, to the inexistence of love. What I had imagined about Juliette was very vague . . . Fired by her beauty, I had mentally credited her with moral qualities, with intellectual superiorities I did not define and that I fancied to be extraordinary. Moreover, Lirat, by groundlessly imputing to her a shameful existence and indecent tastes, had made a veritable martyr of her, and my heart had gone out to her. Taking this madness even further, I thought that by an irresistible sympathy she would confide in me her troubles, the solemn and painful secrets of her soul; I saw myself already consoling her, talking to her of duty, virtue and resignation. In short, I was expecting a series of impressive and affecting things . . . Instead of this poetic vision, I found a ghastly dog that barked at my legs, and a woman just like any other, with no brain, no ideas, solely engaged in pleasure, the limit of whose desires was the Théâtre des Variétés and the caresses of her Spy. Her Spy! Hah! That ridiculous animal that she showered with affection and spoke to in language worthy of a concierge! And as I walked, I kicked out at an imaginary Spy and said in a parody of Juliette's voice, 'Oh, there now, darling! Oh, good dog! Oh, sweet darling little Spy!' Must I admit it, I also felt resentful that she had not said a word to me about my book. That no one spoke to me about it in normal life was of very little concern to me; but a compliment from her would have delighted me! I had hoped to learn that she had felt moved at one page, indignant at another. And nothing! Not the slightest allusion! Yet, I recalled, I had artfully given her the opportunity for this ... politeness.

'There's no doubt about it, she's no better than she should be!' I exclaimed to myself, as I rang at Lirat's door.

Lirat greeted me with open arms.

'Ah, my dear young Mintié,' he exclaimed, 'how very decent of you to come for dinner ... You've picked the right day, let me tell you ... we have cabbage soup.'

He rubbed his hands and seemed very happy ... He wanted to take my coat and hat, and leading me into the little room that served him as a sitting room, he repeated, 'My dear young Mintié, I'm very pleased to see you ... Will you come to the studio tomorrow?'

'Certainly.'

'Well, then, you'll see! You'll see! First of all, I've given up painting, do you understand?'

'You're going to become a businessman?'

'Listen ... Painting is a joke, my dear Mintié.'

He grew animated, paced about the room, waving his arms.

'Giotto! Mantegna! Velasquez! Rembrandt! Well, what about Rembrandt? Watteau! Delacroix! Ingres! Yes, and so what? No, it's not authentic. Painting translates nothing, expresses nothing, it's a joke! It's good for art critics and bankers, and for generals who have their portraits done, on horseback, with a shell exploding in the foreground ... But a patch of sky, the shade of a flower, the rippling of water, the air . . . do you understand? The air! All of impalpable, invisible nature . . . with oils! With oils?'

Lirat shrugged his shoulders.

'With oils that come out of tubes, oils made by the dirty hands of chemists, thick, heavy oil-paint, which sticks to your fingers like jam! Now, I ask you . . . painting . . . what a joke! No really, admit it, my dear Mintié, what a joke! Drawing, etching . . . two colours . . . that's the thing! There's no trickery in it, it's honest . . . besides, art lovers don't care for it seriously, and don't come bothering you . . . it sets no fireworks off in their drawing rooms! Real art, majestic art, artistic art . . . is that what it is? Sculpture, yes . . . when it's good, you feel it in your guts . . . And then drawing . . . drawing, my dear Mintié, without Prussian blue, just ordinary drawing! Will you come to the studio tomorrow?'

'Certainly.'

He went on, in abbreviated sentences, jumbling his words, getting carried away with sound and speech . . .

'I've started a series of etchings . . . you'll see . . . A completely naked woman emerging from a dark hole and rising up, borne on the wings of a beast . . . Lying on her back, heavy-thighed, with rolls of fat, vile wads of flesh . . . a sprawling, overabounding belly, a belly with terrible shadings, a hideous, truthful belly . . . a death's head, but a living death's head, do you understand? Greedy, wide-mouthed, all lips . . . She rises, in front a group of old men in top hats, fur-lined coats and white tie . . . She rises, and the old men lean over her, panting, their mouths hanging open, drooling, their eyes rolling . . . all the faces of lust, all of them!'

Planting himself in front of me with an air of defiance, he went on:

'And do you know what I'm calling it? Tell me, do you know? I'm calling it Love, my dear Mintié. Eh? What do you think of that?'

'It seems too symbolic,' I ventured.

'Symbolic!' burst out Lirat. 'You're talking rubbish, my dear Mintié . . . Symbolic! But that's life! Now let's go and eat.'

Dinner was cheerful. Lirat was delightfully witty, full of original insights on art and literature, free of extremism or contrariness. He had regained the healthy verve of the best days of his life. Several times I thought of confessing to him that I had been to see Juliette . . . A kind of shame held me back, and I dared not.

'Work, work, my dear Mintié,' he said to me, as we parted. 'Produce, keep producing . . . use your hands, your brain to make no matter what . . . if only a pair of boots . . . that's the only thing, you see!'

Six days later I went back to see Juliette, and I fell into the habit of going there regularly to spend an hour before dinner. The unpleasant impression that I formed on my first visit had faded. Gradually, and without my realising it, I had grown so accustomed to the red hangings in the sitting room, the terracotta Cupid, Juliette's childish prattle, even to Spy, who became my friend, that when I spent a day without seeing them, there seemed to be a great gap in my life that day . . . Moreover, the things that had so offended me, no longer offended me; on the contrary, I found them touching, and every time Juliette conversed with her dog, or lavished affection on him, it was a true pleasure to me, repeated confirmation, as it were, of the naiveté and the loving qualities of her heart. Even I ended up speaking this doggy language . . . One evening when Spy was ailing, I felt worried about him, and gently moving aside the blankets and quilts he was wrapped in, I murmured, 'We're not feeling very well, are we, little Spy? Where's it hurting, then?' Only the image of the singer suddenly looming up next to Juliette sometimes disturbed the tranquillity of these meetings, but I had merely to close my eyes for a moment, or turn my head away, and it would immediately disappear.

I persuaded Juliette to tell me her life story. She had always resisted until then.

'No, no,' she would say.

And she would add with a sigh, looking at me with her big sad eyes, 'What's the use, my friend?'

I insisted, I begged her.

'It's your duty to tell me, and it's my duty to know about it.'

Finally convinced by this argument that I never tired of repeating under various persuasive guises, she agreed . . . Ah, the sadness of it!

She was from Liverdun. Her father was a doctor, and her mother, who led a disreputable life, walked out on him. As for Juliette, she was sent to a convent school as a day boarder. Her father drank and came home the worse for liquor every evening . . . then there were terrible scenes, for he was very disagreeable. It became such a scandal that the nuns expelled Juliette, not wanting to have in the school the daughter of a scarlet woman and a drunkard. Oh, what a miserable exist-ence – always shut up in her room, not daring to go out, and sometimes beaten for no reason by her father. Her father came into her room very late one night ('How can explain to you what happened!' said Juliette, blushing. 'Yes, anyway, you understand?') She jumped out of bed, screamed, opened the window . . . but her father took fright and ran away. The next day Juliette left home and went to Nancy, hoping to earn a living . . . It was there she met Charles.

While she spoke in a soft even voice, I took her hand, her lovely hand, and I squeezed it with emotion at the painful parts of the story. I was incensed by her appalling father, and I cursed the mother who had abandoned her child! I felt tremendous devotion and desire for vengeance stirring and brewing within me. By the time she had finished, I was weeping copiously. It was an exquisite hour!

Juliette had few visitors: some friends of Malterre and two or three of their women friends. One of these women, Gabri-elle Bernier, a very attractive tall blonde, always made the same entrance.

'Hello, monsieur . . . Hello, darling . . . Don't get up, I'm not stopping.'

And she would sit on the arm of a chair, briskly smooth-ing down her muff.

'Can you imagine, I've just had another row with Robert . . . If you only knew what he was like! He turns up at my place, whinging: 'My darling Gabrielle, my mother told me this morning I have to stop seeing you – she won't give me any more money!'

"Your mother!' I said to him. 'Well, you can tell your mother from me that I'll stop seeing you the day she stops seeing her lovers ... Until then, she has another think coming ...' Would you believe it, an old trick like that! Robert just guffawed with laughter! Listen, we're going to Amibigu this evening ... Are you coming?'

'No, thanks.'

'Well, I'm off. Don't get up ... Goodbye, monsieur ... Goodbye, darling...'

This Gabrielle Bernier irritated me enormously.

'Why do you do invite women like that here?' I said to Juliette.

'What's the harm in it, my friend? She amuses me.'

As for Malterre's friends, they talked of horse racing and the high life, they always had stories to tell about their clubs and about women, and they went on endlessly about the theatre. I thought that Juliette took more than reasonable pleasure in these conversations, but I forgave her, marking down to politeness this indulgence of hers. Jesselin, an extremely rich young man of much-vaunted seriousness, was the life and soul of the party and they all deferred to his evident superiority. 'What will Jesselin say? We must ask Jesselin ... That's not what Jesselin thinks ...' They pandered to him enormously. Jesselin had travelled a great deal, and was better acquainted than anyone with the best hotels all over the world. He had been to Afghanistan, and all that he retained of his entire trip through Central Asia was this detail: that the Emir of Kabul, with whom he had the honour of playing a game of chess one day, played as quickly as the French. 'I tell you, that emir really amazed me!' Jesselin was also very fond of saying, 'You know, I've made a few trips in my time ... Well, let me tell you, whether I was in a sleeping-car, cabin, or droshky, no matter where, no matter how – at seven thirty every evening I was in dinner dress!'

I was happy only with Juliette. There, in her red drawing

room, under the aegis of her terracotta Cupid, we would sometimes sit for a long while without uttering a word. I watched her; she bowed her head and fiddled pensively with the fringe trimming of her dress or the laces of her bodice. Often my eyes filled with tears – why, I did not know: very sweet tears that flooded over me like a perfume, bathing my soul in a magic liquor. And I felt a sense of fulfilment and delicious languidness throughout my entire being.

'Ah, Juliette, Juliette!'

'Come now, my friend, come now, behave yourself!'

These were the only words of love that escaped us.

A short time afterwards Juliette gave a big dinner party to celebrate Charles' birthday. She seemed nervous and irritable the whole evening. When Charles made some timid remark, she replied harshly in a curt voice I did not recognise. It was two o'clock in the morning when everyone departed. I was left alone in the drawing room. Malterre was at the door with his back to me, chatting to Jesselin, who was putting his coat on in the hall. And I saw Juliette with her elbows resting on the piano, staring at me. A wild gleam of passion appeared, like a new flame, in her suddenly solemn, almost fearsome eyes. The crease in her brow deepened, her dilated and vibrating nostrils quivered; some indefinable shamelessness played on her lips. I pounced. And with my knees seeking her knees, my stomach pressing itself against her stomach, and my mouth on her mouth, I wrapped her in a frenzied embrace.

She yielded, and in a very low choked voice she said, 'Come tomorrow!'

Would that I might not continue with this story, that I might stop there! Ah, would that I might! At the thought that I am about to reveal so many indignities, my courage fails me, I feel a flush of shame rise to my forehead, a feeling of cowardice suddenly overwhelms me, making the pen shake between my fingers . . . And I have asked myself for mercy . . . Alas! I must see through to the very end the painful ascent of this Calvary, even if my flesh is left in bleeding shreds, even if my bare bones shatter on the rocks and stones. Sins like mine, which I make no attempt to explain by the influence of atavistic forces, by the pernicious effects of an upbringing so contrary to my nature, demand a terrible expiation, and the expiation I have chosen is in the public confession of my life: I tell myself that kind and noble hearts will give me credit for my voluntary mortification. I tell myself, too, that my example will serve as a lesson . . .

If even one young man about to go astray were to be inspired with such terror and disgust from reading these pages that he was for ever saved from harm, I feel the salvation of his soul would begin to redeem my own. And even though I no longer believe in God, it is my hope, my earnest hope, that in those peaceful sanctuaries where the sad, consolatory chanting of those who pray for the dead ascends heavenwards in the silence of redemptive nights, I shall have my share of Christian pity and forgiveness.

I had an income of twenty-two thousand francs, and I was convinced that by working I could earn at least as much again as a writer. Nothing seemed difficult to me any more. The road stretched ahead, free of obstacles, and I had only to start walking. My diffidence, fears, doubts, anxieties, writer's block – these were all a thing of the past. One or two novels a year, even a few plays – what was this to a man in love, like myself, I ask you? Did they not say that X and Z, who were known to be hopeless fools, had both made huge fortunes within a few years? A host of ideas for novels, comedies and dramas came to mind, and I noted them down with broad and lofty sweeps of my pen. I saw myself already taking by storm all the bookshops, theatres and newspapers, commanding universal attention. When struggling for inspiration, I would look up at Juliette and her eyes would yield masterpieces like fairy tale kingdoms. I did not hesitate to insist on Malterre's departure, and to assume responsibility for Juliette. Malterre wrote despairing letters, begged and threatened; finally he left. Later, Jesselin, with his native good taste and wit, told us that a very broken-hearted Malterre was travelling in Italy.

'I accompanied him to Marseilles,' he told us. 'He wanted to kill himself, he was always in tears . . . I tell you, I'm nobody's fool, but I really felt sorry for him . . . Honest to goodness!'

And he added, 'You know, he was determined to fight a duel with you. It was his friend, Monsieur Lirat, who prevented him . . . And myself, in fact, because I can't see the point unless it's a duel to the death . . .'

Juliette listened to these details in silence, with apparent indifference. From time to time she ran her tongue round her mouth. There was in her eyes what seemed to be the reflection of some inward joy. Was she thinking of Malterre? Was she happy to know that someone suffered because of her? Alas, I was no longer in any state to wonder about these things.

A new life began.

I did not like the area where Juliette lived. As far as I was concerned, she had undesirable neighbours there, and above all, her apartment held memories that for me were best suppressed.

Fearful that these schemes would not be at all welcome to Juliette, I dared not reveal them to her too suddenly, but at my first mention of them she was jubilant.

'Yes, yes!' she cried joyfully. 'I'd thought of that, too, my dearest. And do you what else I thought of? Tell me, tell me quickly, what else did your little darling think of?'

She placed both hands on my shoulders and smiled. 'You don't know? You really don't know? Well, she thought that you might come and live with her ... Oh, a sweet little apartment, where we could be together, all alone, and love each other, would be so nice, wouldn't it, Jean? You could get on with your work, and meanwhile I would sit quietly beside you, doing some tapestry, and every now and again I would kiss you, to inspire you with wonderful ideas ... My darling, you'll see what a good housekeeper I am, and how well I look after all your little bits and pieces ... For a start, I'll be the one to tidy your desk ... Every morning you'll find a fresh flower on it. And then Spy will have a lovely kennel, won't you, Spy? A lovely, brand new little kennel, with red pompons on it ... And then we'll almost never go out ... and we'll go to bed early ... And then, and then ... Oh, how wonderful it will be!'

Turning serious again, she said gravely, 'Not to mention that it will be much less expensive – half as expensive, in fact!'

We took an apartment in rue Balzac, and we had to furnish it. This was a big job. All day long we were running round the shops, examining carpets, choosing wallpaper, discussing plans and costs. Juliette would have bought everything she saw, but she had a preference for ornate furniture, gorgeous fabrics, and heavy brocades. The dazzle of new gold, the gaudiness of clashing colours attracted her and held her enthralled. If I tried to make any comment, she immediately responded, 'What do men understand about these things? Women know much better.'

She was stubborn in her desire to acquire a kind of Arab sideboard that was appallingly gaudy, encrusted with mother-of-pearl, ivory, and fake stones; it was also huge.

'You can see very well it's too big, we won't be able to get into our apartment,' I told her.

'You think so? But what if we have the legs sawn, darling?'

And she would break off a conversation twenty times a day to ask me, 'You really think that beautiful sideboard's too big?'

In the carriage on the way home Juliette cuddled up to me, offered me her lips, covered me with caresses, radiantly happy.

'Ah, it was naughty of you not to say anything, and to just keep looking at me all the time with those wonderful sad eyes of yours! Yes, those wonderful sad eyes that I love, you naughty boy! I had to be the one to make the first move, after all! Oh, you'd never have dared! I scared you, didn't I? Do you remember, when you took me in your arms that evening? I didn't know where I was any more, I couldn't see . . . I had this strange sensation . . . in my throat, my breast . . . like when you've drunk something too hot . . . I thought I was going to die from being burned . . . burned by you . . . It felt so good, so good! Anyway, I loved you from the very first day . . . No, I loved you before then . . . Ah, you're laughing! You don't think that you can love a person without knowing him and without ever having seen him? I do! I'm sure of it!'

My heart was so full, these things were so new to me, that I was lost for words. I felt choked with joy. I could only hug Juliette, whisper incomplete words, and weep, weep deliciously. Suddenly she became all pensive, the crease in her forehead deepened, she drew hand away from mine. I was afraid I had offended her.

'What's the matter, Juliette, my dear?' I asked her. 'Why are you are being like this? Have I upset you?'

And Juliette, despairing and disconsolate, would moan, 'The corner cupboard, my darling! We forgot the corner cupboard for the sitting room!'

She switched from laughter, from a kiss, to sudden gravity; she combined caresses with the measurements of ceilings; she muddled love-making with wallpapering. It was adorable.

In our bedroom at night all this sweet childishness would disappear. Love gave Juliette's face a kind of austerity, self-absorption, and fierceness, too; it transfigured her. She was not depraved. On the contrary, her passion was strong and healthy, and in her love-making she had the terrible nobility,

116

the roaring heroism of wild beasts. The climactic shudders in her womb were like terrific birth contractions.

My happiness did not last long. My happiness! The extraordinary thing is that I was never, ever, able to savour any joy completely; inevitably, there was always some anxiety that came and troubled the short-lived moments of elation. Disarmed and helpless against suffering, uncertain and fearful in happiness, such have I been all my life. Is it some peculiar tendency of my spirit? A strange perversion of my senses? Or does happiness really deceive everyone, as it does me, and is it nothing but a more importunate and sophisticated form of universal suffering? To take an example . . . the glimmer of the night-light flickers delicately on the curtains and furniture. It is morning – the morning of our first night together – and Juliette has fallen asleep. One of her arms lies naked on the sheet; the other arm, also bare, is tucked loosely under her neck. All around her face that reflects the whiteness of the sheets, a face bruised with great circles of shadow round her eyes, lie scattered the tumbling waves of her loosened black hair. Avidly I gaze at her . . . She sleeps beside me the quiet deep sleep of a child. And for the first time sexual satisfaction leaves me with no regret, no feeling of disgust. For the first time I am able, with a softened and grateful heart, my flesh still quivering with desire, to look at a woman who has just given herself to me. I am at a loss to express my sensations. What I feel is something indefinable, something very sweet, very serious, too, and very religious, a kind of eucharistic ecstasy, like the rapture of my first communion. I feel the same mystic ravishment, the same august and sacred terror. It is, with a dazzling illumination of my soul, a second revelation of God. I feel as if God has descended on me for the second time . . . She sleeps in the silence of the room, her mouth half-open, her nostrils still, she sleeps so lightly that I do not hear the sound of her breathing. There is a flower wilting on the mantelpiece, and I detect a faint whiff of its fading scent . . . I hear no sound from Juliette . . . She sleeps, she breathes, she is alive, and I hear nothing . . . Cautiously, I bend closer, my lips almost touching her, and very softly I call her name.

'Juliette!'

Juliette does not stir. But I smell her breath that is fainter than the flower's exhalation, that is always so fresh and now has a slight stale warmth to it, always so fragrant and now tinged with an almost imperceptible odour of decay.

'Juliette!'

Juliette does not stir. But the sheet that follows the curves of her body, clings to her legs, and rises in a stiff peak at her feet gives me the impression of a shroud. And all at once the idea of death enters my mind and lodges there. Yes, I am afraid that Juliette might be dead!

'Juliette!'

Juliette does not stir. Then my whole being is overwhelmed with dizziness, and while a distant knell rings in my ears, I see around the bed the flames of a thousand funeral candles wavering in the blast from beyond the grave. My hair stands on end, my teeth chatter, and I yell and yell, 'Juliette! Juliette!'

Juliette finally moves her head, sighs, mutters as though in a dream, 'Jean, my dear Jean!'

I seize her in my arms, vigorously, as though to defend her. I draw her against me, and trembling, chilled, I beg her, 'Juliette, my darling Juliette, wake up! Oh, please wake up. You frighten me. Let me see your eyes, and speak to me, speak to me . . . And hug me, too, hug me tight . . . But don't sleep any more, I implore you.'

She snuggles in my arms, mumbles indistinctly, falls asleep again with her head on my shoulders. But, more potent than the revelation of love, the intimation of death persists and, though I listen to Juliette's heart beating regularly against my own, does not fade away till dawn.

How many times since then I have not sensed in her ardent kisses the cold kiss of death? How many times, too, amid love's ecstasy, has the frolicsome image of the Italian opera singer not suddenly appeared to me? How many times has his obscene laughter not come to drown Juliette's words of passion? How many times have I not heard him say, with his horrible sneering face hanging over me, 'Feast on this

118

body, you fool, this body sullied and defiled by me! Go on! Go on! Wherever you place your lips, you will smell the vile odour of my lips. Wherever your caresses wander over this prostituted flesh, they will encounter the foulness of mine ... Go on, go on! Bathe your Juliette, bathe her all over in the cleansing waters of your love. Scrub her with the acid in your mouth. Tear off her skin with your teeth, if you like, you will never obliterate anything, because the imprint of vice I branded her with cannot be removed.'

And I had a fierce desire to question Juliette about this singer, whose image haunted me. But I dared not. I contented myself with being ingeniously devious to find out the truth: often I would throw out a name, suddenly, in the middle of a conversation, hoping – yes, hoping – that Juliette would give a slight start, or blush, that she would grow flustered and I would say to myself, 'He's the one!' So, I went through the names of every singer in every theatre, without Juliette's impenetrable expression revealing the slightest thing to me. As for Malterre, I no longer gave him any more thought.

It was four months before we were able to move in. The decorators seemed to take for ever, and Juliette's whims often required very time-consuming changes to be made. She would return from her daily shopping expeditions with new ideas for the decoration of the sitting room and the dressing room. The wallpapering of the bedroom had to be completely redone three times because she did not like it any more ... At last, one fine day we took possession of the apartment in rue Balzac. It was about time .... This life of perpetual confusion, this constant feverishness, these open trunks, gaping like coffins, this brutal dispersal of familiar belongings, these teetering piles of linen, these pyramids of boxes that got knocked over, these bits of string lying everywhere, this disarray, this profligacy, this brutal disregard for the most cherished, most regretted memories, and above all the uncertainty, the terror, in any departure, and the sad reflections it gives rise to – all these things brought back to me feelings of anxiety, melancholy and – shall I admit it? –

remorse. While Juliette twirled and flew about among her parcels, I wondered if I had not committed an irreparable folly. I loved her. Ah, certainly I loved her, with all my heart. And I did not conceive of anything beyond this love that overcame me even more every day, invading fibres of my being I was unaware of until then . . . Yet, I was sorry to have given in so lightly and so quickly to an impulse fraught, perhaps, with consequences trying both for her and for myself. I was annoyed that I had not been able to resist the desire Juliette had so endearingly expressed for this life together . . . Would we not have loved each other just as well, she in her own home, and I in mine, and avoided the possible vexations of this situation so unedifyingly referred to as 'cohabitation'. And while I was appalled by all this plush tawdriness and brash gilt we were to live with, I felt for my poor discarded pitchpine furniture and for my quiet and austere little apartment, presently standing empty, the sorrowful affection for things we once cherished that are now gone. But then Juliette would come rushing by, looking charmingly busy, giving me a sweet hasty kiss as she passed, and she showed such animated joy, which gave way to such naive astonishment and despair when she could not find something, that my dismal thoughts would vanish, as do the night owls at the first rays of sunlight.

Ah, those wonderful days after we left rue St-Petersburg! First of all, every room had to be examined in detail. Juliette sat on the divans, armchairs, and sofas, making the bouncy, yielding springs creak.

'You try them out as well, my dear,' she said.

She inspected every piece of furniture, ran her fingers over the wallpaper, worked the draw-strings on the door-curtains, moved a chair, rearranged the drop of a fabric, at every moment uttering cries of admiration, going into ecstasies!

She wanted to repeat her examination of the apartment with the windows closed, so as to see the effect with the lights on, never tiring of looking at the same object, rushing from one room to the other, jotting down on a piece of paper things that were missing . . . Then there were the cupboards where she tidied away her linen and mine with meticulous care, elaborate fastidiousness, and the skill of a consummate window-dresser. I scolded her, because she put the most fragrant sachets among my things . . .

'No, no, no! I want my darling to smell nice!'

Of her old furniture and knick-knacks Juliette had kept only the terracotta Cupid, which resumed its place of honour on the drawing-room mantelpiece. I brought nothing but my books and two very fine sketches by Lirat, which I set about hanging in my study. Juliette shrieked with horror.

'What are you doing, my darling? Putting ghastly things like that in a brand new apartment! Please, hide them away somewhere! Oh, hide them away . . .'

'My dear Juliette,' I replied, a little piqued, 'now, you have your terracotta Cupid.'

'I dare say I do have my terracotta Cupid . . . What's that got to do with it? My terracotta Cupid is very, very, very pretty . . . Whereas those things – really! And anyway, they're not respectable! Not to mention that every time I look at that crazy fellow Lirat's paintings, it gives me a stomach ache!'

I used to take pride in my artistic preferences, and would defend them even to the point of getting angry. Feeling it would have been very childish to engage in any discussion about art with Juliette, I simply buried the two pictures at the back of a cupboard without much regret.

The day came when all was in splendid order, with everything in its place: little ornaments daintily arranged on tables, consoles, and in glass cases; broad-leafed plants decorated the room, and books lined the bookstand, within easy reach; Spy was in his new kennel, and everywhere there were flowers. Nothing was missing, nothing, not even a rose on the desk, with its stem immersed in a slender glass vase. Juliette was radiant, triumphant, and kept saying to me, 'Look, you can see how hard your dearest has been working!'

And resting her head on my shoulder, with melting eyes and genuine emotion in her voice, she murmured, 'Oh, my beloved Jean, we're in our own home now, our home, do you realise . . . How happy we're going to be in our pretty nest!'

The next day Juliette said to me, 'It's a long time since you went to see Monsieur Lirat . . . I wouldn't want him to think that I was stopping you from seeing him.'

Yet that was the truth! I had been neglecting poor Lirat for more than five months! Shame held me back. Only shame kept me away from him. I assure you, I would have shouted to the whole world, 'I'm Juliette's lover!' But I dared not utter this word in front of Lirat. At first I thought of telling him everything, at the risk of spoiling our friendship. I said to myself, 'Now then, tomorrow I'll go and see Lirat!' I even became firm in this resolve. And the next day – 'No, not yet, there's no hurry. Tomorrow!' Tomorrow, always tomorrow! And the days, weeks, and months went by . . . Tomorrow! How was I to approach him, now that he been told these things by Malterre, who, before going away, had returned to give Lirat's divan more punishment. What was I to say to him? How could I bear his gaze, his scorn, his anger? His anger, yes! But his scorn, his terrible silences, the disconcerting sneer I could already visualise, curling the corner of his lips? No, really, I dared not! Make him feel sorry for me, take his hand, ask forgiveness for my lack of trust, appeal to all the generosity of his heart – no! I'd play the part badly, and anyway, Lirat would petrify me, check my flow, with a single word . . . So, every day that passed separated us even more, distanced us even further from each other . . . another few months and Lirat would have no place in my life at all! Rather that than cross that threshold, meet those eyes . . .

'Lirat?' I replied to Juliette. 'Yes, yes, one of these days, I have it in mind!'

'No, no,' Juliette insisted. 'Do it today . . . You know what he's like, you know how spiteful he is . . . He must be making up all kinds of tittle-tattle about us!'

There was really no escape. It is a short distance from rue Balzac to the Rodrigues estate. To delay the moment of this painful meeting, I made long detours, dawdling in front of the shop windows of Faubourg St-Honoré. And I thought, 'What if I didn't call on Lirat! I would say, when I got home, that I had seen him, that we had argued. I would make up some story that would save me from this visit for good.'

I was ashamed of this childish notion. Then I hoped Lirat would not be there. How gleefully I would roll up my card and slip it into the keyhole! Comforted by this thought, I finally entered the Rodrigues estate, came to a halt outside his studio door . . . And this door seemed terrifying to me. Nevertheless, I knocked and immediately a voice, Lirat's voice, answered from within.

'Come in!'

My heart was pounding, I felt as if I had an iron bar through my throat . . . I wanted to run away.

'Come in!' the voice repeated.

I turned the handle.

'Ah! It's you, Mintié!' cried Lirat. 'Well, come in . . .'

Lirat was sitting at his table, writing a letter.

'Do you mind if I finish this?' he said. 'I'll be with you in a couple of minutes.'

He returned to his writing. I was somewhat heartened not to feel the coldness of his gaze on me. I took advantage of his back being turned to me to speak, to relieve myself quickly of the burden oppressing my soul.

'It's such a long time since I last saw you, my dear Lirat!'

'Yes, indeed, Mintié.'

'I've moved . . .'

'Ah!'

'I'm living in rue Balzac.'

'A nice area!'

I was choking. I made a supreme effort, gathered all my strength, but by a strange aberration I felt obliged to adopt an offhand manner . . . On my word of honour, I was jocular, yes, jocular!

'I've something to tell you that will amuse you . . . hah! hah! . . . that will amuse you, I'm sure. I . . . I'm living . . . with Juliette . . . hah! hah!.. with Juliette Roux . . . you know, Juliette . . . hah! hah!'

'Congratulations!'

Congratulations! He had this – 'Congratulations!' – in a perfectly calm, indifferent voice. What! No whistle, no fit of anger, no start of surprise! Congratulations! As he might have said, 'Why should I care?' And his back, bowed over the table, remained motionless, without a twitch or shudder! His pen had not fallen out of his hand. He was still writing! What I had just told him, he had already known for a long time. But to hear it from my lips! I was amazed and – must I admit it? – offended that it did not rouse his fury. Lirat got to his feet and rubbed his hands.

'So, what's new, then?' he said.

I could not bear it any more. I rushed towards him with tears in my eyes.

'Listen,' I sobbed, 'Lirat, for pity's sake, listen . . . I've behaved badly towards you, I know . . . and I'm sorry . . . I should have told you everything . . . I didn't dare . . . You frighten me . . . and anyway, you remember Juliette, here, what you told me about her . . . remember? That's what stopped me . . . do you understand?'

'But my dear Mintié,' Lirat cut in, 'I don't blame you at all . . . I'm neither your father nor your confessor. You do what you like, it's none of my business . . .'

I grew excited.

'It's true you're not my father, but you are my friend, my only friend, and I owed you greater trust . . . Forgive me! Yes, I'm living with Juliette, and I love her, and she loves me! Is it any crime to seek a little happiness? Juliette is not the woman you think she is . . . She has been horribly slandered. She's good, honest. Oh, don't smile! Yes, honest! She has a childlike naiveté that you'd find touching, Lirat. You don't like her because you don't know her! If you knew of all the kindness and consideration that splendid woman has for me! Juliette wants me to work. She's proud of what good writing I might produce . . . Listen, she made me come to see you . . . I was ashamed, I didn't dare . . . She made me! Yes, Lirat, have a little compassion for her . . . I beg you, care for her a little!'

Lirat had turned solemn. He placed his hand on my shoulder and gazing at me sadly, he said in emotional voice, 'My dear boy! Why are you telling me all this?'

'Because it's the truth, Lirat! Because I'm fond of you and want to remain your friend . . . Prove that you're still my friend! Listen, come and have dinner with us this evening, as you used to come and have dinner with me. Oh, please come!'

'No!' he said.

And this 'no' was merciless, definitive, and summary, like a pistol shot.

Lirat added, 'Come, yourself, often! And when you feel like blubbing . . . you know . . . the divan is here . . . it's no stranger to poor beggars' tears!'

When the door closed behind me I felt that something enormous and heavy had closed on my past, that walls higher than the sky and deeper than the night separated me for ever from my honourable life, my artistic ambitions. And I felt in my entire being a kind of wrench . . . For a moment I stood there, gaping, with my arms dangling, staring wide-eyed at that fateful door, behind which something had just ended . . . just died.

CHAPTER SIX

It was not long before Juliette grew bored in that lovely apartment where she had promised herself such tranquillity and happiness. Once her cupboards had been put in order and her knick-knacks set out, she did not know what to do and she fretted. Tapestry work irritated her, reading afforded her no enjoyment. She went from one room to the other, not knowing how to occupy her hands, or her mind, yawning and stretching her arms. She took refuge in her dressing room, where she spent long hours getting dressed, trying out new hair-styles in front of her mirror, playing with the bath-taps, which kept her amused for a while; cleaning Spy of fleas, and making elaborate bows for him out of her old hat-ribbons. Running the household might have filled the emptiness of her days, but I soon realised with dismay that Juliette was not the housekeeper she prided herself on being. She had no care or concern and took no responsibility for anything but her underwear and her dog. Everything else was of little importance to her, and things were left to sort themselves out, or rather left to the servants to sort out. Our new staff consisted of a cook – a filthy, grasping and bad-tempered old woman whose talents did not extend beyond tapioca, veal stew and salad; a chambermaid – Celestine, a brazen and vicious girl who had respect only for people who spent a lot of money; and finally a housekeeper, Mère Sochard, who was continually taking snuff and got terribly drunk, in order, she said, to forget her sorrows – a husband who beat her and took advantage of her, and a daughter who had gone to the bad. So there was terrible waste, and we fared very poorly, both at table and in every other respect. If by chance we had visitors, Juliette would order very expensive and pretentious dishes from Bignon. I watched with displeasure as an injudicious familiarity, some kind of friendly relationship grew up between Juliette and Celestine. While helping her mistress to dress, Celestine told stories that Juliette revelled in, disclosed

126

unsavoury secrets of the households where she had worked before, and offered advice . . . At Madame K's they did this, at Madame V's they did that . . . Well, these were 'smart addresses', after all. Juliette would often visit the linen room where Celestine was sewing, and stay there for hours on end, sitting of a pile of sheets, listening to the maid's inexhaustible tittle-tattle. From time to time arguments arose over some missing object, some failure of the chambermaid to do her job properly. Celestine would fly into a rage, hurl the most coarse insults, bang the furniture, screech in her grating voice.

'Well, thank you very much! A fine place this is, where floozies of the sort take the liberty of making accusations against you! Well, let me tell you, sweetheart, I don't give a damn about you or your sapheaded boyfriend over there . . . who looks like a zombie!'

Juliette gave her the sack, and did not even want her to work out her week's notice . . .

'Yes, yes! Pack your bags at once, you horrible girl . . . at once!'

Pale and trembling, she came and took refuge with me.

'Oh, darling, that undeserving creature, that horrible girl! After I'd been so kind to her!'

By the evening everything had been patched up between them. And Celestine's braying voice could be heard above the even great hilarity of their renewed laughter.

'Of course, her ladyship was a real tramp! My, what a tramp!'

One day Juliette said to me, 'Your little darling has nothing to wear any more. All she has left is her birthday suit, poor thing!'

So, there was more shopping, at the dressmaker's, the milliner's, the linen-draper's; and she once again became bright and cheerful and more affectionate. The shadow of boredom that had cast its gloom over her face cleared. Among fabrics and lace, in the midst of feathers, frills and furbelows, she was truly in her element, she blossomed and glowed. Her excited fingers took sensual pleasure in running over the satins, touching the crêpes, stroking the velvets, burying themselves in the reams of milky white muslin. The least bit of silk, from the way she handled it, immediately took on the charming appearance of something alive; she could extract the most exquisite effects from braids and trimmings. Although I was very worried by all these ruinously expensive extravagances, I was incapable of denying Juliette anything, and I succumbed to the joy of knowing her to be so happy, to the pleasure of seeing her look so attractive – a woman whose beauty embellished the inert objects around her, who brought to life everything she graced with her touch!

Every evening for more than a month, there were parcels, boxes, and mysterious bundles delivered to us. There was a succession of dresses, hats and coats. Umbrellas, embroidered camisoles, the most fancy underwear gathered in heaps, spilled out of drawers, cupboards and closets.

'You see, darling,' Juliette explained, catching the look of amazement in my eyes, 'I had nothing left at all . . . That's kitted me out with a complete wardrobe . . . Now I'll only need to replace the odd thing that wears out . . . Oh, you needn't worry! I'm very thrifty! Look, I've had all my dresses made with a high-necked bodice to wear in town, and a décolleté for when we go the opera! Count how many outfits that saves me . . . one . . . two . . . three . . . four . . . five outfits, darling . . . you see!'

She wore for the first time to the theatre a dress that created a sensation. I was the most wretched of men for the whole of that dreadful evening . . . I sensed the lustful gaze of every man in the audience focused on Juliette, staring at her, undressing her, the kind of gaze that defiles with such lewdness the woman it admires. I wished I could hide Juliette at the back of the box and throw a veil of thick dark wool over her. And with bitter hatred in my heart, I wished the theatre might suddenly collapse in a cataclysm, and its chandelier and ceiling come down with tremendous force, crushing all these men, each of whom was robbing me of a little of Juliette's modesty, each taking away from me a little of her love. Revelling in her triumph, she seemed to be saying, 'I love you, gentlemen, for thinking I look beautiful – you're wonderful people.'

We no sooner got home than I drew Juliette towards me, and clutched her to my breast for a long, long time, saying over and over again, 'You do love me, Juliette?' But Juliette's heart was already deaf to me. Seeing my sadness, noticing the tears brimming in my eyes, about to trickle down my cheek, she broke free of my embrace, and said with slight irritation, 'Really! I was the most beautiful woman of all – of all! And you're not pleased! And you're shedding tears! It's not very nice of you! What will it take to satisfy you, then?'

Our first disagreement was about Juliette's friends. Without my inviting them, Gabrielle Bernier, Jesselin and a few other characters brought along by Malterre to rue St-Petersburg turned up again in pursuit of us at rue Balzac. And this did not please me. I meant to detach my mistress from her entire past life. I was quite clear about this to Juliette, who at first seemed very surprised.

'What have you got against Monsieur Jesselin?' she asked. She called the others by their first name . . . But she said Monsieur Jesselin with great respect.

'I've nothing in particular against him, my darling . . . I don't like him, he irritates me, he's absurd . . . Those are good enough reasons, I think, not to want to see that fool . . .'

Juliette was extremely shocked. It had never entered her mind that I might regard as a fool a man of Monsieur Jesselin's importance and reputation. She looked at me, appalled, as though I had just uttered some dreadful blasphemy.

'Monsieur Jesselin, a fool! A man like him, so respectable, so serious, who's been to the Indies! But don't you know that he's a member of the Geographic Society?'

'What about Gabrielle Bernier? Is she also a member of the Geographic Society?'

Juliette never lost her temper. Only, when she was angry, her eyes suddenly became harder, the crease in her forehead became more pronounced, her voice lost some of its sweet resonance. She simply replied, 'Gabrielle is my friend.'

'That's exactly what I have against her!'

There was a moment's silence. Juliette sat in an armchair, twisting the laces of her dressing-gown, thinking. An ironic smile played about her lips.

'So, I'm not to see anyone? That's what you want, isn't it? Well, that's going to be fun! We never go out as it is! We live like real hermits!'

'It's not a question of that at all, my darling. I have friends . . . I'll tell them to come . . .'

'Yes, I know what your friends are like . . . I can already picture them — literary types, artists! People that you can't understand when they talk to you . . . and borrow money from you! No, thank you!'

I was hurt, and replied sharply, 'My friends are honest, do you hear, and they're talented . . . Unlike that cretin and that tramp!'

'Enough said, do you hear!' said Juliette peremptorily. 'If that's what you want, very well then! I'll close my door to them. However, when you insisted on living with me, you should have warned me that you wanted to bury me alive . . . I would have known what I was letting myself in for . . .'

She stood up. I did not dream of telling her that, on the contrary, it was she who had wanted this life together, realising that this would only make matters worse without achieving anything. I took her hand.

'Juliette!' I implored her.

'Well, what?'

'Are you angry?'

'Me? On the contrary, I'm very happy . . .'

'Juliette!'

'Now, let me go . . . stop it . . . you're hurting me.'

Juliette sulked all day long. When I spoke to her, she would not answer, or contented herself with a curt response expressed in infuriating monosyllables. I was miserable and angry. I wanted to take her in my arms and to beat her, to cover her with kisses punches. At dinner she stood on her dignity as the injured woman, with her lips pursed and her eyes full of disdain. In vain I tried to soften her by behaving humbly with sorrowful and repentant looks. Her mask remained pitiless, her brow still crossed with a shadow that worried me. That night, in bed, she picked up a book and turned her back on me. And the nape of her neck, her perfumed neck on which my lips loved to linger, looked as unyielding as a stone wall . . . I felt a secret impatience stirring inside me, and I strove to repress it. As anger overwhelmed me, I tried to make my voice sound more caressing, more gentle and pleading.

'Juliette! Juliette, my love! Speak to me, please! Speak to me! I've upset you, I've been too harsh? It's true . . . I'm sorry, forgive me . . . But speak to me!'

It was as though Juliette had not heard me. She cut the pages of her book, and the rasp of the knife on the paper exasperated me horribly.

'Juliette, my love! Try to understand . . . it's because I love you that I said those things . . . It's because I want you to be so irreproachable, so respected! And those people seem to me unworthy of you . . . If I didn't love you, what would it matter to me? And you think I don't want you to go out? Not at all! We'll go out often, every evening . . . Oh, don't be like that! It was wrong of me! Shout at me, hit me.. but speak to me, say something!'

She went on turning the pages of the book . . .

The words stuck in my throat. 'It's wrong to treat me like this, Juliette . . . I assure you, it's wrong to behave in this way . . . I've said I'm sorry! Ah! What pleasure does it give you to torture me so? I've said I'm sorry! Come now, Juliette, I've said I'm sorry.'

Not a muscle in her body quivered at my entreaties. The back of her neck especially infuriated me. Between the stray locks of her hair I now saw an ironic, inhuman face with eyes that mocked me and a mouth with its tongue stuck out at me. And I was tempted to lay hands on it, to gouge it with my fingers, to draw blood.

'Juliette!' I cried.

And my tautened fingers, splayed and hooked like claws,

moved closer despite myself, ready to pounce on that neck, impatient to tear it to shreds.

'Juliette!'

Juliette turned her head slightly, and looked at me scornfully, without terror.

'What do you want?' she said.

'What do I want? What do I want?'

I was about to start making threats . . . I was half up, out of the sheets, waving my arms about . . . And all of a sudden my anger drained away. I moved over towards Juliette and snuggled up to her, feeling thoroughly ashamed, and kissed that lovely perfumed neck.

'What I want, darling, is for you to be happy . . . to invite your friends round . . . What I was expecting of you was so silly! After all, you're the best woman on earth . . . And you do love me, don't you? Oh, I'll agree to whatever you want in future, I promise you! And you'll see how nice I'll be to them . . . Listen, why don't you invite Gabrielle to come to dinner? And Jesselin too?'

'No, no! You say that now, and tomorrow you'll hold it against me . . . No, no! I don't want to impose on you people that you detest . . . Tramps and cretins!'

'I don't know what I was thinking of . . . I don't detest them . . . on the contrary, I like them very much . . . Invite them both . . . And I'll go and reserve a box at the Vaudeville.'

'No!'

'Please, I beg you!'

Her voice softened. She closed the book.

'Well, then. We'll see tomorrow.'

Honestly, at that moment I loved Gabrielle, Jesselin, Celestine . . . I think even loved Malterre.

I was not working any more. Not that the love of work failed me, but I no longer had any creative ability. Every day I would sit at my desk, with a blank sheet of paper in front of me, searching for ideas, not finding any, and inevitably lapsing back into worries about the present – which meant Juliette – and fears about the future – which also meant Juliette!

Just as a drunkard shakes the empty bottle to extract the last drop of liquor, so I racked my brains, to dredge up some ideas! Alas, my brain was empty! It was empty and it weighed on my shoulders like an enormous ball of lead! My mind had always been slow to awaken: it required stimulation, the lash of a whip. Because of my ill-adjusted sensitivity, my passiveness, I easily succumbed to moral and intellectual influences, good or bad. So Lirat's friendship had been very good for me, in the past. My ideas thawed out in the warmth of his genius; his conversation opened up to me new and unsuspected horizons; what seethed inchoately within me became clearer, assumed a less indeterminate form, which I strove to transcribe. He trained me to see, to understand, to plumb with him the mysteries of the inner life . . . Now, day by day, and as it were hour by hour, the bright horizons I had been reaching out to were closing in, and darkness was falling, a dense darkness that was not only visible but also palpable, for I could actually touch this monstrous darkness. I felt its shadows sticking to my hair, clinging to my fingers, wrapping itself round my body in viscous coils . . .

My study looked out on a courtyard, or rather on a little garden graced with two big plane trees, confined by a trellis-covered wall with ivy growing over it. Beyond this wall, at the far end of another garden, rose the grey, very tall facade of a house, with five rows of windows confronting me. At one of the casements on the third floor, as though framed like an old painting, sat an old man. He wore a black velvet skull-cap and a chequered dressing-gown, and he never stirred. Slumped in a heap, with his head bowed over his chest, he seemed to be sleeping. All I could see of his face were patches of yellow wrinkled flesh pitted with shadow, and wisps of dirty beard, like strange vegetation growing on the trunks of dead trees. Sometimes a woman, visible in profile, bent over him in a sinister manner; and this profile looked like an owl perched on the old man's shoulder. I could make out its curved beak and cruel, avid, blood-thirsty round eyes. When the sun entered the garden, the casement would open, and I heard a harsh, shrill, tetchy voice incessantly nagging. Then the old man would slump even more into a heap, his head would nod slightly, then he became still again, a little more huddled in the folds of his dressing-gown, a little more sunk in his armchair. I spent hours watching the poor wretch, fancying terrible dramas, a tragic love affair, a noble life ruined, wasted, destroyed by that woman with the face of an owl. I pictured this living corpse young, strong and handsome . . . Perhaps he had once been an artist, a scholar, or just a happy and honest man . . . And he used to walk tall, with his eyes full of confidence, advancing towards fame or good fortune . . . One day he had met this woman at a friend's house, and this woman, too, had a perfumed veil, a little muff, a seal-skin hat, a celestial smile, a look of angelic sweetness . . . And he had at once fallen in love with her . . . I followed him step by step through his passion, I counted his failings, his weaknesses, his ever greater decline until he finished up in this armchair, a senile, paralytic old man . . . And what I imagined about him was my own life; it represented my feelings, my dread of the future, my anguish . . . Little by little, the delusion took a purely physical form, and it was myself that I saw under that velvet skull-cap, in that dressing-gown, with that decrepit body, that dirty beard, with Juliette perched on my shoulder like an owl . . .

Juliette! She moped about my study, weary in her body and with boredom written all over her face, letting out yawns and sighs. She had no idea how to amuse herself. More often than not, she would set up a card table by me, and devote herself to a complicated game of patience; or else she would settle down on the divan, spread a towel over herself, with her little tortoiseshell implements and tiny pots of cream, and furiously buff and file her nails, making them shinier than agate. Every five minutes she would examine them, seeking her reflection on those polished surfaces, as though in a mirror.

'Look, darling! Don't they look nice? You, too, Spy, look at your mistress's pretty little fingernails . . .'

The quiet rubbing of her buffer, the slight creak of the

134

divan, the remarks Juliette made, her conversations with Spy were enough to scatter the few thoughts I strove to marshal. My mind immediately returned to its everyday preoccupations, and the dreams I had were painful dreams, the life I led was a distressing one . . . Juliette! Did I love her? This question often confronted me, fraught with terrible doubt. Had I not been deceived by my wonderstruck senses? Was not what I had taken for love the ephemeral, fleeting revelation of a pleasure I had yet to enjoy? Juliette! Of course I loved her . . . But was not the Juliette I loved the one that I had created, who was born of my imagination, who sprang from my brain, the one I had endowed with a soul, a spark of divinity, the one I had fashioned, unrealistically, out of the ideal matter of which angels? And did I not love her as one might love a good book, a fine verse, a beautiful statue, the visible and palpable realisation of an artist's dream? But what about the other Juliette – this one here? This pretty, mindless creature, this ornament, this skirt, this nothing? I studied her closely while she polished her nails. Oh, how I wished I could take her skull apart to examine its hollowness, and open her heart to measure its emptiness.

And I said to myself, 'What kind of life will I have with this woman who has no inclination for anything but pleasure, whose happiness resides wholly in clothes, whose every desire costs a fortune; who, despite her chaste appearance, is instinctively drawn to vice; who, overnight, with no regrets and no memories, walked out on that poor wretch Malterre; who will perhaps walk out on me tomorrow; this woman who is the living denial of my aspirations and admirations, who will never, ever, share my intellectual life; this woman, in short, who already burdens my mind, like a madness; my heart, like remorse; my entire being, like a crime?'

I felt like fleeing, and saying to Juliette, 'I'm going out, but I'll be back in an hour', and then not returning to that house where the ceilings were more oppressive than coffinlids, where the air stifled me and the very objects seemed to say, Go away!'

But no! I loved her! And it was this Juliette I loved, not

the other who had gone the way of all dreams! I loved her for everything that caused my suffering, I loved her for her thoughtlessness, for her frivolities, for the depravity I suspected in her; I loved her with the tormenting love that a mother has for her sick child, for her hunchback child . . . Have you ever encountered, on an icy winter's day, some poor creature crouched in a doorway, with blue lips and chattering teeth, trembling all over in his torn rags? And if so, have you not been overwhelmed with a poignant sense of pity, and have you not thought of taking him and warming him against you, feeding him and covering his shivering limbs with warm clothes? That's how I loved Juliette. I loved her with immense pity . . . oh, don't laugh! . . . a maternal, infinite pity!'

'Aren't we going out, darling? It would be so nice to drive round the Bois.'

And glancing at the blank page on which I had not written a single line, she exclaimed, 'Is that all? Really! You haven't overexerted yourself, have you? And here I was, staying in so that you could work! Well, I knew in the first place that you'd never achieve anything . . . You're far too indolent!'

Soon we were going out every day and every evening. I offered no resistance, being almost happy to escape the mortifying disgust and desperate thoughts our apartment prompted in me, the symbolic vision of that old man, myself . . . Ah, above all to escape myself! In the crowd, the noise, the feverish rush of a pleasure-seeking existence, I hoped to find oblivion and numbness, to quell the rebellion of the spirit, to silence the past whose voice I heard deep inside me, weeping and wailing. And since it was impossible for me to raise Juliette to my level, I was going to lower myself to hers. The serene, sun-blessed heights that I had scaled at the cost of such effort, I would descend again at a stroke, in a sudden irrecoverable fall, even if I were to smash my head on the rocks, or disappear into the deep mire. There was no question of running away any more. If this thought happened to cross my foggy mind, if, without a will of my own, I saw, lying ever more distant, a path of salvation where duty seemed to call me, I would clutch at false pretences of honour to evade that thought and not go dashing down that path ... Was I capable of leaving Juliette — I who had insisted that she leave Malterre? If I went, what would become of her? But no, no, I was lying! I did not want to leave her, because I loved her, because I felt sorry for her, because ... Was it not myself that I loved, that I felt sorry for? Oh, I can't tell any more, I can't tell! So, don't you believe that the abyss into which I fell suddenly caught me off-guard ... Don't you believe it! I saw it from a long way off, I saw that horrible gaping black hole and I rushed towards it. I bent over the edge to breathe the foul stench of its mire. I said to myself, 'It's down there that depraved existences and ruined lives fall and disappear. They never, ever, climb out of there again!' And I threw myself into it ...

Despite the threateningly cloudy sky, the café terrace is swarming with people. There is not a single table free; the café-chantants, the circuses and theatres have disgorged 'the cream' of their audiences. Everywhere are light dresses and dark suits; young women, plumed like horses for a procession, looking bored, pale and unhealthy; bewildered dandies, with their heads bowed over their buttonholes from which the flowers have gone, sucking the tops of their canes with the grimacing gestures of a monkey. Some, with their legs crossed to show off their black silk stockings embroidered with little red flowers, and with their hats slightly tilted back, whistle a tune that is in vogue — the refrain they sang a short while ago at the Ambassadors, accompanying themselves with a banging of plates, glasses and carafes ... The last light has gone out on the front of the Opera. But all around, the windows of clubs and gambling-dens blaze red, like the mouths of hell. In the square, backed up against the pavement, hired carriages — shabby, patched-up affairs — stand in line, three deep. Coachmen doze, lying on their seats; others, gathered in groups, a comic sight in their improvised livery, chat together, chewing on the ends of cigars, swapping salacious stories about their clients, with broad laughter. And the insistent cry of newsvendors is to be heard constantly, as they pass to and fro, throwing out in the midst of their racy patter a famous woman's name, news of a scandal, while some grimy, sly street-urchins slip between the tables like cats, offering obscene photographs, which they half reveal to whip up dormant desires, to rekindle slaked curiosity. And little girls whose precocious vice has already blighted their thin, childish faces, come up to you with flowers, smiling an ambiguous smile, making eyes with the knowingness and ghastly lewdness of old whores. Inside the café all the tables are taken . . . There is not one empty seat . . . You sip at a glass of champagne, or nibble at a sandwich. Every minute curious passers-by drop in on the way to their club, or before going to bed, out of habit, or because it's the done thing, and also to see whether there isn't 'something happening'. Slowly strutting, they make their rounds, stopping to chat with friends, greeting someone, here, there, with a quick wave of the hand, looking at themselves in the mirrors, rearranging their white scarves that show over the top of their light-coloured overcoats; then they're gone, their minds furnished with some new libertine-slang expression, the richer for some piece of gossip gathered in passing that will sustain their idleness for a whole day. The women, leaning on their elbows in front of a soda-water, resting their drooping heads – with little pink love-bites on their necks – on their long-gloved hands, affect the languid looks, and soulful, dreamy expressions of consumptives. They exchange masonic winks and secret smiles with neighbouring tables and, smug and silent, the gentlemen accompanying them tap the toes of their shoes with their canes. This is a brilliant social gathering, embellished with frills and laces, braids and pom-poms, with coloured feathers and full-blown flowers, with blonde locks and brown tresses and the glitter of diamonds. And everyone is at battle stations, young and old, beardless novices, white-haired veterans, artless dupes and hardened hangers-on; here are social deviancy, equivocal relationships, wild depravity, base cupidity, squalid bargains – all the

138

flowers of corruption that germinate, commingle, grow and flourish in the warmth of the Parisian dungheap.

It was into this atmosphere fraught with boredom and anxiety, and heavy with scent, that we came every evening after this. In the daytime we would be at the dressmakers, the Bois, the races; in the evening, at restaurants, theatres, and fast parties. Wherever the denizens of this particular world paraded themselves, you could be sure of seeing us appear — we were even greatly courted, because of Juliette's beauty, which was beginning to get talked about, and because of her dresses, which excited the envy and emulation of other women. We never dined at home any more. Our apartment served only as a dressing room. When Juliette was dressing, she became hard, almost fierce. The crease in her forehead cut across her skin like a scar. She spoke in broken snatches, lost her temper, seemed bent on destruction. Around her was a scene of pillage: with open drawers, petticoats strewn on the carpet, fans taken out of their cases lying scattered on the chairs, opera-glasses cluttering the furniture, muslin garments billowing in corners, flowers dropped on the floor, towels stained with rouge, gloves, stockings, and veils hanging from the branches of the candelabras. And Celestine, quick, bold, and cynical, moved round, sprang about, glided through this chaos, kneeling at her mistress's feet, putting pins in here, adjusting a fold there, knotting bows, her clammy limp hands, made to mess with dirty things, lovingly cleaved to Juliette's body. She was happy, no longer answering back to cutting remarks or hurtful reproaches, and her eyes, lit up with a gleam of low-minded vice, stared at me with persistent irony. It was only in public, in the glitter of lights, under the crossfire of men's gazes, that Juliette recovered her smile and the slightly surprised and candid expression of joy she retained even in these loathsomely debauched circles. And we would come to this night-spot with Gabrielle, with Jesselin, with people we had met God knows where, introduced to us by God knows whom, fools, crooks, princes, a whole pack of international pleasure-seekers that trailed round after us. We were generally referred to as 'the Mintié crowd'.

'What are you doing this evening?'

'I going out with the Mintié crowd.'

Jesselin would tell us about those who patronised the place; there was nothing he did not know about the seamier side of this fast life, and he spoke of it with a kind of admiration, despite all the shameful or tragic details he revealed to us.

'You see that man with a crowd gathered round, listening to him respectfully?'

He had been a valet. His master sacked him for theft. But he went on to be a croupier and worked all the clandestine dives, became a club cashier, then cleverly disappeared for a few years. Now he had shares in gaming houses, stakes in racing stables, credit with the stock-brokers, his own horses and a town house where he entertained. He secretly loaned money, at one hundred percent interest, to young ladies in financial difficulties whose talents and wiles he had already put to the test. Ostentatiously open-handed when it suited him and buying very expensive paintings, he passed for an honourable man and a patron of the arts. His name was quoted with reverence in the newspapers.

'And that enormous chubby-cheeked fellow, with a perpetual idiotic grin on his fat crumpled face? A mere child! Eighteen years old, if that. He has a stunning mistress with whom he appears in the Bois on Mondays, and a tutor-priest whom he drives to the lake on Tuesdays in the same carriage. This is his mother's idea of educating her son, having him simultaneously schooled in religious beliefs and carnal intrigues. Anyway, he is drunk every evening and bullies his crazy old mother. A real character!' Jesselin concluded.

'That fellow over there is a duke who bears one of the great names of France!'

Ah, what a fine duke! The king of freeloaders! He comes in timidly, like a nervous dog, looks through his monocle, sniffs out a supper, sits down and devours some ham and pâté de foie gras. The duke has perhaps not dined; he has probably returned unsuccessful from his daily rounds of the Café Anglais, the Maison Dorée and Bignon's in search of a friend and a meal. Very much at ease with the ladies and with horse-dealers, he runs their errands and mounts their beasts. He is required to say wherever he goes, 'Ah, what a charming woman! Ah, what a fine beast!' In exchange for these services he receives a few gold coins with which he pays his valet.

'And there's another great name that has gradually and irredeemably fallen into the cesspool of despicable professions and covert pimping. He was once a splendid-looking fellow. Despite the stoutness he has developed, despite the puffiness of his flesh, he still retains an elegant demeanour and an air of chicness. In the evil haunts and strange circles in which he operates, he plays the same role, for a fee, that fifty years ago was played by army officers sitting at the table d'hôte. His politeness and education are an asset that he trades on to perfection. He knows how to take advantage of others' dishonour as skillfully as he has of his own, for no one is more adept at exploiting his conjugal misfortunes.

'That ghastly pale face framed with greying whiskers, that thin lip and dull eye?'

Didn't we know? For a long time sinister rumours circulated about this person, tales of violence . . . At first people were afraid and kept away from him . . . But that's an old story, after all! And he spends a lot of money . . . What do a few drops of blood matter, on piles of gold! Women were crazy for him!

'That very attractive young man with the elegantly curled moustache?'

One day, having completely run out of money, and being cut off by his family, he had the ingenious idea of pretending to repent, made a great show of leaving an old mistress, and went back home. A young girl, a former childhood companion, adored him. She was rich. He married her. But on the very night of his wedding he ran off with the dowry and returned to his old mistress.

'That's a good story!' Jesslin concluded. 'No, really, that's a very good story!'

Complaisant husbands, those who had been drummed out

of their clubs, or banned from the race-tracks, or hammered on the Stock Exchange, strangers from the devil knows where, brought here by one scandal, driven away by another, those living beyond the pale, social outcasts who consider themselves Parisian royalty, to whom others bow – vainglorious and depraved, they all swarmed here with impunity!

Juliette listened, amused by these accounts, attracted by this blood and mire, flattered by the ignoble homage she sensed being paid to her in the eyes of these imbeciles and villains. But she retained her air of decorum, her virginal charm, a manner at once haughty and shameless, for which I had traded my soul one day at Lirat's . . .

And then these faces grow pale, their features become drawn, and their eyes are made puffy and red by tiredness . . . One by one they leave the bar, weary and apprehensive . . . Do they know what tomorrow holds in store for them? What awaits them at home? What ruin stalks them? At the bottom of what pit of misery and ignominiousness they, poor devils, are to languish? Sometimes a pistol-shot creates a gap in our crowd . . . Will it be their turn tomorrow? Tomorrow! Will it not be my turn, too? Ah, tomorrow! Always the threat of tomorrow!

And we went home without saying a word to each other, dazed and dispirited.

The boulevard was then deserted. A great silence weighed heavily on the city. Only the windows of the gambling-houses gleamed like the eyes of giant beasts crouched in the darkness.

Without knowing precisely how my finances stood, I felt close to ruin. I had paid out large sums of money, my debts were accumulating, and far from decreasing, Juliette's demands became ever more numerous and more extravagant. Gold ran through her fingers like water from a fountain, in a continuous stream.

'She must think me richer than I am,' I thought, trying to delude myself. 'I should tell her, and perhaps she would be more restrained in her desires.'

The truth is, I systematically dismissed any such idea; I

dreaded more than any misfortune in the world the probable consequences of this kind of disclosure. In my rare moments of lucidity, of honesty with myself, I realised that, behind the apparent sweetness and ingenuousness of a spoilt child, behind that strong, vibrant, sexual passion, Juliette concealed a terrible will to be forever beautiful, adulated and courted, an appallingly selfishness that would not shrink from any cruelty or moral crime. I saw that she loved me less than the least of her clothes, that she would have sacrificed me for a coat, a scarf, a pair of gloves. Caught up in this way of life, she would stop at nothing . . . So what? Then a great shiver would run through me from head to toe . . . That she should leave me – no, no, that was what I did not want! The most difficult moment for me was in the morning, waking up. Pulling the blankets over my head, with my eyes closed and my body curled up in a ball, I considered my situation, in terrible agonies . . . And the more fast and loose Juliette seemed to play, the more desperately I clung to her. It was no good telling myself that the money would suddenly run out, that the credit on which I might dishonestly prolong for a week or two the agony of my hopes would eventually be withdrawn; I persisted, determined to find impossible expedients . . . I imagined myself achieving tremendous tasks within a week . . . I dreamt of finding millions in a hackney cab . . . Extraordinary bequests turned up out of the blue . . . My thoughts dwelt on robbery . . . Gradually all these delusions gained substance in my deranged mind . . . I gave Juliette palaces and châteaux, I buried her under the weight of diamonds and pearls; gold flowed and blazed around her; and I raised her on swathes of purple to dizzy heights above the earth . . . Then reality would suddenly return . . . I would burrow deeper into my bed, seeking voids into whose depths I could disappear, trying to fall sleep. And all of a sudden, wild-eyed and panting, with sweat on my brow, I would cling to Juliette, and hug her with all my strength.

'Juliette, you'll never leave me!' I would sob. 'Say it, say that you'll never leave me . . . Because, you see, it would be the death of me ... it would drive me mad ... I'd kill myself! Juliette,I swear I'd kill myself!'

'Now, what's come over you? Why are you shaking? No, my darling, I won't leave you ... Aren't we happy together? And besides, I love you so much ... when you're being nice to me, like this!'

'Yes, yes, I'd kill myself... I'd kill myself!'

'Are you being funny, darling! Why do you say that?'

'Because ...'

I was going to tell her everything ... I did not dare. And I went on, 'Because I love you. Because I don't want you to leave me! I don't want you to!'

I had to let her know eventually ... Juliette had seen a pearl necklace in the window of a jeweller's on rue de la Paix, which she kept talking about. One day when we happened to be in that area, she said to me, 'Come and see this pretty necklace!'

And with her nose pressed against the glass, and her eyes shining, she stared for a long time at the triple row of pink pearls displayed on the dark-red velvet of the jewellery case. I sensed shivers running over her skin.

'Isn't it beautiful? And not at all expensive! I asked how much ... fifty thousand francs. It's an exceptionally good price.'

I tried to draw her away, but she cajolingly held me back, clutching my arm. And she sighed, 'Ah, how nice it would look round your little darling's neck!'

She added with an air of deep dejection, 'And it's true ... every other woman has heaps of jewellery ... I don't have anything ... If you were kind, really, really kind, you'd give it to your poor little Juliette! And that's a fact.'

I stammered, 'Of course, I will ... but later ... in a week's time!'

Juliette's face darkened.

'Why in a week's time? Oh, straightaway, please, straightaway!'

'The thing is, you see, right now, I'm short of money ... very short ...'

'What? Already? You haven't any money left? Well, really! Where's it all gone, then? You haven't any money left?'

'Well, yes . . . yes! Only just at the moment I'm short.'

'So, what? What difference does that make? I asked about payment . . . They'll accept promissory notes . . . five notes for ten thousand francs . . . It's no big deal!'

'I dare say . . . later . . . I promise you . . . let's go . . .'

'Ah!' was all Juliette said.

I looked at her. The crease in her brow terrified me. I saw a dark gleam in her eyes . . . And in the space of a second I was overwhelmed by a whole multitude of extraordinary sensations I had not previously experienced. Very baldly, with perfect lucidity, with cold deliberation, with a lightning succinctness of judgement, I put to myself this twofold question: 'Juliette and dishonour; Juliette and prison?' I did not hesitate.

'Let's go in,' I said.

She carried off the necklace.

That evening, with her pearls round her neck, she sat on my lap looking radiant, and with her arms wrapped round my neck she spent a long time lulling me with her sweet voice.

'Ah, my poor darling,' she said. 'I've been naughty . . . Yes, I know . . . I'm sometimes a little crazy . . . But that's the end of it now! I want to be good and behave responsibly . . . And anyway, you'll work hard . . . you'll write a fine book, a wonderful play . . . And then we'll be rich, very rich . . . And then, when you're too hard-up, we'll sell the lovely necklace! Because jewels aren't like dresses . . . Jewels are money . . . Give me a big hug . . .'

Ah, how quickly that night flew past! How the hours raced by, no doubt terrified to hear the doomed voices of the damned howling their love.

Financial crises came thick and fast. Promissory notes made out for Juliette's purchases remained unpaid, and, borrowing from everywhere, I could barely the find the money we needed for our daily needs. My father had left a few unclaimed debts at St-Michel. Generous and kind-hearted, he liked to oblige small farmers in difficulty. I mercilessly set the bailiffs on these poor devils, forcing them to sell their hovels, their bit of land, their means of eking out a wretched existence, doing without everything. In the places where I still had credit, I bought things that I immediately sold off cheaply. I resorted to the most dubious second-hand dealers ... Outrageous blackmail schemes came into my mind, and I wore out Jesselin with my perpetual requests for money. Finally, I went once to Lirat. I needed five hundred francs that evening, and I wilfully, brazenly went to Lirat. Yet in his presence, in that studio so full of regretful memories, my confidence dropped, and I felt a belated sense of shame ... I hung round Lirat for a quarter of an hour, unable to tell him what I expected of his friendship. His friendship! And I got ready to leave.

'Ah, well, goodbye Lirat!'

'Goodbye, my friend.'

'Ah, I almost forgot ... You couldn't lend me five hundred francs, could you? I was counting on my rent-roll – it's late coming in.'

And hastily I added, 'I'll pay you back tomorrow ... tomorrow morning.'

Lirat fixed his eyes on me for a moment. I still remember the look he gave me ... It was actually full of sorrow.

'Five hundred francs!' he said. 'Where the devil do you expect me to find them? Have I ever had five hundred francs?'

I insisted. 'I'll pay you back tomorrow ... tomorrow morning.'

'But, my poor Mintié, I don't have that much money ... I've two hundred francs left ... Would that help?'

I thought, the two hundred francs he was offering me was his food for a whole month. Broken-hearted, I replied, 'Well, yes! Damn it! I'll pay you back tomorrow ... tomorrow morning.'

'That's fine, that's fine!'

At that moment I wished I could have thrown my arms

round Lirat's neck, asked his forgiveness, shouted, 'No, no, I don't want the money!' And like a thief, I took it.

The properties I owned, the Priory itself, the old family home, which had been mortgaged up to the hilt, were sold off! Ah, what a sad journey it was that I made on that occasion! It was a long time since I had been back to St-Michel. And yet when I felt sick and weary, amid the noxious excitement of Paris, the thought of this quiet little village was a balm, a relief to me. The pure breezes that reached me from there cooled my congested brain, eased the burning in my chest caused by the corrosive acids borne on the filthy air of cities. I had often promised myself that, when I tired of chasing dreams all the time, that was where I would take refuge, in the peace and serenity of my native surroundings. St-Michel! The place had never been so dear to me as since I had left. It seemed to contain beauties and riches I had been unable to enjoy before, and that I was suddenly discovering . . . I liked to look back on my memories of them, I especially liked to recall the forest, the beautiful forest where, as a restless, dreamy child, I had so often lost my way . . . Breathing in the pungent smell of sap, my ears charmed by the melody of the wind in the copsewood and timber trees, made to vibrate like harps and cellos, I would plunge down the broad straight avenues that came to an abrupt end far off in the distance and, like a church bay, opened onto the dazzling brightness of an ogive-framed patch of sky . . . In these dreams I saw the boughs of the oak trees, happy to see me again, reaching towards me with their greenest clusters. The young saplings greeted me with a joyous rustling as I passed by.

'Look how tall we've grown,' they said, 'how smooth and strong our trunks are, how good the air is in which we spread our delicate, well-spaced branches, how generous the soil where we grow our roots, which are constantly glutted with invigorating juices.'

The mosses and ferns called out to me, 'We've made you a good bed, young man, a good, sweet-smelling bed, the like of which is not to be found in the gilded miserliness of town

147

houses . . . Lie down, and roll over. If you're too hot, the ferns will fan their airy fronds above your head; if you're too chilly, the beeches will part their branches to let a sunbeam through to warm you.'

Alas, these voices had gradually fallen silent since I had been in love with Juliette. These memories no longer came back to me, like guardian angels, to comfort my sleep and flutter their white wings in the ruined azure of my dreams! Ashamed of me, the past was growing distant!

The train sped on, having crossed the Beauce plains, a gloomier sight now than in the harrowing days of war . . . And I recognised my little hummocky fields with their thick hedges, my straggling apple-trees, my narrow vales, my poplars with their crests bowed in the shape of cowls, looking like strange processions of novice Penitents through the countryside, my farms with their high mossy roofs, my rock-strewn sunken footpaths bordered with hornbeam pollards and overhung with dense foliage; my forest, over there, black in the sunset . . . It was dark when I arrived in St-Michel. This was just as well. I would have found it painful to walk down the road in broad daylight beneath the curious gaze of all these good people who had known me as a child . . . I felt that I was so covered in shame they would have turned away in horror, as though from a mangy dog . . . I quickened my pace, turning up the collar of my raincoat. The grocer, who was called Madame Henriette and in the past used to stuff me with cakes, was in front of her shop, chatting with some neighbours. Quaking at the thought that they might me talking about me, I stepped off the pavement into the roadway. Luckily, a cart went by, making a noise that drowned the women's words. The presbytery . . . the convent . . . the church . . . the Priory! By that time the Priory was nothing but an enormous black mass against the sky. And yet my heart stopped . . . I had to lean against one of the gate pillars to catch my breath. A few yards away the forest groaned, its deep voice swelled in anger, like the fury of the waves . . .

Marie and Felix were waiting for me . . . Marie older and

more wrinkled, Felix more stooped, his head wagging even more than before . . .

'Ah, Monsieur Jean! Monsieur Jean!'

And at once, taking my case, Marie said, 'You must be ever so hungry, Monsieur Jean! I've made a soup – you used to like that – and I've put a nice tasty chicken on the spit.'

'Thank you,' I said, 'I shan't be wanting any supper.'

I wanted to hug them both, to fling my arms round them and let my tears fall on their old shrivelled faces . . . And instead, my voice was harsh and curt. I'd said 'I shan't be wanting any supper' in an ominous tone of voice.

They stared at me, somewhat alarmed, and kept saying, 'Ah, Monsieur Jean! It's been such a long time! Ah, Monsieur Jean! What a handsome young man you are!'

Then Marie, thinking to interest me, began to retail the local news.

'As you know, poor Father Blanchetière died, and the new priest isn't going down well . . . it comes of being too young and fanatical . . . Baptiste was killed by a tree . . .'

I cut her short.

'Yes, yes, Marie . . . you can tell me all that tomorrow . . .'

She led to me my room, and asked, 'Will you be wanting your bowl of milk, Monsieur Jean?'

'As you wish.'

Once the door was closed I collapsed in an armchair and sat there, sobbing, for a long, long time. The next day I was up at dawn. The Priory had not changed; there were just a few more weeds on the paths, some moss on the steps, and a few trees had died. Once more I saw the gate, the scruffy lawns, the stunted rowans, the age-old chestnut-trees; I saw the pond with floating lilies where the kitten had been killed, the screen of firs that concealed the outhouses, the abandoned office; I saw the park with its gnarled trees and stone benches resembling old tombs . . . Felix was in the vegetable garden, hoeing a flowerbed . . . Oh, how decrepit the poor man was!

He pointed out to me a hawthorn bush, and said, 'That's

where you came with your dear departed father to stalk blackbirds . . . Do you remember, Monsieur Jean?'

'Yes, yes, Felix'

'And thrushes, too, by God!'

'Yes, yes, Felix.'

I moved away. I could not stand the sight of the old man who expected to die at the Priory, and whom I was about to drive out of there. And where he was to go? He had served us faithfully, was virtually a member of the family; and now that the poor man was unable to earn his living any more, I was going to drive him out! Oh, how could I!

Marie seemed nervous at lunch. She hovered round my chair with unusual restlessness.

'Forgive me, Monsieur Jean,' she said at last, 'there's something I've got to know . . . Is it true that you're selling the Priory?'

'Yes, Marie.'

The old woman's eyes widened in amazement, and resting both hands on the table, she repeated, 'You're selling the Priory?'

'Yes, Marie.'

'The Priory, where all your family was born . . . where your father and mother died . . . Lord Jesus, the Priory?'

'Yes, Marie.'

She shrank away from me, as though terrified.

'But you're a wicked young man, then, Monsieur Jean!'

I made no reply. Marie left the dining room and never spoke to me again.

I left two days later, once my affairs were settled and the legal papers signed . . . Of my fortune, all that remained was barely enough to live on for a month. It was gone, all gone! Nothing but debts, crippling debts, shameful debts! Ah, if only the train could have carried me on and on, and never arrive! It was not until I got back to Paris that I realised I had not been to kneel at the graves of my mother and father.

Juliette gave me a loving welcome. She kissed me passionately.

'Ah, my darling, my darling! I thought you'd never come

back! Five days! Just imagine! Now, if you make any more trips, I want to go with you . . .'

She was so affectionate, so genuinely upset, her caresses gave me so much confidence, and, besides, the sadness in my heart seemed such a heavy burden that I did not hesitate to confess all to her. I took her in my arms and sat her on my lap.

'Listen to me,' I said, 'listen carefully. I'm ruined, bankrupt . . . Bankrupt, do you understand? Bankrupt! All we have left is four thousand francs!'

'Poor dear!' sighed Juliette, resting her head on my shoulder. 'Poor dear!'

I burst into sobs, and cried out, 'You realise that I'll have to leave you . . . And it will kill me!'

'Don't be silly! You're crazy to talk like that . . . Do you think I could live without you, my darling? There, now, don't cry, don't get all upset . . .'

She dried my eyes and went on in a voice that grew gentler every moment, 'After all, we've four thousand francs . . . that will keep us going for four months . . . During those four months you'll be working . . . Now, in four months you'll have time to write a wonderful book! But don't cry . . . because if you do, I won't tell you a big secret . . . a big, big secret . . . Your little loved one had a bit of suspicion about all this, and do know what she's been doing? Do you? Well, for the last three days she's been going to a riding school and taking riding lessons . . . and next year, she'll be so good that Franconi will take her on. Do you know what a horsewoman at a top-class riding establishment earns? Two or three thousand francs a month . . . So, you see, there's no reason to be so upset, poor dear!'

I was prepared to accept any foolishness, or craziness. I clung to them desperately, as the drowning sailor clings to the unsound wreckage driven by the waves. As long as they sustained me for a moment, I did not ask myself towards what reefs of even greater peril, towards what darker depths they would carry me. Consequently, I retained the absurd hope of the man condemned to death who even on the bloody platform, even under the blade, expects some impossible event, an instant revolution, a planetary catastrophe, that will deliver him from execution. I allowed myself to be lulled by the pretty drone of Juliette's words! Resolutions for heroic work filled my mind and threw me into transports of enthusiasm . . . I envisaged panting crowds bowed over my books, and theatres where grave and grease-painted gentleman stepped forward, proclaiming my name to the frenetic applause of the public. Overwhelmed with tiredness, shattered by the emotion, I fell asleep . . .

We've had our supper . . . Juliette has been even more loving than on my return. Yet I detect some anxiety, some preoccupation in her. She is at once sad and gay. So what's going on behind that forehead with clouds passing across it? Despite her protestations, has she decided to leave me, and is she trying to make our parting less painful by lavishing on me all the wealth of her caresses?

'Oh, what a bore, my darling!' she said. 'I have to go out.'

'What do you mean, you have to go out? Now?'

'Well, yes, actually . . . Poor Gabrielle is very ill . . . She's on her own . . . I promised to go and see her. Oh, I shan't be long . . . An hour at most . . .'

Juliette talks very naturally. And I don't know why, I think she's lying, that she's not going to see Gabrielle . . . and I am seized with a vague, ghastly suspicion . . .

'Couldn't you wait till tomorrow?' I say.

'Oh, that's impossible! Don't you see, I promised!'

'Please! Tomorrow . . .'

'It's impossible! Poor Gabrielle!'

'Well, I'll come with you, then . . . I'll wait for you at the door!'

Slyly I watch her. Her face does not twitch . . . No, truly, she is not in the least betrayed by her nerves. She replies sweetly.

'That's unreasonable! You're tired, my darling . . . Go to bed!'

I see the train of her dress slip like a snake through the door-curtain that closes behind her. Juliette is in her dressing room. And keeping my gaze fixed on the tablecloth, on which the red reflection of a bottle of wine flickers, I reflect that some women have been here recently, fat, louche women, reminiscent of bitches sniffing at rubbish . . .

I asked Juliette, 'Who are these women?'

Juliette replied, on one occasion, 'She's my stay-maker.' And on another, 'She's my embroideress . . .'

And I believed her!

One day I picked up a visiting-card that was lying on the carpet . . . Madame Rabineau, 114 rue de Sèze . . .

'Who's this Madame Rabineau?'

Juliette replied, 'It's nothing. Here, give it to me . . .'

And she tore up the card. And I, like a fool, did not even go to rue de Sèze to find out! I remember all this . . . Ah, why didn't I realise? Why did I not fly at the throats of those ugly peddlers of human flesh? And a great veil lifts, allowing me to see Juliette, looking exhausted and hideous, and her body defiled, prostituting herself to dirty old men! Juliette is there, before me, drawing on her gloves, before me, dressed in a dark outfit . . . with her thick veil hiding her face . . . The shadow of her hand flits across the cloth, lengthens, broadens, narrows, disappears and returns . . . I shall always see that diabolical shadow, always!

'Hug me tight, my darling.'

'Don't go out, Juliette, don't go out, I beg you.'

'Hug me . . . tight . . . tighter . . .'

She is sad . . . Through the thick veil I feel the wetness of a tear on my cheek.

'Why are you crying, Juliette? Juliette, for pity's sake, stay with me!'

'Hug me . . . I adore you, Jean, I adore you!'

She's gone . . . Doors open and close again . . . She's gone . . . I hear the noise outside of a carriage in motion . . . The sound grows more and distant, and dies away . . . She's gone!

And now I'm in the street, too. A cab comes by. '114 rue de Sèze!'

Ah, my decision was quickly taken! I thought I had time to get there before her . . . She realised all too well that I was not taken in by Gabrielle's illness ... My gloominess and insistence has no doubt prompted in her the fear of being spied on and followed, and she probably will not have made her way there straightaway ... But why has this appalling idea struck me all of a sudden, like a bolt from the blue? Why this, and not something else? I still hope that my apprehensions have deceived me, that Madame Radineau is 'nothing', that Gabrielle is ill!

A kind of small mansion squashed between two tall buildings; a narrow doorway set back in the wall, at the top of three steps; a dark facade whose closed windows let no light filter through ... This is the place! This is where she's coming, where she has perhaps already been! And waves of fury drive me to this doorway. I feel like setting fire to this house; I feel like making all the doomed bodies inside scream and writhe in an infernal blaze. Just now, a woman in a light-coloured jacket, with her hands in her pockets and her elbows out, went inside, swinging her hips and singing. Why did I not spit in her face? An old man got out of his brougham. He passed right by me, snorting and puffing, supported under the arms by his valet. His trembling legs could not carry him, Between his swollen and flaccid eyelids flashed a gleam of sadistic debauchery. Why did I not slash the hideous face of that invalid old goat? Could he be waiting for Juliette? The gate of hell closed behind him, and for a moment my eyes penetrated the abyss. I thought I saw red flames, smoke, dreadful couplings, the flounderings of frightfully entangled human bodies ... No, it's a bleak deserted corridor, lit by the pale glow of a lamp, and at the far end there's a blackness, like a dark hole, seemingly infested with foul things ... And carriages halt, vomiting their load of human dung into this cesspool of love.

A little girl of scarcely ten years of age follows me. 'Lovely violets! Lovely violets!'

I give her a gold coin. 'Go away, little girl, go away! Don't stay here. They'll get you!'

My mind is in a frenzy, and I feel the pain of a thousand fangs, a thousand claws relentlessly probing and tearing my heart. Murderous desires stir inside me and teach my arms how to kill . . . Ah, would that I could rush, whip in hand, into the midst of these satyrs, and lash their bodies, leaving indelible wounds, and splatter the mirrors, carpets, beds, with rivulets of warm blood, with bits of living flesh! And nail the Rabineau woman to the door of her squalid house, naked, disembowelled, with her guts hanging out, like an owl on the door of a country barn!

A cab stops and a woman gets out. I recognise the hat, the veil, the dress.

'Juliette!'

She utters a cry as she sees me. But she quickly recovers. Her eyes defy me.

'Let me go!' she cries. 'What are you doing here? Let me go!'

Squeezing her wrists, I say to her in a choking, rasping voice, 'Listen . . . if you take another step, if you say a single word . . . I'll throw you on to the pavement and crush your head under the sole of my shoes.'

'Let me go!'

I bring my hand down heavily on her face and in a fury I rake her forehead and cheeks with my fingernails, drawing blood.

'Jean! Oh, Jean! Please, have pity on me! Jean! Spare me, spare me! Be good! You're killing me . . .'

Brutally I force her over to the cab . . . and we return home. She's here in front of me, bent double, sobbing . . . What am I going to do? I have no idea . . . Truly, I have no idea . . . I have no thoughts, my mind is a blank. I feel as though a mountain of rocks has collapsed on top of me. I have the impression that heavy boulders have flattened my skull, crushed my flesh . . . Why, in the darkness where I am, do these tall pale walls go reaching up into the sky? Why are there sinister birds flying in sudden patches of light? Why is this thing, in a heap beside me, crying? Why? I don't know . . .

CHAPTER SEVEN

I'm going to kill her! She's lying in her room in the dark. I'm in the dressing room, pacing round and round, breathing heavily; my head's very hot and my fists are clenched, impatient for justice . . . I'm going to kill her! Every so often I stop at her door and listen. She's crying. And soon I'll go in . . . I'll go in and haul her out bed, I'll drag her by the hair, I'll bloody her belly, I'll smash her skull against the marble corners of the fireplace . . . I want the room to be red with her blood. I want her body to be just a bundle of bruised flesh that I shall throw on to the rubbish heap, which the dustcart will collect tomorrow . . . Go on, cry! In a moment you'll be screaming, my precious!

Have I been stupid? To have thought of everything but that! To have been afraid of everything but that! To have said to myself constantly, 'She'll leave me', and never, ever, 'She'll deceive me.' Not to have had any inkling of that brothel, that old man, all that vice! No, really, it never entered my mind, blind fool that I was . . . She must have been laughing up her sleeve when I begged her not to leave me. Leave me, ah, yes, leave me! She didn't want to leave me! I understand now . . . I don't represent to her decency and respectability, but rather a seal of approval, a label . . . a cachet! Yes, if she's seen on my arm, she's worth more, she can sell herself more dearly than if she went streetwalking, a nocturnal ghoul preying on the obscene darkness of the gutter . . . She gobbled up my fortune in one bite, her lips sucked my mind dry with one kiss . . . Now, it's only logical she should be looking to make the most of my honour. My honour! How would she know I'm left with none? So, am I going to kill her? Once you're dead, that's the end of it! Men take their hats off to a criminal's coffin, people show deference to a prostitute's corpse . . . In churches, the faithful kneel and pray for the souls of those who have suffered, for those who have sinned . . . In cemeteries, the tombs are held in respect and the cross is their protector ... To die is to be forgiven! Yes, death is beautiful and holy and solemn! Death is the beginning of the great eternal brightness. Oh, to die! To lie down on a mattress softer than the softest mossy nest. Not to think any more! Not to hear life's din any more! To experience the infinite voluptuous delight of nothingness! To be a soul! I shan't kill her ... I shan't kill her, because she must suffer, horribly, for ever ... she must suffer in her beauty, her pride, in her flaunted prostituted sexuality! I shan't kill her, but I shall brand her with such ugliness, I shall make her so repulsive that everyone will run away in terror at the sigh of her. And I shall force her, with her nose cut off and her eyes bulging out of scar-ringed eyelids, to display herself, every day, every night, on the street, in the theatre, everywhere ...

Suddenly my sobs are choking me. I roll on the divan, chewing the cushions, and I weep and weep! Ah, Juliette, monstrous Juliette! Why did you do it? Why? Couldn't you have said, 'You're not rich any more, and money's what I want from you ... So, get lost!' That would have been less excruciating. It might perhaps have killed me – what does that matter? It would have been better ... How can I possibly look you in the eye any more? How can our lips ever meet again? That damned brothel now stands between us! Ah, Juliette! Poor Juliette!

I remember when she went out ... I remember everything! I can see her in the outfit she was wearing, and the bizarre shadow of her hand dancing on the grey fabric of dress ... I can see her as clearly as if she were before me now, even more clearly ... She was sad, she was crying ... I did not imagine it – she was crying, since her tears wet my cheeks! Was she crying for me, or for herself? Ah, who knows? I remember ... I said to her, 'Don't go out, Juliette!' She replied, 'Hug me tight, much tighter!' And there was greater sorrow, tenseness, and fear in her kisses, as though she were trying to cling to me, tremulously seeking protection in my arms ... I can see her eyes, her entreating eyes ... They implored me, 'Something diabolical is impelling me to go ... Make me stay! You have me in your embrace ... Don't

157

let me go! And instead of taking her, carrying her away, hiding her, loving her enough to make her dizzy with happiness, I opened my arms and she went! She sought refuge in my love, and my love rejected her. She cried out to me, 'I adore you, I adore you!' And I stood there, stupidly, as astonished as a child whose caged bird has just escaped with an unexpected whir of its wings . . . I didn't understand the meaning of that sadness, those tears and kisses and fond words, those tremors, and it's only now that I can hear that silent, doleful language: 'My dear Jean, I'm a poor little woman, who's a little crazy and very weak! I've not much idea about anything . . . Who taught me what modesty, duty and virtue were! I was contaminated as a child by the spectacle of vice, and shown evil by the very people responsible for looking after me . . . I'm not wicked though, and I love you . . . I love you now more than ever before! My beloved Jean, you're strong, you know such wonderful things that I'm totally unaware of . . . So, protect me! A more urgent desire is luring me there . . . For I've seen jewels and dresses and very expensive, delightful little things that you can't give me any more, and that they've promised me! I can sense that it's bad and will cause you pain . . . Well, bring me to heel! I'm all for being good and virtuous . . . Teach me how . . . If I don't do as you say, beat me.'

Poor Juliette! It's as though she were kneeling beside me, with her hands joined . . . Tears flow from her eyes, from those big, meek and gentle eyes tears flow constantly, as they once used to flow from my mother's eyes. And at the thought that I wanted to kill her, that I wanted to disfigure this darling, penitent face with horrible mutilations, I am assailed with remorse, my anger melts into pity . . .

She goes on: 'Forgive me! Oh, Jean, you must forgive me. It's not my fault, I assure you. Just think . . . Did you ever warn me? Did you ever show me the path I should follow? Out of feebleness, out of fear of losing me, out of excessive and criminal complaisance, you yielded to all my whims, even the worst of them . . . How could I possibly realise that it was bad, since you didn't say anything . . . When I was racing towards the abyss, instead of stopping me on the edge of it, you actually urged me on. What examples have you placed before me? What guidance have you given me? When did you ever tear me away from this alarmingly dissolute world? Jesselin, Gabrielle, all those depraved creatures whose presence gave encouragement to my folly – why didn't you throw them out of the house? What you should have done was inspire me with some of your knowledge, cast a little light into the darkness of my mind! Yes, you should have recreated me, given me a second life! I'm at fault, Jean! And I feel so ashamed I don't expect to be able to redeem the disgrace of this black hour even with a whole lifetime's sacrifice and repentance. But are you so sure of having fulfilled your duty? I've no fear of expiation. On the contrary, that's what I want . . . But what about you? Can you set yourself up as the judge of a crime admittedly mine, but also yours, since you failed to prevent it? My beloved, listen to me . . . This body I tried to defile inspires you with horror. You could never look at it again without anger and despair. Well, let it disappear, then! Let it be sent to rot in a cemetery and consigned to oblivion! My soul will remain with you. It belongs to you. For it has not left you; it loves you. Look, it's pure white . . .'

A knife glints in Juliette's hands. She is about to strike herself with it . . .

Then I reach out my arms and cry, 'No, Juliette, no, don't . . . I love you . . . No, no, don't . . .' My arms close round, and I'm embracing nothing but space. I look round, terror-stricken. The room is empty! I look again. The gas burns yellower in the dressing-table lamps. Discarded petticoats and ankle-boots lie strewn on the carpet. And daylight very wanly steals through the slats of the shutters. I'm afraid that Juliette might really have killed herself, for why should that vision have risen before me? I tiptoe quietly to the door and listen. I hear a faint sigh, then a moan, and a sob. And I burst into the room like a madman. A voice speaks to me in the darkness, Juliette's voice.

'Oh, Jean, my poor little Jean!'

And with a chaste kiss upon her brow, such as Christ gave Mary Magdalene, I embraced her.

CHAPTER EIGHT

'Lirat! Ah, you, at last! I've been looking for you for a week, writing to you, calling you, waiting for you . . . Lirat, my dear Lirat, save me!'

'Good heavens, man! What's the matter?'

'I want to kill myself!'

'Kill yourself! I know all about that . . . Never mind, it's not dangerous.'

'I want to kill myself! I want to kill myself!'

Lirat looked at me, winked, and strode into my study.

'My poor Mintié,' he said, 'if you were a minister, a stock-broker . . . I don't know . . . a grocer, an art critic, a journal-ist . . . I'd say to you, 'So you're unhappy and tired of life, my boy? Well, go ahead and kill yourself!' And I'd leave you to get on with it! But you have the rare good fortune of being an artist, you have the divine gift of being able to see, understand and feel what others don't see, understand and feel! There are in nature strains of music meant for none but you, that others will never hear. The only joys in life – the noble, grand, pure joys that console you for what men are, and make you almost godlike – you have them all . . . And you're going to renounce all this just because a woman has deceived you? She has deceived you, of course she has. What do you expect? And what difference can it possibly make?'

'Don't laugh at me, I beg you! You just don't know, Lirat . . . you have no idea . . . I'm ruined, disgraced!'

'Disgraced, my friend? Are you so sure? You've some bad debts? You'll pay them off!'

'It's not that! I'm disgraced! Disgraced, do you under-stand? Listen, I haven't given Juliette any money for four months. Four months! And I live here, eat here, I'm a kept man! Juliette gets home late, every evening, before dinner . . . tired out, pale and dishevelled . . .What den of iniquity, whose bed, whose arms has she just left? On whose pillow has she rolled her head? Sometimes I see threads of bed linen dangling, shamelessly, from the ends of her hair . . . She doesn't care any more, she doesn't even bother to lie . . . it's as though it were a matter agreed between us . . . She undresses and I think she gets a sinister pleasure out of letting me see her ill-tied petticoats, her unlaced bodice, all the disarrangement of her crumpled clothes, of her unfastened underwear falling scattered around her, filling the room with the smell of other men! I'm overcome with fits of rage, and want to bite her; bursts of anger blaze and rumble inside me, and I want to kill her . . . and I say nothing. In fact I often go to kiss her, but she pushes me away. 'No, leave me alone, I'm exhausted!'

'In the early days of this dreadful existence I beat her . . . for there's no depth to which I've not sunk, Lirat, no shameful deed I've not committed . . . Yes, I beat her, and she submitted to it, barely complaining. One evening I grabbed her by the throat and held her down. Oh, I was quite determined to make an end of it . . . As I squeezed her neck, I turned my head away, in the fear of being moved to pity, and kept my gaze stubbornly fixed on a flower in the carpet, and so as not hear any moan or rattle in her throat, I yelled out incoherent words like a man possessed. How long did I go on doing that? Soon she was no longer struggling. Her contracted muscles relaxed. I felt the life being choked out of her beneath my fingers. Another few shudders, then nothing . . . she was no longer moving. And all of a sudden I saw her purple face and bulging eyes, her mouth, wide open, her rigid body, her inert arms.

Like a madman, I went rushing through every room in the apartment, calling the servants, shouting, 'Come quickly, I've killed madame! I've killed madame!'

I raced downstairs, without a hat, into the porter's lodge. 'Get up there quickly, I've killed madame!'

And then I was out in the street, bewildered . . . I ran and ran, all night long, without knowing where I was going, down endless boulevards and across bridges, I collapsed on to benches in the squares, and always kept returning, automatically, in front of our building . . . I thought I could see candles flickering through the closed shutters, and priests in their cassocks and surplices flurrying past with the last sacraments; that I could hear funeral chants, the sound of organ pipes, the rasp of cords on the wood of the coffin. I imagined Juliette lying on her bed in a white gown, with her hands joined together and a crucifix on her breast and flowers all around her. And I was surprised that there weren't yet any black drapes over the door and a catafalque in the entrance hall, with bouquets and wreaths and crowds of people in mourning vying for the holy water sprinkler . . .

'Ah, Lirat, what a night that was! How I didn't throw myself under the wheels of carriages, smash my head against the walls of houses, or jump into the Seine, I just don't know! It grew light. I thought of giving myself up to the police. I felt like going up to police officers and saying to them, 'I killed Juliette! Arrest me!'

But the most outrageous ideas came into my mind, contended with each other and gave way to others. And I ran and ran, as if a pack of dogs were chasing me. It was a Sunday, I remember . . . There were a lot of people on the sunny streets . . . I was convinced all eyes were upon me, that all these people were crying with horror as they saw me running, 'That's Juliette's murderer!' By evening, when I met Jesselin, I was exhausted and ready to collapse on the pavement.

'Hey, there!' he shouted. 'You've certainly been excelling yourself!'

'You've already heard?' I asked, trembling.

Jesselin laughed and replied, 'Have I heard? But, my dear friend, the whole of Paris has heard . . . Just now, at the races. Juliette was showing us her neck and the marks your fingers left on it. She said, 'It was Jean who did this to me . . .' Heavens alive! You really go at it, don't you?'

And as he left, he added, 'It has to be said, she's never looked more attractive . . . And what a success!'

So, there was I thinking she was dead, and all the time she was out parading herself at the racetrack! More attractive than ever!'

Lirat listened to me, looking very solemn. He had stopped walking around and sat down, nodding his head. 'What do you expect me to say?' he murmured. 'You must go away . . .'

'Go away?' I echoed. 'Go away? But I don't want to! A glue that grows thicker every day keeps me stuck to these carpets. A chain that grows daily heavier rivets me to these walls. I can't! Listen, right now, I have dreams of insane heroism . . . I would like to purge myself of all this despicableness, I would like to hurl myself at the blazing mouths of a hundred canons. I feel I have the strength to defeat fearsome armies with my bare fists. When I wander the streets, I am on the lookout for runaway horses, fires, any terrible challenge I might take on. There isn't a dangerous, superhuman feat I lack the courage to perform. But that's something I'm incapable of! At first I came up with the most ridiculous excuses, the most preposterous reasons. I said to myself that if I went away, Juliette would sink even lower, that my love was in some way her last shred of decency, that I would eventually succeed in retrieving her, in rescuing her from the mire in which she wallows . . . I actually tried to afford myself the luxury of pity and sacrifice. But I was lying! I can't! I can't, because I love her, because the more vile she is, the more I love her. And because I want her, do you understand, Lirat? And if you knew what this love consists of, of what rage, what ignominy, what torture! If you knew to what infernal depths passion can sink, you would be appalled! In the evening, when she's in bed, I prowl round the dressing room, opening drawers, raking the ashes in the hearth, piecing together fragments of torn letters, sniffing the underwear she has just taken off, indulging in the most squalid spying, in the most shameful investigations. I'm not satisfied any more with knowing, I need to see for myself! Indeed, I'm no longer a mind, or a heart, or anything . . . I'm a raging sexual maniac with a ravenous appetite, demanding his ration of live flesh, like the wild beasts that howl in the heat of their nights of bloodshed.'

I was exhausted. The words that came out of my throat were no more than whistling sounds. Yet, I continued.

'Ah, there's no understanding it! Sometimes Juliette falls ills . . . her pleasure-taxed limbs refuse to work. Her organism, shaken with nervous tremors, rebels. She takes to her bed. If you could see her then? A child, Lirat, a sweet and engaging child! She dreams only of the countryside, of little brooks, green fields, simple joys. 'Oh, my darling,' she cries, 'how happy we could be with an income of ten thousand francs!' She makes delightful, Virgilian plans. We are to go and live far, far away, in a little house surrounded by big trees . . . she will keep chickens that will lay eggs she herself will collect every morning; she will make cream cheese and jam . . . toss hay and visit the poor, wear aprons like this and straw hats like that, and trot along the paths on a donkey that she will call Joseph . . . 'Gee up, Joseph, gee up! Oh, it would be wonderful!'

'Listening to her, I feel hope returning, and I surrender to this impossible dream of a rural existence with Juliette dressed up as shepherdess. Landscapes of haven-like peacefulness, of heavenly enchantment, pass before us . . . And we go into raptures, into ecstasies . . . Juliette cries: 'My poor darling, I've caused you a lot of pain, but, honestly, it's over now, I promise you . . . And I'll have a pet sheep, won't I? A big, white sheep, with a red bow that I'll tie around its neck, won't I? And it'll follow me everywhere, with Spy, won't it?'

'She insists that I have my supper on a little table by her bed. And she fusses over me like a nurse, treats me with a mother's attentiveness . . . she feeds me like a child, repeating all the time, in a voice touched with emotion, 'Poor darling!'

At other times she becomes pensive and serious.

'My love, I want to ask you something that's been worrying me for a long time . . . swear that you'll tell me.'

'I swear.'

'Well . . . when you're dead, in the coffin, do your feet touch the side of the box?'

'What an idea! Why talk about that?'

'Tell me, tell me, please, tell me!'

'But, my dear Juliette, I don't know.'

'You don't know? It's true, actually, whenever I ask a serious question you never know the answer . . . . because, you see, I don't want my feet to touch the side of the box . . . When I'm dead, I want you to make sure I have a cushion . . . and a white dress . . . you know . . . with pink flowers . . . my Grand Prix dress! Will you be terribly upset, poor darling? Kiss me . . . come here, close to me, closer . . . I adore you!'

'How I wished that Juliette were always ill! As soon as she recovers, she doesn't remember anything. Her promises, her resolutions turn to nothing, and our hellish life resumes with a vengeance, more frenetic than ever before . . . And from that little corner of sky where I had stopped for a while, I plunge, even more appallingly dashed, into the blood and mire of this love! Ah, but that's not all, Lirat! I should stay at home, lurking in the apartment, alone with my shame, wouldn't you say! Shouldn't I be heaping such darkness and oblivion on myself that people might think me dead? Well, yes, indeed! Go the Bois and you will see me there every day . . . At the theatre, there again, you'll see me, in a stage-box, wearing a dress-coat, with a flower in my buttonhole . . . me everywhere! Juliette is in her element among those flowers, feathers and jewels. She looks delightful, in a new dress that everyone admires, with her increasingly virginal smiles and the pearl necklace I've not paid for, with which she elegantly and remorselessly toys with her fingertips . . . And I haven't a cent, not a cent! And I'm as deep as can be in debt, swindle and fraud! I often shudder . . . Because I've thought I could feel the heavy hand of a policeman bearing down on me. Already I hear distressing whispers, I catch oblique glances filled with contempt . . . gradually the gap widens and extends around me, as if I were plague-stricken . . . Old friends pass by, turn their heads away, avoid me so as not to greet me . . . And despite myself, I adopt the shifty, servile demeanour of discredited people who go about fearfully hunched, casting sidelong glances, in search of an outstretched hand! The horrible thing, you see, is that I realise very clearly that it's only Juliette beauty that protects me. It is the desire that she excites, her mouth, the exposed and profaned mystery of her body that in this world of pleasure covers me with false respect, with a false appearance of esteem . . . A handshake, an obliging look means, 'I've slept with your Juliette, and I owe you this at least . . . Perhaps you would prefer money . . . Would you?' Yes, I have only to leave Juliette, and I'll be booted out of this very world, this promiscuous, complaisant, depraved world, and reduced to the dubious friendship of croupiers and pimps!'

I burst into sobs. Lirat did not stir, did not look up at me . . . He sat motionless, with his hands crossed, staring at I don't know what . . . nothing probably . . .

After a few minutes' silence I went on.

'My dear Lirat, you remember our chats in your studio! I used to listen to you, and what you told me was so wonderful! Without it perhaps, you instilled me with noble desires and grand enthusiasms . . . You fired me a little with the beliefs, ambitions and lofty impulses of your own soul. You taught me to read nature, to understand its passionate language, to feel the sentiment dispersed in things . . . you brought me into contact with immortal beauty. You said to me, 'Love? But it exists in the earthenware jug, in the verminous beggar I paint . . . Recreating a sensibility, a joy, a pain, a tremor, a certain light, a quiver, anything fleeting that has been part of life, capturing it in colours, words or sounds – that's loving! Love is man's striving towards creation!'

'And I dreamed of being a great artist. Ah, do you remember my dreams, the thrill of imagination I felt, my doubts, my blessed anguish? Now you see what I've made of all that! I wanted love, and I went to a woman, the killer of love. I set off, on wings, delirious with space, blue skies and brightness! And now I'm nothing but a filthy pig, wallowing in its filth, with a voracious lust in its belly, its sides jiggled by indecent rutting. You can see very well, Lirat, that I'm lost, lost, lost, that I must kill myself.'

Then Lirat came over to me and laid both his hands on my shoulders.

'You're lost, you say. Come now, is the life of a man, if he's one of your kind, ever lost? You must kill yourself? Does a person sick with typhoid fever cry, 'You must kill me?' He says, 'You must cure me . . .' You have typhoid fever, my poor child. Cure yourself . . . Lost! But there's no crime in existence – do you hear? – no crime however monstrous and vile, that forgiveness cannot redeem. Not the forgiveness of God, nor the forgiveness of men, but self-forgiveness, which is much more difficult to obtain, and better by far . . . Lost! I was listening to you, my dear Mintié, and do you know what I was thinking? I was thinking you have the finest and noblest soul I know of . . . No, no, a man who accuses himself as you do . . . no, a man who puts into his confession the heart-rending accents you've put into yours . . . no, that man is not lost. On the contrary, he's finding himself again, and he's close to redemption. Love has passed over you, leaving all the more mud on you because of your more generous and sensitive nature . . . Well, you must wash off this mud, and I know where there's water that will remove it . . . You have to go away . . . leave Paris . . .'

'Lirat,' I implored, 'don't ask me to leave! I've tried twenty times already, and failed.'

'You have to go away,' repeated Lirat, whose face suddenly darkened. 'Otherwise, I've been mistaken, and you're a worthless nobody!'

He went on, 'In the wilds of Brittany, there's a fishermen's village called Le Ploc'h. The air there is clean, the landscape superb, the people tough and honest. That's where you'll go and live . . . for three months, six months, a year if necessary. You'll walk across the beaches, the moors, through the pine forests, over the rocks. You'll dig the earth, you'll collect wrack, you'll lift boulders, you'll holler in the wind . . . Eventually, my friend, you will subdue this poisoned body that's been maddened by love . . . At the beginning, it will be hard for you, and you will experience fits of nostalgia, and rebellion, you will feel desperate urges to return . . . Don't be discouraged, I beg you. On days that oppress you, do more walking, spend the nights at sea with those honest folk there, and if you feel heavy-hearted, go ahead and cry, but on no account give in to daydreaming, reading, writing her name on the rocks or tracing it in the sand ... Don't think, don't think of anything ... In such instances, literature and art are bad counsellors; they would lead you back to love in no time. You need constant physical activity, some heavy labour, to have your flesh worn down by overwhelming tiredness, your mind lashed and dazed by wind, rain, and squalls ... I tell you, you'll come back from there not only cured but stronger than ever, better armed for battle ... And you will have paid your debt to the monster. You will have paid with your fortune? What's a fortune? Ah, you know, I envy you, and I wish I could go with you ... Now then, my dear Mintié, a bit of courage! Come on!'

'Yes, Lirat, you're right. I must leave ...'

'Well, come along then!'

'I'll leave tomorrow, I swear to you.'

'Tomorrow? Ah, tomorrow! She's coming back, isn't she? And you'll throw yourself in her arms ... No, come on!'

'Let me write to her! I can't just leave her like that, without a word, without saying goodbye. Lirat, have some thought! Despite the suffering, despite the shame, there are some happy memories, some blessed moments ... She's not wicked ... she doesn't know, that's all ... but she loves me ... I'll go, I promise you I'll go ... Give me a day! A single day! A day's not much, when I shan't be seeing her again! Ah, just one day!'

'No, come on!'

'Lirat! My dear Lirat!'

'No!'

'But I haven't any money! How do you expect me to leave with no money?'

'I've enough for your journey ... I'll send you some more there ... Come on.'

'Let me pack a suitcase at least!'

'I have some woollens and berets ... everything you need ... Come on!'

He dragged me away. I moved through the apartment

169

without seeing anything, almost without understanding what was happening, bumping into the furniture as I went. It did not upset me, because I was not aware of anything. I walked behind Lirat with that lumbering pace, in that passive way, of beasts being led to slaughter.

'What about your hat?'

It is true! I was going out hatless . . . I did not feel that I was abandoning anything, that I was leaving behind a part of myself; that the things I could see, among which I had lived, were dying one after the other, as I passed in front of them.

The train was leaving at eight o'clock in the evening. Lirat remained with me for the rest of the day. In an effort, probably, to keep my mind occupied and my will in check, he talked to me, accompanying his speech with grand gestures, but all I heard was a confused, irritating noise, buzzing in my ears like a cloud of flies . . . We dined in a restaurant near Montparnasse station. Lirat went on talking to me, stupefying me with his words and gestures, tracing strange geographical lines on the table with his knife.

'Look, that's where it is! So you follow the coast and . . .'

He gave me, I think, information relating to my journey, to my exile there . . . mentioning the names of villages, of people . . . The word 'the sea' kept recurring, with a scraping of pebbles moved by the waves.

'Will you remember?'

And without knowing exactly what he was talking about, I replied, 'Yes, yes, I'll remember.'

It was only at the station, that huge station, full of hustle and bustle, that I became truly aware of my situation . . . And I experienced a dreadful anguish. So I was about to leave! So it was all over! I would never see Juliette again, ever! At that point I forgot the suffering, the shame, my ruin, Juliette's irremediable behaviour, recalling only the brief moments of happiness, and I rebelled against the injustice that was separating me from my beloved . . .

Lirat was saying, 'And then if you knew what a pleasure it is to live among humble folk . . . to study their poor and dignified life, their martyr-like resignation, their . . .'

I thought of giving him the slip, of running away all of a sudden. A crazy hope restrained me. I kept saying to myself, 'Celestine will have told Juliette that Lirat called, that he carried me off by force. She'll guess straightaway that something horrible is going on, that I'm in this station, that I'm going to leave . . . And she'll come running . . .' I seriously believed this . . . so much so that I looked out through the big open bay-windows, examining those who came in, scanning the people in groups, searching the tightly packed queues of travellers standing in front of the ticket counters. And if an elegant woman appeared, I would give a start, ready to rush towards her.

Lirat went on, 'And there are some people who have described these heroes as brutes . . . Ah, you'll see them, those magnificent brutes with their callused hands, their eyes filled with infinity, and their backs that make you weep . . .'

Even on the platform I was still hoping Juliette would come. Surely, in a second, she would be there, pale, distraught and imploring, her arms reaching out to me. 'Jean, Jean, I've been a bad woman, forgive me! Don't be angry with me, don't abandon me. What do you expect will become of me without you? Oh, come back, Jean, or take me with you!'

And figures took fright and disappeared into carriages, fantastic shadows crept up the walls and came to grief on them, long trails of smoke swirled beneath the vaulted roof.

'Hug me, my dear Mintié, hug me.'

Lirat clasped me to his breast. He was weeping.

'Write to me as soon as you get there. Farewell!' He shoved me into a carriage and closed the door.

There is a whistle, then a rumbling sound . . . then lights following each other in succession, things flying past, then nothing but black night . . . Why did Juliette not come? Why? And I have a clear vision of her, in her dressing room, with her petticoats strewn over the carpets, bare-shouldered at her mirror, dusting her face with a powder-puff. Celestine, with her clammy limp fingers, sews a strip of soft crêpe to the neck of a bodice, and a man I don't know, semi-reclining on the divan, with his legs crossed, gazes at Juliette with desire gleaming in his eyes . . . The gas lamp burns, the candles blaze, a bunch of roses that has just been delivered mingles its more subtle fragrance with the strong scents of the dressing table. And Juliette takes a rose, breaks off the stem, smooths the leaves, and tenderly, with a smile, sticks it in the man's buttonhole. A little bonnet, with it strings dangling, sits in splendour on top of a candelabrum.

And the train speeds on, huffing and puffing . . . The night remains black, and I settle into nothingness.

CHAPTER NINE

Lying flat on my stomach in the dune, with my elbows in the sand, my head in my hands, my gaze lost in the distance, I dream ... The sea lies before me, a vast bluey-green, streaked with broad purple shadows, churned up by deep waves whose crests, poised here and there, show white. And from the breakers of the Gamelle that from time to time reveals the dark tips of its rocks comes the muffled sound of distant cannon fire. Yesterday there was a raging storm; today the wind has dropped, but the sea is not yet resigned to the calm. The surge advances, swells, rolls, rises, shakes its mane of crimped foam, bursts into a seething spume and with a terrific roar of anger comes crashing down in ruins over the shingle. Yet the sky is tranquil, with azure showing through the rents in the clouds that are quickly swept away, and with seagulls flying very high. The fishing boats have left port; they sail off, grow smaller, scatter, fade away and disappear ... On my right, the strand, dominated by collapsing sand dunes, runs all the way to Le Ploc'h, of which the roofs of the nearest houses, the openwork stone belltower, then the enormous granite mound of the pier with the lighthouse standing on the end of it, are visible behind a fold in the land, against a bleak green background. Beyond the pier, the eye has an impression of indistinct spaces, pink beaches, silver-grey coves, cliffs of soft blue misted with spray, of such lightness they seem nebulous, and always the sea, and the sky, blending into one another, over there, in a mysterious and poignant fading to nothingness.

On my left, the dunes, where the broomrape displays its corymbs of purple flowers, suddenly end. The ground rises, slopes steeply, and tumbling heaps of rock yawn with booming pits, or else plunge into the sea, brutally cutting through it like the prows of giant ships. On that side there is no beach. The sea hugging the coast beats upon the rocks with a vengeance, leaps up at them in a constant fury, white with foam. And the coastline continues, made jagged, indented, eaten away by the eternal effort of the waves, collapsing here in monstrous chaos, rising there and projecting disquieting silhouettes against the sky. Flocks of linnets fly over me, and above the anger of the waves, the wind brings to my ears the plaintive cries of gannets and curlews.

This is where I come every day ... Whether there is wind, or rain, whether the sea is roaring or singing, clear or sombre, this is where I come ... Yet it is not that these spectacles move me and impress me, that I get any consolation from this horrible and attractive scenery. I hate this scenery. I hate the sea, the sky, the cloud that passes, the wind that blows, the bird that wheels in the air. I hate everything around me, and everything I see, and everything I hear. I come here out of habit, driven by the instinct that takes animals back to a familiar place. Like the hare, I have dug my form on this sand and I return to it ... On sand or moss, in the shade of forests, at the bottom of pits, or out in the sun on lonely beaches – it's all the same! So where is the man in pain to find refuge? Where is the voice that soothes? Where is the pity that dries eyes that weep? Ah, I know those chaste dawns, those cheerful noons, those pensive evening and starry nights! Those distances in which the soul dilates and sorrows mingle. Oh, do I know them! Beyond the line of this horizon, beyond this sea, are there not places like any other? Are there not men, trees, noise? Nowhere is there rest, and nowhere silence! I wish I could die! But who is to say that the thought of Juliette won't come and join the worms in devouring me? One stormy day I came face to face with death, and I made my entreaty. But death turned away from me ... It spared me – a person good for nothing, of no use to anyone, whose life is more of a torture to him than the condemned man's iron collar, the convict's chains – and it went and carried off a strong, brave and honest fellow who had poor relatives waiting for him! Yes, the sea once took me, tossed me in its waves, and then spewed me up again, alive, onto the beach, as if I were unworthy of disappearing in its depths ...

174

The clouds break up, even whiter. Sun shines like a brilliant rainfall upon the sea, whose changing green softens, turns golden in places, and in other places grows opalescent, and near the shore, above the line of seething foam, is subtly shaded with every hue of pink and white. The reflections of the sky, infinitely fragmented by the waters, chopped up into a multitude of little slices of light, shimmer on the turbulent surface. The slender masting of a cutter, towed by men hauling on the bowline, glides slowly behind the mole, then the hull comes into view, the hoisted sails swell, and the boat gradually moves away, dancing on the main. A fisherman hurries to find limpets on the strand uncovered by the falling tide, and some cabin boys come running along, bare-legged, splashing in puddles, lifting seaweed-covered rocks in search of sea slugs and crabs. Soon the cutter is only a grey speck on the horizon, which grows blurred, shrouding itself in a pearly mist . . . It looks as if the sea is calming down.

And I've been here for two months! Two months! I've roamed along the paths, in the fields, on the moors. I'm familiar with every blade of grass, every stone, every one of the crucifixes standing at the crossroads. Like the tramps, I've slept in ditches, my limbs stiff with cold, and I've huddled among the rocks, on beds of dead leaves; I've walked along the beaches and cliffs, lashed by the spray, dazed by the wind; with bleeding hands and lacerated knees, I've climbed rockfaces inaccessible to humans and visited only by cormorants. I've spent dramatic nights at sea and seen sailors in terror of death crossing themselves. I've rolled enormous boulders, and collected wrack in dangerous currents with water up to my waist; I've grappled with trees, and hacked deep into the soil with a pick. People said I was crazy . . . My arms are aching with fatigue, my flesh is all bruised . . . Yet, all the same, not for one minute, not for one second has love released me; I'm even more in its possession. I feel it choking me, mashing my brain, crushing my chest, gnawing my heart, burning through my veins . . . I'm like the little creature the polecat pounces on; no matter how much I roll on the ground, struggling desperately to escape its fangs, the polecat hangs on to me, and does not let me go. Why did I leave? Could I not have skulked in some furnished room? Juliette would have visited me from time to time, no one would have known that I existed, and there, in that obscurity, what divine and abominable pleasures I would have tasted . . .

Lirat spoke to me of honour, of duty, and I believed him! Lirat said, 'Nature will console you . . .' And I believed him! Lirat lied. Nature is soulless. Completely intent on its work of eternal destruction, it inspires me only with thoughts of crime and death. Never has it ministered to my burning brow, to cool it, or my heaving chest, to calm it . . . And the infinite has only brought me closer to pain! I don't offer resistance any more and, defeated now, I surrender to suffering without trying to fend it off. Let the sun rise amid crimson dawns, let it set in purple glory, let the sea display its jewels, let everything glisten and sing and smell fragrant, I don't want to see anything, or hear anything . . . all I want is to see Juliette in the fleeting form of a cloud, hear Juliette in the wandering lament of the wind, and I want to kill myself embracing her image in things! I see her in the Bois, smiling, happy in her freedom; I see her showing off in stage-boxes at the theatre; I see her most of all at night, in her room. Men enter and leave, others come and go, all sated with love. By the glow of the night-lamp, obscene shadows dance and grimace around her bed; laughter, kisses, muted convulsions are smothered in her pillow, and with the whites of her eyes showing and her mouth quivering, she yields her body, never weary of pleasure, to every lust. With my head feeling feverishly hot, digging my fingernails into my throat, I cry, 'Juliette! Juliette!' as if Juliette could possibly hear me at that distance. 'Juliette! Juliette!' Alas, the only answer I get is the cry of the seagulls and the boom of the waves breaking on the rocks: 'Juliette! Juliette!'

And evening comes. Mists rise, all pink and light, shrouding the coast and the village, while the jetty, almost black, looks like the hull of a big ship with its masts taken down.

The bronze orb of the sun sinks towards the sea, casting a trail of choppy, blood-red light upon the vast expanse. On either side, the water darkens, and sparkles dance on the crests of the waves. It is at this melancholy time of day that I make my way home cross country, always meeting the same carts drawn by oxen in grey linen dust-coats, seeing the same figures of peasants bowed over the meagre soil in a bleak struggle with sandy moor and rock. And on the heights of St-Jean, where the windmills turn their crazy sails against the brightness of the sky, is the same wayside cross, Christ with His arms spread in agony.

I was staying on the far side of the village, at the house of Mère Le Gannec, a good-hearted old woman who took care of me as best she could. The house, which looked out over the harbour, was clean and well-kept, with shiny new furniture. The poor old woman went out of her way to please me, wracking her brains to think of something to remove the frown from my brow, to bring a smile to my lips. She was a real treasure. When I came down in the morning, I would find her, with the housework done, knitting socks or making nets, looking bright and alert, almost pretty in her flat Breton head-dress, short black shawl and green serge house-coat.

'Our Mintié,' she would cry, 'I'm going to fry some tasty scallops for your supper. If you prefer a good eel soup, I'll make a good eel soup . . .'

'As you wish, Mère Le Gannec.'

'But you always say the same thing . . . Ah, glory be to Jesus! Our Lirat wasn't like you . . . Mère Le Gannec, I want clams . . . Mère Le Gannec, I want periwinkles . . . And, to be sure, I'd give him clams and periwinkles! And then, he wasn't sad like you . . . No, to be sure, he wasn't . . .'

And she would tell me stories about Lirat, who had spent an entire autumn with her.

'My, what energetic and adventurous soul ! Even in the wind and rain, he'd go out 'to look at the view' . . . The weather didn't bother him . . . He'd come back soaked to the skin, but always cheerful, always singing! And you should have seen the way he ate! I tell you, he would have eaten the sea itself!'

Sometimes, to distract me, she would tell me about her misfortunes, simply, without complaint, repeating with sublime resignation, 'We must bend ourselves to the will of God ... It won't do us any good to spend the whole time weeping . . .'

And in that sing-song voice that Breton women have, she said, 'Le Gannec was the best fisherman in Le Ploc'h, and the most fearless sailor of all, along this coast. There was nobody whose boat was better equipped, nobody who knew as well as he did where the fish were. When a boat went out in rough weather, you could be sure it was the *Marie-Joseph*. Everyone respected him, not only because of his courage, but because he was irreproachable and dignified in his behaviour. He avoided any bar like the plague, couldn't abide drunkards, and it was an honour to be associated with him ... It should also be said that he was in charge of the lifeboat ... We had two strong, fearless boys, our Mintié, two strapping lads, one of eighteen, and the other twenty, that their father had brought up to be good sailors just like himself . . . Ah, you should have seen them, our Mintié, those two fine boys of mine! And we were doing well, so well that with our savings we been able to build this house and buy this furniture . . .. Anyhow, we were happy!

'One night two years ago, the boys and their father didn't come home! I didn't wonder at it ... He'd sometimes go a long way, as far as Croisic, Les Sables, L'Herbaudière ... To be sure, he'd be following the fish, you see? But the days went by and no sign of them! And then more days went past, and still no sign! Then every morning and every evening I went out on to the mole, and watched out for them ... I would question sailors, 'You haven't seen the *Marie-Joseph*, then?' 'No, ma'am.' 'How is that she hasn't come home?' 'That I don't know.' 'Could there have been some mishap?' 'To be sure, it's possible, ma'am.'

'And they would cross themselves as they said this ... Then I lit three candles to Our Lady of Safe Voyages! Finally, one day, they came back, all three of them, in a big cart, black, bloated, half eaten by crabs and starfish . . . Dead, what! All three of them, my husband and my two fine lads, dead, our Mintié . . . The keeper of Penmarc'h lighthouse had found them washed up on the rocks.'

I was not listening. I was thinking of Juliette: where is she? What is she doing? Those eternal questions!

Mère Le Gannec went on: 'I know nothing of your affairs, our Mintié, and I don't know what's making you unhappy! But you haven't lost your husband and your two sons all at once! And even if I don't shed any tears, our Minté, believe me, it doesn't mean I don't grieve for them.'

And if the wind was blowing, if the sea was booming in the distance, she would add in a grave voice, 'Blessed Virgin! Have pity on our poor children out at sea . . .'

I meanwhile would be thinking, 'Maybe she's dressing . . . Maybe she's still sleeping, after a tiring night!'

I would leave the house, walk through the village, and go and sit on a milestone on the road to Quimper, at the foot of a long rise, waiting for the postman to arrive. The road, which has been carved out of the rock, is bordered on one side by a high embankment crowned with fir trees and thin clumps of oak shoots; on the other side it looks down on to a small sound surrounding the flat, open moorland, in the midst of which glisten pools of water. Cone-shaped pillars of grey rock rise from the ground at intervals, and a few stone-pines open their blue parasols in the hazy sky. Crows fly past, incessantly, in endless black lines, hurrying towards who knows what carnivorous revels, and the wind carries the sad tickling of the small bells hung round the necks of scattered cows grazing on the sparsely growing grass on that sandy moor. As soon as I saw the two little white horses and the yellow-bodied carriage come rattling and jangling down the hillside, my heart would start pounding . . .

'There may be a letter from her in this van!' I would say to myself.

And this rickety old vehicle, squeaking on its springs, was more splendid to me than any coronation coach, and the driver with his collapsible hat and red face appeared to me like a liberator . . . How could Juliette have written to me, since she didn't know where I was? But I always hoped in miracles . . . I would then hurry back to the village, convincing myself, with a series of irrefutable arguments, that I would receive a long letter that day, in which Juliette would announce that she was coming to Le Ploc'h, and I read in anticipation her fond words, her passionate declarations, her expressions of repentance. I saw the still wet traces of her tears on the paper, for at moments such as this I imagined that Juliette spent her whole time weeping. Alas, nothing came but the occasional letter from Lirat, a wonderful paternal that bored me . . . With a heavy heart, feeling even more devastated by the plight of being abandoned, my mind entertaining countless possibilities, each one crazier than the next, I would return to my sand dune . . . From this short-lived state of hopefulness I would plunge back into acute anguish, and spend the day invoking Juliette, calling her name, addressing my search for her to the pale flowers of the sands, the froth on the waves, to all of unfeeling Nature that denied her to me, reflecting an incomplete image of her, eroded by everyone else's kisses!

'Juliette! Juliette!'

One day on the pier I met a young girl accompanied by an old man. She was tall and slender, and seemingly pretty under the thin white veil covering her face, the ends of which, tied behind her grey felt hat, fluttered in the wind. Her supple and gracious movements were reminiscent of Juliette. Truly, in the carriage of her head, in the delicate curve of her waist, in the sweep of her arms, in the airy sway of her dress, I recognised something of Juliette! I gazed at her with emotion, and two tears rolled down my cheek. She went right to the end of the pier. I sat on the parapet, charmed and pensive, observing the young girl's silhouette. As she walked away, I was moved to tenderness. Why had I not met her sooner, before the other woman? I might perhaps have loved her! A young girl who had never felt the foul breath of men on her, whose ears were chaste, her lips innocent of filthy kisses. How delightful it would be to love her, in the same way that angels love! The white veil fluttered over her, like a seagull's wings. And all of a sudden she disappeared behind the lighthouse. At the foot of the pier the movement of the sea was like that of a child's cradle rocked by a nurse singing lullabies, and the sky was cloudless; it extended over the still surface of the waves like a vast trailing veil of white muslin.

It was not long before the young girl returned, passing so close that her dress almost brushed against me. She was blonde; I would rather she had been dark-haired, like Juliette. She walked away, left the pier, took the road into the village, and soon all I could see of her was the white veil bidding me, 'Farewell! Farewell! Don't be sad any more, I shall return!'

Come evening, I asked Mère Le Gannec about her.

'That's Mademoiselle de Landudec,' she replied. 'A thoroughly good and very deserving child, our Mintié. The old man is her father. They live in that big château on the road to St-Jean ... You know, you've been there many times ...'

'How is it I've never seen them before!'

'Ah, Jesus! That's because the father's always ill, and the daughter stays and takes care of him, poor child! He's probably better today, and she's taking him out for a while.'

'Her mother's no longer alive?'

'No, she's been dead a long time now.'

'Are they wealthy?'

'Wealthy! Not particularly! Give to everybody, they do. If you only went to mass on Sunday, our Mintié, you'd see the young lady.'

That evening I lingered to chat with Mère Le Gannec.

I saw the good young lady again on the pier on several occasions, and on those days the thought of Juliette was less burdensome. I roamed around the château, which seemed to me as desolate as the Priory; there was grass growing in the courtyard, the lawns were ill kept, the park drives were rutted by the heavy carts of the neighbouring farm. The grey stone facade, flaked by the weather and mossed by the rain, was as dismal a sight as the big granite rocks on the moors. The following Sunday I went to mass, and I saw Mademoiselle de Landudec praying among the peasants and seamen . . . Kneeling at her stool, her slim body inclined as in early depictions of the Virgin, her head bowed over a book, she prayed fervently. Who knows? She may have realised that I was unhappy and perhaps included me in her prayers? And as the priest tremulously recited mass, and the nave of the church filled with the clatter of clogs on the paving-stones and the mutterings of pious lips, and the incense from censers rose to the vaulted ceiling, along with the shrill voices of the choirboys, and the young girl prayed, as Juliette might have, had she been given to praying, I dreamed . . . I was in a park, and the young girl came towards me, all bathed in moonlight. She took me by the hand and we walked across the lawns and beneath the soughing trees.

'Jean,' she said, 'you're suffering and I've come to you . . . I've asked God if I might love you, and God granted me permission . . . I love you!'

'You're too beautiful, too pure and holy to love me! You mustn't love me!'

'I love you! Take my arm. Rest your head on my shoulder, and let us stay for ever so.'

'No, no! Can the swallow love the owl? Can the dove that flies in the sky love the toad that lurks in the mire of stagnant waters?'

'You're not an owl, and you're not a toad, since you're my choice . . . The love for which I have God's permission washes away all sins and is a comfort against all sorrows. Come with me and I shall make you pure again. Come with me and I shall give you happiness.'

'No, no! My heart is rotten, and my lips have drunk the poison that kills souls, the poison that is the damnation of virgins like you . . . Don't come so near me; I shall sully you. Don't look at me like that ; my eyes will defile you, and you will be just like Juliette!'

The mass ended and the vision faded. A great noise

erupted in the church made by the scrapping of chairs and tramping feet, and the choirboys put out the candles on the altar. Still kneeling, the young girl continued to pray. All I could see of her face was a profile shrouded in the soft shadow of her white veil. She stood up, having crossed herself. I had to move my chair to let her through. She passed by me. And I felt genuine satisfaction, as if I had just accomplished a great duty by refusing the love that the young girl had offered me in my dream.

She occupied my thoughts for a week. I resumed my punishing walks across the moors, and along the beaches. I wanted to be cured. As I walked, exhilarated by the wind, in the grip of that peculiar sense of elation a lashing coastal rain gives you, I imagined romantic conversations with Mademoiselle de Landudec, nocturnal adventures that took place in enchanting lunar landscapes. Like characters in an opera, we vied with each other in sublime thoughts, heroic sacrifices, extraordinary devotion. To passionate rhythms and moving ritornelles, we extended the limits of human self-denial. The sobbing strains of the orchestra mingled with the heartbreak in our voices.

'I love you! I love you!'

'No, no, you mustn't love me!'

She, in a very long white gown, wild-eyed, with outstretched arms . . . I, a dark man of destiny, with swelling calves in purple silk tights, and tousled hair . . .

'I love you! I love you!'

'No, no, you mustn't love me!'

Never had violins sounded so plaintive, and the oboes moaned while the double basses and dulcimers boomed like stormy winds and rolling thunder.

O, what a histrionic display of sorrow!

The curious thing is that Mademoiselle de Landudec and Juliette were now indistinguishable. I could no longer separate them, I confused them in the same extravagant and melodramatic dream. They were both too pure for me.

'No, no! Leave me, I'm a leper!'

183

They insisted on kissing my wounds, spoke of dying, cried, 'I love you! I love you!'

And defeated, overcome, redeemed by love, I fell at their feet. The old dying father extending his hands over us and blessed all three of us!

This madness did not last long, and I soon found myself on the dunes face to face again with Juliette.

Juliette! Juliette!

There were no more violins or oboes; there was just a bellow of anguish and protest, the cry of a wild beast in captivity demanding its prey.

'Juliette! Juliette!'

One evening I came home feeling more on edge than ever, with dark delusions haunting my mind, my arms and hands itching, as it were, with a passion to kill, to choke . . . I wanted to feel living beings writhe under the pressure of my fingers, draw their last gasp and die. An anxious Mère Le Gannec was on the doorstep, knitting her perpetual pair of socks.

'How late you are today, our Mintié! I've got a fine lobster ready for you!'

'Stop bothering me, you senile old woman!' I shouted. 'I don't want your lobster, I don't want anything, do you hear?'

And spluttering words of rage, I brutishly made her get out of the way to let me past . . . The poor good-hearted woman threw up her arms in amazement and moaned, ' Oh, my goodness! Oh, sweet Jesus!'

I went to my room and shut the door.

At first I rolled on the bed, broke two chairs, banged my forehead on the walls, and then I started writing Juliette an impassioned, crazy letter, full of terrible threats and humble pleas; a letter in which I wrote, in incoherent phrases, of killing her, and forgiving her; I begged her to come before I died, describing in melodramatic terms a rock from which I would throw myself into the sea . . . I compared her to the worst of whores, and two lines later to the Blessed Virgin. I started the letter more than twenty times over, allowing myself to be carried away, weeping, switching from frenzies of rage to raptures of tenderness. At some point I heard a noise outside the door, like the scratching of a mouse. I went and opened it. Mère Le Gannec stood there, trembling, completely pale, staring at me with a look of alarm in her kindly eyes.

'What are you doing here?' I shouted. 'Why are you spying on me? Go away!'

'Our Mintié,' the saintly woman moaned, 'our Mintié, don't be angry! I can tell you're unhappy, and I came to see if there was anything I could do for you.'

'Well, yes, I am unhappy. So there! Is it any business of yours? Here, take this letter to the post office and leave me alone.'

For four days I did not go out. Mère Le Gannec came to my room to make my bed and serve my meals. She was humble and fearful, fussing over me more than ever, and sighing, 'Oh dear! Oh dear!'

She was so kind to me, and I realised I had behaved badly towards her, and I wanted to for my churlishness. My feelings were stirred by her white head-dress, her black shawl, her sad face of a bereaved mother. But a kind of stupid pride froze the words on my lips. She tottered around me, resigned, with an air of infinite, maternal compassion, and from time to time she kept saying, 'Oh dear! Oh dear!'

The day was drawing in. While Mère Le Gannec swept the room, having cleared away my meal, I gazed out from the open window, with my elbows resting on the sill. The sun had disappeared below the line of the horizon, of its radiant glory leaving in the sky only an reddish glow, and the sea, dense and heavy, without a single reflection, turned a dismal grey. Night was approaching, slow and silent, and the air was so still that you could hear the rhythmic beat of oars upon the water in the port and the distant whine of the yard-ropes on the mast-heads. I saw the lighthouse light up, its red beacon turning in space like some crazy star. And I felt extremely unhappy!

Juliette had not replied. Juliette would not come! My

letter had probably scared her, and she had remembered those angry scenes when I had come close to strangling her brutally. She had been frightened, and she would not come! And after all, did she not have parties and dinners and the races to go to? Were there not impatient queues of men at her door claiming her, who had paid for the promised night in advance? And besides, why should she come? There was no casino on this desolate strand. There was no one on this god-forsaken Atlantic coast to whom she could have sold her body. She had already taken everything I had – my money, my intellect, my honour, my future, the lot! What else could I give her? Nothing. So why would she come? I should have told her I had ten thousand francs left, and she would have come running. And what would have been the good of that? Ah, better that she didn't come! My anger had calmed and was replaced by a horrible feeling of self-disgust.

How was it possible that in such a short time a man who was not a wicked person, whose aspirations in the past were not without pride or nobility, should sink so low into such a thick mire that no human power was capable of rescuing him. What pained me then was not so much the folly and baseness of my actions, my crimes, as the unhappiness I had caused around me. Old Marie! Old Felix! Those poor souls! Where were they now? What were they doing? Had they even enough to eat? By getting rid of them – and they so old, so good, so trusting, more helpless and forlorn than a dog without its master – had I not made them beg for their bread? I pictured them, bent over walking sticks, horribly thin and exhausted, coughing, sleeping at night under whatever shelter they chanced to find. And what about saintly Mère Le Gannec, who mothered me and cosseted me with the comfortingly affectionate ways that humble folk have? Instead of kneeling before her and thanking her, had I not maltreated her, almost hit her? Oh, better she didn't come! Better she didn't!

Mère Le Gannec lit my lamp and I was about to close the window when I heard harness-bells on the road, then the rattle of a carriage. I automatically looked out. A carriage was indeed coming up the hill, which was very steep here, a kind of omnibus that looked high and was loaded with trunks.

A sailor was walking by. The coachman called out to him, 'Hey! Mère Le Gannec's house, please?'

'It's there, in front of you,' replied the sailor, pointing to the house, and he continued on his way.

I had turned completely white . . . and by the light of the carriage-lamp I saw a little gloved hand reaching out for the door-handle.

'Juliette! Juliette!' I cried wildly. 'Mère Le Gannec, it's Juliette. Quick, quick. It's Juliette!'

Racing headlong down the stairs, I rushed out into the road.

'Juliette! My darling Juliette!'

Arms enfolded me, lips were planted on my cheek, a voice sighed, 'Jean! My little Jean!'

And I fainted in Juliette's embrace.

I soon regained consciousness and found myself lying on the bed with Juliette bent over me, in tears, kissing me and calling my name.

'Ah, poor darling! What a fright you gave me! How pale you are still! Do you feel better now? Speak to me, Jean!'

I gazed at her without saying anything. It was as if my whole body, lying inert and chilled, suddenly struck down by great suffering or happiness − I could not tell which − were channelling back into my gaze the life that was ebbing away from me, draining from my limbs, veins, heart, and brain . . . I gazed at her! She was still beautiful, a little paler than she used to be, but otherwise just the same, with her gentle shining eyes, her amorous mouth, her delightfully child-like clear voice.

I searched her face and gestures, her bearing, and her words for distressing traces of her secret life, some blemish, some disfigurement, something new and more faded about her! No, in truth, she was a little paler, but that was all. And I burst into tears.

'I never thought to see you again, my little Juliette!'

She drank in my tears, weeping herself, and held me in her arms.

'Jean! My dearest Jean!'

Mère Le Gannec came and knocked on the bedroom door. She did not address Juliette, and pretended not to see her.

'What's to be done with the trunks, our Mintié?' she asked.

'They're to be brought upstairs, Mère Le Gannec!'

'All those trunks can't be brought up here,' the old woman replied sternly.

'Do have you many, then, darling?'

'No, not many! There are six of them . . . These people are stupid!'

'Well, Mère Le Gannec,' I said, 'keep them downstairs for tonight. We'll deal with them tomorrow . . .'

I was up by then, and Juliette was rummaging round the room, exclaiming at every moment, 'Well, isn't this charming? It's very quaint, my darling . . . And you have a bed, a real bed . . . And I thought that people in Brittany slept in wardrobes. Ah! What's this? Don't move, Jean, don't move!'

She had taken a big sea-shell from the mantelpiece and was pressing it to her ear.

'Strange!' she said disappointedly. 'Strange! Your shells don't go shhh . . ... Why not, I wonder?'

Then she suddenly threw herself in my arms and covered me with kisses.

'Ah, your beard! You're letting your beard grow, naughty! And how long your hair is! And how thin you are! Have I changed at all? Am I as beautiful as I used to be?

She clasped her hands round my neck and rested her head on my shoulder.

'Tell me what you do here, how you spend your days, what you think about . . . Tell your little darling . . . And don't lie . . . Tell her absolutely everything!'

So I told her about my frantic walks, my fits of despondency on the dunes, my sobs, about how I kept seeing her, and calling for her like a madman, out in the wind and rain . . .

'Poor little love!' she sighed. 'And I bet you don't even have a mackintosh?'

'And you? And you, my darling Juliette? Did you even think of me?'

'Ah! When I found you'd left the house, I thought I was going to die. Celestine told me that a man came to take you away. Yet I waited . . . He'll come back, he'll come back . . . And you didn't come back . . . And I went rushing to see Lirat the very next day. Ah, if you knew how I was received there . . . the way that he treated me! And I asked everybody, 'Do you know where Jean is?' And no one could tell me. Oh! you wicked thing, going off like that, without a word! So you didn't love me any more? Well, you see, I yearned for oblivion . . . I was so upset!'

Her voice took on a ring of curtness.

'As for Lirat! Don't worry, my darling, I'll get my revenge! And you'll see! It'll be such fun! What a heel your friend Lirat is! But you'll see, you'll see!'

One thing tormented me: how many days, weeks, was Juliette going to spend with me? She had brought six trunks, so she intended to stay in Le Ploc'h at least a month, perhaps longer . . . My great joy at having her with me was mingled with acute anxiety . . . I had no money, and I knew Juliette too well not to that she would not be content to live like me, and I foresaw expenses that I was in no position to meet. Now what was I to do? Not daring to question her directly, I said, 'We can think about that, my darling, in three months' time, when we return to Paris . . .'

'In three months' time? But my poor dear, I'm only staying a week . . . It's such a nuisance!'

'Stay, my little Juliette, I beg you, stay for ever . . . for longer . . . a fortnight!'

'It's impossible, you see . . . Oh, don't be sad, my darling. Don't cry . . . because if you cry, I shan't tell you my news, my good news.'

She became even more affectionate, snuggled up closer to

me, and went on, 'Now listen, my darling. I've only one thought in my mind: to live with you. We'll leave Paris and move to a little house so hidden away, you see, that no one will know whether we're still alive or not . . . But we need an income of twenty thousand francs . . .'

'Where do expect me to find that now?' I cried in despair.

'Just listen!' said Juliette. 'We need an income of twenty thousand francs. Oh, I've made all the calculations! Well, in six months, that's what we'll have.'

Juliette looked at me with an air of mystery. She said again, 'That's what we'll have.'

'Please, darling, don't talk like that. You don't know how much it upsets me . . .'

Juliette raised her voice and the crease on her brow grew harsh.

'So you'd prefer me always to belong to other men?'

'Ah, stop it, Juliette, stop it! Never, ever, say such things!'

'You're a strange fellow! Now, be good and kiss me!'

As she dressed the next day, very much at a loss without her maid, with her trunks lying open around her and her clothes strewn everywhere, she made various plans for the day. She wanted to walk along the pier, climb up to the top of the lighthouse, do some fishing, go out on the dunes and sit at the spot where I wept so bitterly. She was thrilled to see so many Breton woman prettily attired in local costume, just like on stage, and to drink milk straight from the farm!

'Are there any boats here?

'Yes, indeed.'

'A great many?'

'Yes, indeed.'

'Oh, good! I do so love boats!'

Then she told me the news from Paris. Gabrielle was not with Robert any more . . . Malterre was getting married . . . Jesselin was away on a trip . . . There had been some duels! And there were stories about everybody! This rank whiff of Paris made me feel miserable again and brought back painful memories.

Seeing my dejection, she broke off, kissed me, and affected to be very upset.

'I suppose you think I like living like this!' she complained. 'That all I think about is having fun, being flirtatious. If you only knew . . . You see, there are some things I can't tell you, but if you knew what a torture it is to me! So you're unhappy? What about me? Let me tell you, I often feel so sickened that, but for the hope of living with my beloved Jean, I would kill myself!'

Then, dreamy and cajoling, she returned to her pastoral idylls, her leafy lanes, the tranquillity of a quiet, reclusive life with flowers, animals and love . . . Ah, meekly devoted love, eternal love, love that would burn brightly, like a hot sun, until death.

We went out after lunch, which Mère Le Gannec served us without once opening her lips. No sooner had we gone out than, with the freshening wind flattening her hair, Juliette wanted to go back.

'Ah, the wind, darling! The wind, you know, I can't stand it . . . It messes my hair and puts me out of sorts!'

She fretted with boredom all day long, and our kisses were insufficient to fill the time on our hands. She spread a towel over her dress, just as she used to in my study, and on the towel she laid out her tiny brushes and files, and gravely began to polish her nails. I felt terribly oppressed, and was haunted by the image of the old man at the window.

The next day Juliette announced that she had to leave that very evening.

'Ah, what a pity, my darling! I'd forgotten . . . Quick, quick, order a cab . . . Oh, what a pity!'

I did not try to detain her. Gloomy and motionless, sunk in a chair with my head in my hands, I witnessed her preparations for departure without uttering a word, letting no entreaty pass my lips. Juliette went to and fro, folding her dresses, packing her vanity case, closing her trunks, and I heard and saw and understood nothing.

Some men came in, their heavy footsteps making the floorboards creak. I realised they were carrying out the trunks. Juliette sat on my knees.

'My poor darling,' she wept, 'you're upset that I should go away like this . . . I have to . . . Be good . . . Anyway, I'll be back soon . . . for a long time . . . Don't be like this . . . I'll be back, I promise . . . I'll bring Spy with me . . . I'll bring a horse, too, to go out riding – you'd like that, wouldn't you? You'll see how well your little Juliette can ride . . . Now, kiss me, Jean! Why don't you kiss me? Come on now, Jean! Goodbye! I adore you! Goodbye!'

It was dark when Mère Le Gannec came into my room. She lit the lamp and quietly came up to me.

'Our Mintié! Our Mintié!'

I looked up at her, and she was so sad, so full of generous pity, that I threw myself in her arms.

'Ah, Mère Le Gannec! Mère Le Gannec!' I sobbed. 'And that's what's destroying my life . . . That!'

And Mère Le Gannec murmured tenderly, 'Our Mintié, why don't you pray to the good Lord? It would comfort you.'

I have not been able to sleep for a week. My skull is helmeted in red-hot metal. My blood is boiling – it feels as though my distended arteries are bursting and great flames are licking my back. Whatever humanity survived in me, whatever traces of shame, remorse, respect, and vague hope were left of my moral anguish under the heap of dross, whatever kept me affiliated, by however weak a link, with the category of thinking beings has all been swept away by a mad brutish frenzy. I have no concept any more of good, truth, justice, of the strict laws of nature. I am no longer mindful of the sexual aversion of one kingdom for another, which keeps their separate worlds in constant harmony. Everything is shifting, joining in sterile, mass fornication, and in my sensual delirium I dream of nothing but outrageous couplings. Not only is the image of Juliette prostituting herself no longer a torture to me, on the contrary it excites me. It is an image I seek out and hold on to, and try to fix indelibly in my mind: paired with objects, animals, and monstrous mythological beasts; driven, by me, to criminal debauchery, having been lashed into a frenzy by iron-hard rods. Nor is Juliette the only woman whose image tempts and obsesses me . . . Gabrielle, the Rabineau woman, Mère Le Gannec, Mademoiselle de Landudec are always passing before my eyes in unspeakable postures. Neither virtue, nor goodness, nor misfortune, nor the sanctity of age are any bar to me, and as a setting for these dreadful excesses my preference falls on sacred and holy places – church altars, cemetery tombs . . . My suffering is not of the soul any more, only of the flesh . . . My soul died with Juliette's last kiss, and now all I am is a casting mould of impure and impressionable flesh that demons are bent on pouring molten metal into. Ah! I had not anticipated this punishment!

The other day I met a fisherwoman collecting clams along the seashore. She was dark, dirty, and smelly, like a pile of

rotting seaweed. I approached her, gesticulating wildly . . .
And suddenly I fled, for I felt a diabolical temptation to fall
on that body and copulate with it, there on the shingle, amid
the pools of water. I walk and walk, cross country, my nose
to the wind, like a hunting dog, scenting females. One night
I ventured down the winding lanes of the village, my throat
burning and my mind crazed with dreadful visions, and I
knocked at the door of a sailors' whore. And I went inside
that hovel. But as soon as I felt that alien flesh against my
own, I let out a cry of rage, and tried to leave. She held me
back.

'Let me go!' I shouted.

'Why don't you stay?'

'Let me go!'

'Stay . . . I'll love you . . . I've often followed you along
the shore . . . Often, I've hung about the house where you
live . . . I wanted you . . . Stay!'

'Just let me go! Can't you see that you disgust me!'

And since she clung round my neck, I hit her.

She groaned. 'Ah, my God, he's mad!'

Mad! Yes, I am mad! I looked at myself in the mirror and I
was frightened by what I saw. My eyes in their sunken sock-
ets look big and scared, the bones show through under my
yellow skin, my mouth is pale, trembling and hangs open
like the mouths of lewd old men. My gestures are wild and
my fingers, constantly twitched with nervous spasms, crack,
predatorily groping the air.

Mad! Yes, I am mad! When Mère Le Gannec moves
around, when I hear her slippers shuffling across the floor,
when her dress brushes against me, wicked thoughts occur to
me, obsess me, goad me, and I cry out, 'Go away, Mère Le
Gannec, go away!'

Mad! Yes, I am mad! I have often spent hours at night
outside her bedroom door, with my hand on the latch, on
the point of rushing into the darkness. I don't know what
held me back . . . Fear, probably. For I would say to myself,
'She'll struggle, and call for help, and I shall be forced to kill
her!'

Once, alerted by the noise, she got up. Seeing me bare-legged, in my nightshirt, she was dumbfounded for a moment.

'Oh, it's you, our Mintié! What are you doing here? Are you ill?'

I stammered out some incoherent excuse, and went back upstairs.

Ah, I should be chased, and hunted, and pursued, like a rabid dog, with pitchforks and stakes and scythes! Will there not be men coming in soon who will fall upon me, and gag me, and carry me off into the eternal darkness of the lunatic asylum.

I must get away! I must see Juliette! I must vent on her this accursed rage!

When it gets light, I shall go downstairs and say to Mère Le Gannec, 'Mère Le Gannec, I must get away! Give me some money . . . I'll pay you back later . . . Give me some money . . . I must get away!'

Juliette had found me a room on the second floor of a small hostel in Faubourg St-Honoré, very close to rue Balzac. The furniture was rickety, opening the drawers made them squeal, and an acrid smell of musty wood and old dust clung to the curtains and bed covers. But by placing a few knick-knacks here and there, she had managed to lend a touch of intimacy to this cold anonymous room so many strangers had passed through without leaving any trace behind. Juliette had also insisted on tidying my things away in the wardrobe, which she stuffed with sachets of orris.

'Look, darling . . . Here are your socks . . . there are your night-shirts . . . I've put your ties in the drawer . . . your handkerchiefs are here . . . See what a tidy person your little sweetheart is . . . And every day I'll bring you a flower that smells nice . . . Now, don't be sad . . . Just remember I love you, nobody else but you, and that I'll come often . . . Ah, I've forgotten your underpants! I'll send Celestine over with them, together with my photograph in a red plush frame . . . Don't get bored, poor dear. And you know, if I'm not back by twelve thirty this evening, don't wait up for me . . . Go to bed . . . Sleep well . . . Promise?'

And casting a final glance around the room, she was gone.

Juliette did indeed call by every day, on her way to the Bois and before dinner on the way home again. Restlessly anxious to get away, she would only stay a few minutes – just long enough to kiss me and open the wardrobe to see if things were as tidy as she had left them.

'Well, I'm off now . . . Don't be sad . . . I can see you've been crying again . . . That's not very considerate of you. Why upset me?'

'Juliette, can I see you this evening? Oh, please come this evening.'

'This evening?'

She reflected for a moment.

'Yes, my dear. But don't wait up too late for me . . . Go to bed . . . Sleep well . . . Above all, don't cry. You drive me to despair! Really, there's no knowing how to deal with you!'

And I lived there, sprawled on the divan, almost never going out, counting the minutes that ticked away very, very slowly, in endless waiting.

The frenzied excitement of my senses had given way to great despondency. I spent entire afternoons without stirring, my flesh aching, my limbs feeling leaden, and my mind sluggish, as if I were suffering a hangover. My life was like a heavy slumber invaded by distressing dreams, broken by sudden awakenings even more distressing than the dreams, and in the collapse of my will and the obliteration of my intellect, I felt even more keenly the horror of my moral decline. In addition, Juliette's way of life kept me in perpetual anguish . . . As in the past, on the dune at Le Ploc'h, I was incapable of dispelling her squalid image that grew, became more distinct, and took on more terrible forms.

To lose someone you love, someone responsible for all the joy you have ever known, whose memory is associated with nothing but happy memories, is a heartrending grief . . . But where there is grief, there is also consolation, and the pain is to some extent soothed by its own sweetness. I was losing Juliette every day, every hour, every minute, and all I could attach to these successive deaths, these impenitent deaths, were excruciating memories and defilement. Scour though I might the turbulent mire of our two hearts, I could not find a single flower, not even the tiniest little flower, whose perfume it would have been so good to smell. And yet I could conceive of nothing without Juliette. All my thoughts began with Juliette, and ended with Juliette. And the more she eluded me, the more bent I became on the absurd idea of winning her back. I had no hope that, caught up as she was in this life of unsavoury pleasures, she would ever stop. Yet despite myself, despite her, I planned for a better future. I said to myself, 'It's impossible that she won't one day be overcome with disgust, that one day sorrow won't awaken in her some remorse, some pity. And she will come back to

197

me. Then we'll move into working class accommodation, and I shall drive myself like a slave . . . I'll go into journalism, I'll publish novels, I'll beg for jobs as a copyist . . . Alas, I strove to believe in all this, to ameliorate the abject state into which I had fallen.

From the sale of Lirat's two sketches, a few pieces of jewellery I had, and my books, I had acquired the sum of four thousand francs, which I treasured away for that illusory possibility. Once when Juliette was more pensive and loving than usual, I dared to tell her of this wonderful plan. She clapped her hands.

'Yes! Yes! Oh, that would be such fun! A teeny, weeny, little apartment! I could keep house. I'd have some pretty bonnets and a pretty apron. But with you, it's impossible. What a pity! It's impossible!'

'Now, why is it impossible?'

'Because you won't work and we'll starve to death. It's just the way you are. Did you ever work at Le Ploc'h? Will you work now? You've never worked!'

'How can I? Don't you realise that I can never for one moment get you out of mind? It's everything I don't know about your life, the atrocious agony of what I sense, what I guess about you, that gnaws away at me, consumes me, sucks my bones dry! When you're not here, I don't know where you are, and yet I'm always with you, wherever you are. Ah, if that was what you wanted! To know that you were with me, quiet and loving, far from that which corrupts and torments . . . But I'd have the strength of a god! Money! Money! But I'd earn it for you by the bucketful, by the cartload. Ah, Juliette, if that was what you wanted!'

She gazed at me, excited by the loud jingle of gold that my words set ringing in her ears.

'Well, earn some quickly, my dear . . . Yes, lots, piles of it. And don't think about the nasty things that upset you . . . Men are so peculiar! They just won't understand!'

Affectionately she sat on my lap.

'You know I adore you, my dearest! You know how I

hate all the others, and that they have no claim on me at all . . . none, do you hear . . . You know how unhappy I am!'

Her eyes were filled with tears as she tried to snuggle up to me, making herself as small as possible, and she repeated, 'Yes, very, very unhappy!' It was horrible, and pitiful.

'Ah, he thinks I like what I do!' she cried, sobbing. 'That's what he thinks! But if I didn't have my Jean to comfort and cuddle and hearten me, I couldn't go on . . . no, I couldn't . . . I'd rather die.'

Suddenly changing tack, and in a voice in which I thought I could detect a wail of regret, she said, 'Anyway, to do that . . . to get the little apartment . . . we'd need money, and you haven't any!'

'But I have, darling . . . I have,' I protested triumphantly. 'I do have some money! We've enough to live on for two or three months, until I make a fortune!'

'You have some money? Let me see . . .'

I laid out the four one-thousand franc notes in front of her. Juliette grabbed them, fiercely, one by one, counted them, examined them. Her eyes gleamed in amazement and delight.

'Four thousand francs, darling! You mean, you have four thousand francs! But you're rich! Well . . .'

She fastened her arms lovingly round my neck.

'Well,' she continued, 'seeing as you're very rich . . . I have a fancy for a little travelling case that I've seen on rue de la Paix! You'll buy it for me, won't you, darling?'

'What does it cost?'

'Two thousand francs, darling.'

'Fine. Take two thousand francs . . . You can buy it yourself.'

Juliette kissed me on the forehead, took two thousand-franc notes, which she hastily stuffed into the pocket of her coat, and with her eyes fixed on the two remaining ones, which she no doubt regretted not having asked for, she said, 'Really? Are you sure? Oh, how sweet of you! That means that if you go back to Le Ploc'h, I'll come and see you with my brand new case.'

When she had gone, I gave way to a violent fit of rage against her, against myself most of all, and when my anger had calmed I was astonished all of a sudden to feel no more pain. Yes, truly, I breathed more freely, I extended my arms with strength in my movements, I had a new spring in my calves. In short, it was as though someone had just relieved me of the crushing weight I had been carrying on my shoulders for such a long time. I took a very keen pleasure in loosening my limbs, in working my joints, in stretching my nerves, as one leaping out of bed in the morning. And was I not actually waking up from a sleep as heavy as death? Was I not emerging from a kind of catalepsy, in which my whole torpid body had experienced the ghastly nightmares of non-existence? I was like someone who rediscovers the light after being buried, like a starving person given a piece of bread, a prisoner condemned to death who receives a pardon . . . I went to the window and looked out into the street. Golden sunlight cut across the houses on the pavement opposite, people went hurrying about their business with happy faces, carriages drove cheerily past each other in the roadway. This bustle and activity, this hum of life exhilarated and thrilled me, and touched my feelings, and I inwardly exclaimed, 'I don't love her any more! I don't love her any more!'

In the space of a second I had a very clear vision of a new life of work and happiness. I was eager to cleanse myself of this filth, to resume my interrupted dreams. I wanted not only to redeem my honour, but to win glory, a glory so great, so undisputed and universal that Juliette would die of resentment at having lost a man like me. I already saw myself in the distant future, in bronze and marble, raised on columns and on symbolic pedestals, filling the centuries to come with my immortalised image. And what delighted me most was the thought that Juliette would not have an ounce of glory, that I would mercilessly deny her any share of mine.

I went downstairs and for the first time in more than two years it gave me delicious pleasure to be out in the street. I walked quickly, with an easy stride and an air of victory, taking an interest in the most ordinary sights, which appeared as new to me. And I wondered in amazement how I could possibly have been unhappy for so long, and how it was that my eyes had not opened sooner to the truth. Ah, despicable Juliette! How she must have laughed at my submission, my blindness, my pity, my inconceivable folly! No doubt she told her casual lovers of my idiotic anguish, and they spurred each other on in their love-making by mocking me. But I would have my revenge, and it would be a terrible revenge! Juliette would soon be grovelling at my feet, begging; she would implore my forgiveness.

'No, no, wretched woman, never! When I wept, did you comfort me? Did you spare me any suffering at all? Did you even for one moment agree to resign yourself to my poverty, to share my life? You're unworthy of sharing my glory . . . No, go away!'

And to show my adamant scorn I would throw millions in her face.

'Here! You want millions? Well, then, take them!'

Juliette will twist her arms in despair. She will cry, 'Jean, have pity on me! Oh, it's not money I want! What I want is to live secluded and inconspicuous in your shadow, happy if just one ray of the light that surrounds you were to fall on your poor Juliette! For pity's sake!'

'Did you ever show me any pity when I asked it of you? No! Women like you are to be pelted with gold! Look, here's more. And more!'

I strode along, talking to myself out loud, gesticulating as if I were throwing millions into the air.

'Here, take that, you wretch!'

Yet my impassiveness at the thought of Juliette was not so grim that the glimpse of any woman did not disconcert me, and that I did not cast an impatient glance into the carriages constantly passing in the street. When I reached the boulevard, my confidence collapsed and I was overcome with all of my former anxiety. Again I felt an intolerable weight on my shoulders, and the devouring beast, momentarily driven away, fell on me even more ferociously, digging its claws even deeper into my flesh. For this to happen, I had only to see the theatres and restaurants, those accursed places of such mystery in Juliette's life. The theatres said to me, 'Your beloved Juliette was here last night! While you agonised, calling for her, waiting for her, she was adorned with flowers, happily flaunting herself in a box, without a thought for you.' The restaurants said to me, 'Last night your beloved Juliette was here. Her eyes drunken with debauchery, she lay sprawled on our broken-backed divans, and men reeking of wine and cigars had their way with her . . .'

And all the proud, dashing young men I encountered said to me, 'We know your beloved Juliette . . . Does she bring you any of the money she costs us?'

Every house, every object, every sign of life – all shouted at me with frightful jeers, 'Juliette! Juliette!' The sight of roses in the florists' was a torture to me, and I felt enraged just from looking at the shops with their displays of tantalising wares. It seemed to me that Paris spent all its energy, exerted all its charm solely to seduce Juliette from me, and I wished to see it disappear in a catastrophe, and I regretted the retributive days of the Commune, when petrol was poured on the streets and death was sent out abroad.

I made my way home . . .

'Has no one called?' I asked the concierge.

'No one, Monsieur Mintié.'

'There's been no letter either?'

'No, Monsieur Mintié.'

'You're sure no one went up to my room while I was out?'

'The key has not moved from its place, Monsieur Mintié.'

I scribbled the following words on my visiting card: 'I want to see you.'

'Take this to rue Balzac . . .'

I waited in the street, impatient and nervous. It was not long before the concierge reappeared.

'The maid told me that madame had not yet returned.'

It was seven o'clock . . . I went up to my room and lay down on the sofa.

'She won't come . . . Where is she? What is she doing?'

I had not lit any candles. The street lamps outside the

window cast a dim light into the room and projected a yellow brightness on to the ceiling, where the shadow of the curtains loomed and trembled.

And the hours went by, slow and endless, so slow and endless that time seemed suddenly to have stopped.

'She won't come!'

From the street came the continuous sound of passing vehicles: the heavy rumble of omnibuses, the rattle of way-worn hackney carriages, the swish of the lighter, swifter broughams. Whenever one of them clipped the pavement or slowed down, I rushed over to the window, which I had left half open, and I leaned out into the street. None of them stopped.

'She won't come!'

And even as I said, 'She won't come!', I was still hoping that Juliette would arrive in a few minutes. How many times had I rolled on the sofa, crying, 'She won't come!', and Juliette had arrived! Always, just when I most despaired, I would hear a carriage stop, then footsteps on the stairs, then a creak in the hall, and Juliette would appear, smiling, all dressed up, filling the room with a heady scent and a rustle of silk.

'Come on, get your hat, darling.'

Irritated by her smile, her clothes, her perfume, exasperated at being kept waiting, I often treated her harshly.

'Where have you been? What dens of iniquity have you been trawling through? Go on, tell me!'

'Oh, if it's a row you want, thank you very much, I'm going. Good night! After I took so much trouble to free myself to come and see you!'

Then clenching my fists, with all my muscles tensed, I yelled, 'Very well, go away! Go to the devil! And don't ever come back!'

As soon as the door closed behind Juliette, I ran after her.

'Juliette! Juliette!'

She would be going down the stairs.

'Juliette, come back, please! Juliette, wait, I'm coming with you!'

On she went without a backward glance. I caught up with her.

Once I was close to her, to that dress, to those feathers, flowers, and jewels, I would be overcome with rage again.

'Now, come back up to my room, or I'll smash your head on the stairs!'

And back in the room, I would fall at her feet.

'Yes, my little Juliette, I'm in the wrong, I'm in the wrong. But I'm in such agony! Have a little pity for me! If you knew what a hell my life is! If you could with your hands move aside the walls of my chest and see what is in my heart! Juliette! I can't take any more of this, I can't live like this any longer! I tell you, a beast would take pity on me. Yes, a poor beast would have pity!'

I squeezed her hands, I kissed her dress.

'Juliette! I haven't killed you . . . I would have been within my rights to, I swear to you. I haven't killed you! You ought to credit me with that . . . It's an act of heroism, for you just don't know what terrible vengeful things a man who is suffering, and alone the whole time, can conceive of . . . I haven't killed you! I was hoping, I'm still hoping! Come back to me. I'll forget everything, I'll wipe the slate clean, of my sorrows and our shame. For me, you'll be the purest, most radiant of virgins. We'll go far away from here, wherever you like . . . I'll marry you! That's not what you want? You think I'm only saying it in order to have you more to myself? Swear that you'll turn over a new leaf and I'll kill myself right now, in front of you! Listen, I've sacrificed everything for you! I'm not talking about my wealth, but what was once the pride of my life, my honour as a gentleman, my dreams as an artist, I gave up all that for you, without any regret. Surely you can now sacrifice something for me? What is that I want of you? Nothing . . . the joy of being good and honest . . . Self-sacrifice, my dear Juliette, dedication – this a great and noble thing! Ah, if you only knew the pleasure of making a sacrifice! Listen, Malterre is a rich man . . . he's a decent fellow, better than the others . . . he loved you . . . I'll go to him and say, 'Only you can save Juliette, and rescue her from the world that she's living in ... Go back to her ... you've nothing to fear from me ... I'll go away ...' Is that what you want?'

Juliette would look at me in total amazement, an anxious smile hovering on her lips. She murmured, 'Now, you're talking nonsense, darling ... Don't cry. Let's go.'

And on the way I continued to wail, 'A beast would have pity! Yes, a beast ...'

There were other times when she sent Celestine to fetch me, and I found her lying in bed looking fresh and sad and languid. I could tell that someone had been there only a short while ago, and had just left. I could tell from the softer look in Juliette's eyes, from everything around me – the remade bed, the over-meticulously tidied wash-stand, all the traces that had been removed and which I saw reappear in their horrible and painful reality. I lingered in the dressing room, rummaging in drawers, scrutinising everything, sinking to a disgraceful examination of familiar objects ... Now and again, Juliette called out from the bedroom.

'Come here, darling! What are you doing?'

Oh, if only I could recreate his image, catch a smell of him! I sniffed the air with flaring nostrils, thinking I could detect strong male odours; and I had the impression that the shadow of powerful torsos loomed on the hangings, that I could see athletic shoulders, heroic arms, nervous and hairy thighs with bulging muscles.

'Are you coming?' said Juliette.

On those nights Juliette talked only of the soul, of heaven, and birds. She had a need of transcendency, of airy fantasies ... She sighed, all curled up in my arms, as innocent as a child.

'Oh, isn't this bliss! Jean, say some lovely, tender things to me, like in poetry. I do so love your voice ... it has the sound of an harmonium ... talk to me for a while ... You're so good, you comfort me so well! I'd like to live like this, always in your arms, not moving, and listening to you! And do you know what else I'd like? Ah, I dream of it! To have a little girl by you, all pink and blonde, like a cherub! I would nurse her ... and you would sing her very pretty songs to send her to sleep! Jean, when I'm dead, you'll find a little pink notebook with a gilt binding in my jewellery box. It's for you ... you're to take it ... I've written down my thoughts in it, and you'll see how much I loved you! You'll see! Oh, what a bore – I have to get up tomorrow, and go out. Hold me, speak to me, tell me how you love my soul ... my soul!'

And she fell asleep. And she was so pure and white that the bed curtains looked as if they were two wings attached to her.

The night wore on. The neighbourhood was falling quiet again. Every now and then, some belated carriage would pass by on its way home, and two policemen plodded along the pavement, their pace never changing! The door of the building had opened and closed several times. I had heard creaks, the rustle of a dress, voices whispering in the corridor – but it wasn't Juliette! And the silent building had long seemed to be asleep. I got up from the sofa, lit a candle and looked at the clock: it was three in the morning.

She won't come! It's too late now ... she won't come!

I went and stood and the window. The street was deserted and the total blackness of the sky above weighed down on the houses like a leaden lid. Heavy carriages came along, over in the direction of Boulevard Haussmann, shattering the night with their resonant rumbling. A rat ran across from one pavement to the other, and disappeared down a drain. I saw a poor dog go past, head down, with its tail between its legs, stopping in doorways, sniffing in the gutter, then slinking off ...

I was feverish, my head was burning, my hands were sweaty, and I felt a tightness in my chest.

'She won't come! Where is she? Has she gone home? Or else, in what corner of this great unchaste darkness is she wallowing?'

What infuriated me most was that she had not contacted me ... She had received my card ... she knew that she would not be coming ... and she had sent no word! I had wept and implored her, I had clung to her knees . . . and not a word! What tears, what blood did a man have to shed to soften that heart of stone? How could she go running after pleasure, her ears still filled with the sound of my sobs, her mouth still wet with my entreaties? The loosest of women, the most damned to perdition sometimes take a break from their debauched and rapacious lives. There are moments when they let the sun warm their hearts that have grown cold, when with their eyes turned heavenward they beseech the love that forgives and redeems! Juliette, never! Something more unfeeling than destiny, more ruthless than death drove her, swept her along, eternally tossed her, without let or respite, from sordid amour to bloody amour, from that which is dishonourable to that which kills! The more time passed, the more debauchery branded her flesh. Her passion, once strong and healthy, was now mingled with appalling sexual curiosity and that chronic insatiability, that unslakeable addiction to love-making that result from indulgence in unnatural and sterile pleasures. Apart from those nights when exhaustion took on the unexpected guise of absolute purity, she seemed to bear the imprint of innumerable refined and various depravities, innumerable perverse fantasies of surfeited lovers and old men. She would let slip words and cries that suddenly opened up vistas of diabolical degeneracy in her life. And though she had conveyed to me the consuming ardour of her depravities, though I took a kind of fiendish, criminal delight in them, often I could not look at Juliette without shuddering with terror! Leaving her embrace, in shame and disgust, I felt the condemned man's need to gaze on quiet, restful scenes, and I envied, how I envied, with such bitter regret, those superior beings who have made virtue and chastity the unbending rules of their lives! I dreamed of monasteries devoted to prayer, of hospices dedicated to serving others . . . I was overwhelmed with a mad desire to enter brothels in order to convert the wretched women that for want of a good word languished in vice. I vowed to follow at night the prostitutes lurking in the shadows at crossroads, and to comfort them, to talk to them of virtue, with such passion, so affectingly, that they would be moved, and weep, and say to me, 'Yes, yes, save us . . .'

I liked to spend hours on end in the Parc Monceau, watching the children play, seeing blissful happiness in the eyes of their young mothers. It touched me to imagine those lives, so removed from my own; to relive, in their company, those sacred delights for ever lost to me . . . On Sundays I would wander through the stations, in the midst of joyous crowds, among the office clerks and working men out with their families in search of a little fresh air for their choked-up lungs, gathering a little strength to endure the strains of the week. And I would dog the footsteps of one working man whose appearance interested me, wishing I had his resigned stoop, his twisted hands blackened by hard work, his doltish look, his trustful gaze like that of a faithful mastiff. Alas! I wished for everything I did not have, and to be everything that I was not. Those walks, which made even more painful the realisation of how low I had sunk, none the less did me good, and I always came home afterwards making brave resolutions. But in the evening I would see Juliette again, and Juliette meant forgetting honour and duty . . .

A faint glow lit the sky above the houses, announcing the arrival of dawn. And I saw two bright dots in the darkness at the end of the road, two carriage lamps swinging and swaying and advancing like two wandering street-lights. And for a moment I was hopeful . . . The carriage came closer, dancing over the cobblestones, the lights getting bigger and the noise quickening. I thought I the familiar rattle of Juliette's brougham. But no! All of a sudden the carriage turned left and disappeared. And in an hour it would be light!

'She won't come! This time, it really is too late, she won't come!'

I closed the window and lay down again on the sofa, my temples throbbing, and with an aching in every limb. In vain I tried to sleep . . . I could only weep and sob and cry, 'Oh, Juliette! Juliette!'

My chest was burning, and I felt as if there were seething lava inside my head . . . My thoughts wandered, giving way to hallucinations. Weasels pursued each other along the walls of my room, leaping about and disporting themselves in obscene playfulness . . . And I hoped that I would be struck down with a fever that would confine me to bed, that would carry me off . . . Oh, to be ill! Yes, to be ill for a long time, for ever! With Juliette sitting at my bedside, watching over me, raising my head to give me medicine, and seeing the doctor out, talking to him in an undertone; the doctor's expression would be grave.

'No, no, madame, all hope is not lost! Don't worry!'

'Oh, doctor, save him, save my poor Jean!'

'You alone can save him – it's because of you that he's dying!'

'Ah, what can I do? Tell me, doctor, tell me!'

'You must love him, be kind to him . . .'

And Juliette would throw herself in the doctor's arms.

'No! It's you I love . . . come!'

And she would lead him away, hanging from his lips . . . and in the bedroom, they would grapple with each other, leap up to the ceiling, and fall back on my bed, entwined.

'Die, Jean, please die . . . Oh, why are you so long in dying?'

I had dozed off . . . When I awoke, it was broad daylight . . . The omnibuses were running again, the street-hawkers were yelling out their morning cries, and I could hear the scratching of a broom against my door, in the corridor, where people were walking by.

I went out and made my way to rue Balzac. I really meant only to set eyes on Juliette's house, to look up at her windows, and perhaps run into Celestine, or Mère Sochard . . . I paced back and forth more than a dozen times on the pavement opposite. The dining room windows were open, and I could see the chandelier brass gleaming in the shadows. A carpet hung over the balcony. The bedroom windows were closed.

What lay behind those sealed shutters, that expanse of blank impenetrable wall?

A disorderly, ransacked bed, the heavy smell of love-making, and two sprawled sleeping bodies – Juliette's . . . and the other? Everyman's body. The body Juliette had happened to pick up, from under a night-club table, out on the street! They slept, sated with lust. The concierge emerged to shake her rugs out on the pavement. I moved away, for since leaving the apartment I had avoided the old woman's ironic gaze, and I blushed every time my eyes met her two puffy and malicious little eyes that seemed to deride my misfortunes. When she had finished, I went back and stood for a long time fretting about that wall behind which some dreadful thing was happening, and which retained the cruel impassiveness of a sphinx crouched against the sky. Suddenly, as though struck by a thunderbolt, I was seized by an insane fury galvanised me from head to toe, and without considering what I was going to do, without even knowing, I entered the house, climbed the stairs, and rang at Juliette's door . . . It was Mère Sochard who answered.

'Tell madame,' I shouted at her, 'tell madame that I want to see her, right away, to speak her . . . And tell her that if she doesn't come, I shall go and get her, and drag her out of bed, do hear? Tell her!'

All pale and trembling, Mère Sochard stammered out, 'But my poor Monsieur Mintié, madame is not here . . . Madame's not back yet.'

'I'm warning you, you old witch, don't try and fool me, do hear? And do as I say . . . Otherwise I'll kill and destroy everything – Juliette, you, the furniture, the house . . .'

The old servant raised her arms to the ceiling in a gesture of terror.

'But it's God's truth!' she exclaimed. 'As I said, madame's not come home, Monsieur Mintié! Go and look in her bedroom! You'll see! It's just as I said!'

With two strides, I burst into the bedroom . . . it was empty . . . the bed had not been slept in. Mère Sochard followed on my heels, saying, 'Really, Monsieur Mintié! Really! At this hour! Seeing as you're not together any more!'

I went into the dressing room. Everything was in order

there, just as it used to be when we came home late at night
... with Juliette's things laid out on the divan, and the kettle,
filled with water, standing on the gas stove ...

'So where is she?' I asked.

'Ah, monsieur!' replied Mère Sochard. 'Who knows
where madame goes? Some valet or other came this morning
who talked to Celestine, and then Celestine went off with a
change of clothes for madame ... That's all I know!'

And prowling round the dressing room, I came upon the
card I had sent the day before.

'Has madame read this?'

'Well, probably not ...'

'And you don't know where she is?'

'Lord, no! To be sure, madame doesn't discuss her private
affairs with me!'

I went back into the bedroom and sat on the chaise-
longue.

'Very well, Mère Sochard, I shall wait for her ... And let
me tell you, this is going to be good for a laugh. Ha! Ha!
You see, Mère Sochard, in the end there comes a point ...
I've been patient ... I've been ... Well, not any more!'

I shook my fists in the air.

'It'll be good for a laugh, Mère Sochard! And you'll be
able to boast that you were a witness to an extraordinary
spectacle that you'll never, ever, forget! And at night you'll
dream of it, by God, in terror!'

'Ah, Monsieur Mintié ... Monsieur Mintié!' pleaded the
old woman. 'For the love of the good Lord, calm down ...
Go away! You're bound to make trouble! What will you do,
Monsieur Mintié, what will you do?'

At that moment Spy emerged from his basket and came
towards me, arching his back and mincing along on his frail,
spidery legs. And I stared at Spy long and hard ... And it
occurred to me that Spy was the only living thing Juliette
loved, and that to kill Spy would be the greatest sorrow
anyone could inflict on Juliette. The dog stretched out its
legs towards me and tried to climb up on my lap. It seemed
to say, 'Even if you're suffering terribly, it's not my fault ...

211

It would be despicable to take revenge on me, seeing as I'm so small, and weak, and trusting . . . And anyway, she's not all that fond of me, you know! I amuse her, as a plaything, I provide her with a moment's entertainment, that's all . . . If you kill me this evening, she'll get another little dog just like me, that she'll call Spy, the same as me, on which she'll lavish her affection, as she does on me, and nothing will have changed!'

I did not listen to Spy, just as I never listened to any of the voices that spoke to me when I felt a criminal urge to commit some wicked deed. Brutally, savagely, I grabbed the little dog by its hind legs.

'What will I do, Mere Sochard?' I shouted. 'Watch this!' And I whirled Spy in the air and smashed his head with all my strength against the corner of the mantelpiece. Blood spurted over the mirror and curtains, bits of brain splattered the candlesticks, a detached eye fell on to the carpet.

'What will I do, Mère Sochard?' I repeated, tossing the dog into the middle of the bed, on which a creeping red stain appeared. 'What will I do? Ha! Ha! You see this blood, this eye, this brain, this corpse, this bed! Ha! Ha! Well, Mère Sochard, I'll do the same to Juliette. To Juliette, do you hear, you old soak!'

'Oh, bless my soul!' stammered Mère Sochard in terror. 'Oh, Lord, bless my soul, I . . .'

She did not finish her sentence. With her mouth wide open in a horrible grimace, she stared, round-eyed, at the dog's black body on the bed, and the blood soaking into the sheets, its crimson stain growing bigger and bigger . . .

CHAPTER TWELVE

When I came to my senses, killing Spy seemed to me a monstrous deed and horrified me, as though I had murdered a child. Of all the despicable things I had done, I considered it the most cowardly and the most odious. Killing Juliette – that would certainly have been a crime, but perhaps it was possible to find in a revolt against my suffering if not an excuse at least an explanation for this crime . . . But killing Spy – a dog, a poor inoffensive beast! Why? Oh, yes, why? Only a brute would have done it, someone with a savage and irresistible instinct for murder! During the war I had killed a good and strong young man. I had killed him at the very moment when, with his eyes charmed, and his heart stirred, he was overcome with emotion at the sight of the rising sun. I had killed him in a cowardly manner, hidden behind a tree, under cover of shadow. He was a Prussian? So what! He was also a man, a man like me, a better man than I . . . On his life depended the lives of those who were weak, of women and children. Somewhere anguished creatures were praying for him, waiting for him. In that powerful young body of his, in those strong loins, there were perhaps the seeds of higher beings that humanity was hoping for. And with one stupid fearful gunshot I had destroyed all that! And now I'd killed a dog! And I'd killed it when it was coming to me, and trying with its little paws to climb on to my lap! So I really was a murderer! That little body haunted me. I kept seeing that hideously smashed head, the blood spurting over the pale fabrics in the room, and the bed, indelibly stained with blood!

What also tormented me, was the thought that Juliette would never forgive me for the loss of Spy. She must surely detest me . . . I wrote repentant letters, assuring her that I would agree to whatever she wanted, that I would not complain, or criticise her behaviour any more; letters so demeaning, so abject, so grovellingly submissive, that any other woman but Juliette would have sickened to read them . . . I had a messenger take them round and anxiously awaited his return on the corner of rue Balzac.

'There's no reply.'

'You didn't go the wrong address? You did delivered it to the first floor?'

'Yes, monsieur . . . The maid actually said to me, 'There's no reply!'

I went and called on her in person. The door opened only the length of a security chain, which Juliette, out of fear of me, had had fitted the very evening of that horrible scene . . . and in the opening I saw Celestine's mocking and cynical face . . .

'Madame is not at home!'

'Celestine, my dear Celestine, let me in!'

'Madame is not at home!'

'Celestine! My dear sweet Celestine . . . let me wait for her . . . And I'll give you a lot of money!'

'Madame is not at home!'

'Celestine, I beg you! Go and tell madame that I'm here . . . that I'm quite calm . . . that I'm very ill . . . that I'm dying! And a hundred francs is yours, Celestine . . . a hundred francs!'

Celestine gave me a furtive look, happy above all to see a man lower himself before her, to plead cringingly with her.

'One brief moment, Celestine . . . just to see her, and then I'll leave.'

'No, no, monsieur! I'll get into trouble!'

A bell rang. I heard its rings grow more urgent.

'You see, monsieur, I'm being summoned!'

'All right! Celestine, tell her that if she hasn't come to see me by six o'clock, if she hasn't written, tell her that I'll kill myself! Six o'clock, Celestine . . . don't forget . . . tell her that I'll kill myself!'

'Very well, monsieur!'

And the door closed on me, with a rattling of the chain.

I had the idea of calling on Gabrielle Bernier, to tell her of my woes, ask her advice, and use her as a mediator. Gabrielle was just finishing lunching with a friend, a thin little woman with a sharp, rodent-like face, who, when she talked, seemed to be munching hazel nuts the whole time. Dressed in a dirty, creased, white silk wrap, with her hair pinned up on top of her head with a crookedly inserted comb, Gabrielle was smoking a cigarette and sipping a glass of chartreuse, with her elbows on the table.

'Ah, Jean! So you're back?'

She led me into her very untidy dressing room. At my first mention of Juliette, Gabrielle cried, 'You mean you don't know? But we fell out a month ago ... when she stole a consul from me, my dear, an American consul who was giving me five thousand a month! Yes, that baggage stole him from me! Well, now, what about you? You've shaken her off, I hope?'

'Oh, me!' I said, 'I'm pretty miserable! So it's a consul who's her lover now!'

Relighting her cigarette that had gone out, Gabrielle shrugged her shoulders.

'Her lover! What woman like that is capable of keeping a lover? Not even the good Lord himself could stand it, my dear! I'm telling you, there's no man that stays long with her ... it's here today and gone tomorrow, thank you very much! It's all very well fleecing them, but it has to be done subtly, eh! And you're still in love with her, poor boy!'

'Yes, more than ever! I've done everything to cure myself of this shameful passion that's turned me into the basest of men, that's killing me ... and I've failed! And of course her behaviour's disgraceful!'

'True enough,' exclaimed Gabrielle, blowing a stream of smoke into the air. 'You know, I'm no prude. I enjoy myself as much as the next person ... But, word of honour, I swear on my mother's life, I'd blush to do what she does!'

With her head tilted back, she released two smoke rings that rose to the ceiling, quivering ... And to emphasise what she had said, she repeated, 'Ah, true enough!'

Although I was suffering horribly, although Gabrielle's

every word stabbed through my heart like a knife, I went up to her, adopting a coaxing manner.

'Come now, my dear Gabrielle,' I begged her, 'tell me.'

'Tell you! Listen, you know the Borgsheim brothers – those two beastly Germans! Well, Juliette was going with both of them at the same time! I tell you, I saw it myself. At the same time, my dear! One evening she'd say to one, 'Well, it's you I love.' And she'd take him home. The next day, she'd say to the other, 'No, actually it's you.' And she'd take him home. If only you'd seen that! Two wretched Prussians who always quibbled over the bill! There's lots more I could tell you . . . but I won't let on, because I can see I'm upsetting you . . .'

'No,' I cried, 'no, Gabrielle, tell me . . . because, you see, eventually the disgust . . . the disgust . . .'

I was choking . . . I burst into sobs.

Gabrielle consoled me. 'There, there! Poor Jean, now, don't cry. Is she worth getting into such a state over? A real gent like you! Would you believe it? I was always saying to her, 'You don't understand him, my dear, you've never understood him . . . a man like that – he's a gem!' Ah, I know plenty of women who'd be jolly pleased to have a young fellow like you . . . and they'd treat you well, you can be sure of that!'

She sat on my lap and tried to dry my tears. Her voice had become caressing, and her eyes gleamed.

'Now, be brave . . . and leave her! Get yourself another woman . . . someone good and kind, who would understand you . . . There, now!'

And suddenly she folded me in her arms and pressed her mouth to mine. A naked breast that had spilled out of her lace wrap was crushed against my chest. This kiss, this flaunted flesh filled me with horror. I violently broke free of Gabrielle's embrace and pushed her away.

Recovering her balance and repairing her state of undress, she said, 'Yes, I understand . . . I've been through the same thing myself . . . But you know, my dear . . . When you feel like it . . . come and see me . . .'

I left. My legs were weak, and it was as though I had iron bands round my head. My face was bathed in a cold sweat that trickled down my back. I had to lean against the walls of the houses in order to be able to walk. Since I was almost fainting, I went into a bar and avidly knocked back a few mouthfuls of rum. I cannot say I was in great agony . . . It was stupor that made my limbs feel heavy, a state of physical and moral examination, in which the thought of Juliette occasionally infiltrated a sharp shooting pain. And in my distraught frame of mind, Juliette became impersonalised: she was no longer a woman with her own individual existence, she was prostitution itself, sprawled vastly all over the world, the eternally sullied, unchaste idol that panting crowds rushed after, in hideous darkness lit by monstrous torches fashioned in the image of the androgynous demon Baphomet.

I sat there for a long time, with my elbows on the table, staring at a wall-panel with painted flowers on it, set between two mirrors. I eventually left the bar and just kept walking, without knowing where I was going. I walked and walked . . . After covering considerable ground, I found myself, with no intention of going there, on avenue du Bois-de-Bologne, near the Arc de Triomphe. Daylight was beginning to fade. Above the purpling slopes of St-Cloud, the sky turned a glorious crimson, and little pink clouds drifted in extremely pale-blue space. The forest gathered itself in more darkly. A fine dust reddened by the reflections of the sinking sun rose from the avenue that was black with carriages. And those compact vehicles kept passing, following closely on each other in endless lines, taking predatory whores to wreak nocturnal havoc. There they were, stretched out on their cushions, indolent and disdainful, masked with stupidity, their flesh flaccid and steeped in filth, all so alike that I recognised Juliette in every one of them. The procession appeared to me more dire than ever. Looking at those horses and that finery, that blood-red sun making the sides of the carriages glisten like armour, that blazing array of fabrics, of red, yellow, and blue, all those plumes quivering in the breeze, I had the impression I was seeing enemy regiments, conquering regiments crazed with pillage, moving in on a defeated Paris. And truly I was outraged not to hear cannons roaring, not to hear death-spraying machine guns sweeping the avenue. A workman on his way home had stopped on the edge of the pavement. Round-shouldered, with his tools on his back, he watched the spectacle. Not only was there no hatred in his eyes, but a kind of ecstasy was detectable in them.

I was overcome with anger. I felt like going up to him, grabbing him by the collar and shouting at him, 'What are you doing here, you fool? Why are looking at those women like that? Those women are an insult to your torn overalls, your tired and aching arms, the whole of your poor body crushed by its daily tribulations. When the revolution comes, you think that by killing soldiers and priests, and those who are poor and suffering, like yourself, you'll be revenged on the society that oppresses? And it's never occurred to you to erect scaffolds for these wicked creatures, for these savage beasts that rob you of your bread, your sunshine ... Can't you see? The society that grinds you down, that strives to make ever more heavy the chains that shackle you to eternal poverty, protects and enriches them. It transforms your drops of blood into gold to cover the slack breasts of these wretches. It's so that they can live in palaces that you wear yourself out, that you die of hunger, or get your skull cracked on the barricades. Can't you see? Poor devil, when you go out on the streets demanding bread, you get beaten up by the police! Look how the same police keep the way clear for their coachmen and horses! Can't you see? Yet what a good harvest! What fine vintage blood! And what a bumper crop of wheat will grow, tall and nourishing, in the earth where they rot!'

All of a sudden I saw Juliette. I caught a momentary glimpse of her profile. She was radiant and smiling, in a pink hat. She looked happy, nodding slightly in response to those who greeted her. Juliette did not see me. She drove past.

218

'She's going to call on me. She's remembered. She going to call on me.'

I did not doubt it . . . An empty cab came by. I climbed in. Juliette had already disappeared.

'I only hope I get there when she does . . . For she going to my place! Hurry, coachman, hurry now!'

No sign of a carriage at the entrance to the building . . . Juliette had already left! I rushed in to the concierge's lodge.

'Someone just asked for me? A lady? Madame Juliette Roux?'

'No, Monsieur Mintié.'

'Then there's a letter for me?'

'Nothing, Monsieur Mintié.'

'She'll be here soon,' I thought. And I waited, feverishly pacing the sidewalk, repeating out loud, to reassure myself, 'She'll be here soon.'

I waited. No one came. I waited longer. Not a soul. Time passed . . . And still no one came.

'The wretch! And she was smiling! And her face was cheerful! And she knew that I was to kill myself at six o'clock!'

I ran over to rue Balzac. Celestine assured me that madame had just gone out.

'Listen to me, Celestine . . . you're a fine person . . . I like you . . . You know where she is? Go and find her, and tell her that I want to see her.'

'But I don't know where madame is.'

'Yes, you do, Celestine, you do . . . I beg you . . . Go on! It's too much to bear!'

'On my word of honour, monsieur, I don't know.'

I insisted. 'Perhaps she's with her lover? Or at a restaurant? Oh, do tell me!'

'But I don't know!'

I was growing impatient. 'Celestine, I'm being polite to you . . . Don't provoke me, or else . . .'

Celestine folded her arms, nodded her head, and said with a churlish drawl, 'Or else what? You're beginning to get on my nerves, you no hoper! And if you don't make yourself

scarce, I'm going to end up calling the police, do you hear?'
And pushing me roughly towards the door, she added,
'Would you believe it! Worse than dogs, they are, these
devils!'

I had enough sense not to start arguing with Celestine,
and I went down the stairs, covered in shame.

It was midnight when I returned to rue Balzac. I had been
hanging round restaurants, looking for Juliette, peering
through windows and gaps in the curtains. I had been into
several theatres. At the Hippodrome, where she was a regular
on the days for season-ticket holders, I had walked round,
checking the boxes ... That large space, those blinding
lights, especially that orchestra, playing a sad and mournful
piece of music – all contrived to calm my nerves, and I wept!
I was drawn to groups of men, thinking they would talk
about Juliette, and I would learn something. And of all those
dandies in evening dress, I said, 'That might be her lover!'

What was I doing here? It seemed it was my destiny to be
for ever running round, spending my whole time on the
street, outside some unsavoury places, waiting for Juliette to
arrive! Exhausted with tiredness, and with my head buzzing,
unable to find Juliette anywhere, I ended up in the street
again, waiting! What for? To be honest, I did not know. I
was waiting for everything, and nothing. I was there to immo-
late myself, yet again, or to commit a crime ... I hoped that
Juliette would return home alone. Then I would go up to
her and make her feel sorry for me. I was also afraid of seeing
her with a man. Then I might kill her ... I wasn't planning
anything. I'd come, that's all! I hid in the corner of the
doorway of the house next to hers, the better to catch her
unawares.

From there, I could see everything without being seen, if
it suited me not to reveal myself. I had not long to wait. A
cab coming from Faubourg St-Honoré turned into rue
Balzac, veered over to my side of the road, and grazing the
pavement, stopped outside Juliette's house! I was gasping for
breath ... My whole body was trembling as a shudder ran
through it. Juliette climbed out first. I recognised her. She

ran across the pavement, and I heard her pull the bell. Then a man climbed out, and I thought I recognised the man as well. He approached the lamp, fumbled in his purse, clumsily extracted some coins, which he examined in the light, with his elbow raised. And his angular, foolish shadow was cast on the ground! I wanted to rush forward. A heaviness kept me rooted to the spot. I wanted to cry out. The sound died in my throat. At the same time a chill rose from my heart to my brain. I had the feeling that my life was failing me . . . I made a superhuman effort and staggered towards the man. The door had opened and Juliette had disappeared, saying, 'Well, are you coming?'

The man was still fumbling in his purse.

It was Lirat! I could not have been more surprised if the buildings, or the sky, had fallen on my head. Lirat coming home with Juliette! It wasn't possible! I was mad . . . I went closer.

'Lirat!' I cried. 'Lirat!'

He had finished paying, and was staring at me, terrified! Standing motionless with his feet apart, he stared at me, gaping, without saying a word.

'Lirat! Is it you? It's not possible . . . It isn't you, is it? You look like Lirat, but you aren't!'

Lirat remained silent.

'Come, now, Lirat! You wouldn't do this . . . or else I'd say that you sent me to Ploc'h to steal Juliette from me! You, here, with her! But that's insane! Lirat, remember what you told me about her . . . remember the fine things with which you nurtured my spirit . . .. the fine things you instilled in my heart! That wretched girl! It's all right for me, I'm a lost cause . . . But you! You're generous, you're a great artist! Is it to get even with me? A man like you doesn't do such a thing . . . He doesn't sully himself! If I haven't been to see you, Lirat, it's because I didn't dare, so as not to incur your anger. Come on, speak to me, Lirat! Answer me!'

Lirat remained silent. Juliette called to him from the corridor.

'Well, are you coming?'

I grabbed hold of Lirat's hands.

'Listen, Lirat . . . she's making a fool of you . . . Don't you? One day she said to me, 'I'll be revenged against Lirat, for his contemptuous behaviour, for his harsh high-handedness . . . and it'll be comic!' She's take her revenge . . . you're going up to her place, aren't you? And tomorrow, tonight, before long, she will disgracefully throw you out! Yes, that's what she wants, I swear to you! Ah, I understand! She pursued you! However foolish, and appallingly stupid, and far removed from you she might be, she infatuated you . . . She has the touch of evil, and you were pure! She's poured poison into your veins. But you're strong! After what's passed between us, you can't do this! Either you're a wicked man, or you're a dirty pig! You, whom I admire! A dirty pig? Come now!'

Lirat suddenly broke free of my grasp and pushed me aside with his two clenched fists.

'All right then!' he cried. 'I'm a dirty pig! Leave me alone . . .'

There was a hollow sound that rang out in the night like a clap of thunder. It was the door closing behind Lirat. The houses, the sky, the lights in the street spun round and round . . . And I could not see any more. I stretched my arms out in front of me and fell on to the pavement.

Then I saw, in the midst of peaceful countryside, a very white road with an extremely weary man walking along it. The man feasted his eyes on the splendid crops ripening in the sun, the big meadows with contented herds grazing on them, their noses buried in the grass. Apple-trees offered him their branches laden with crimson fruit, and springs purled in mossy secrecy. He sat at the roadside where the bank was bedecked with small fragrant flowers, and listened in delight to the divine music of things. From all round came the sound of voices, rising from the earth, descending from the sky, very sweet voices that murmured, 'Come to us, you who have suffered, you who have sinned. We are the comforters who restore to the lives of the unfortunate restfulness and peace of mind . . . Come to us, you who want to live!'

And the man, with his arms lifted to heaven, implored them, 'Yes, I want to live! What must I do not to suffer any more? What must I do not to sin again?'

The trees swayed, the wheat ruffled its stalks, a rustling emerged from every blade of grass, the tiny flowerheads of the little flowers danced on the end of their stems, and from all those there rose a single voice. 'Love us!' said the voice.

The man continued on his way. Birds whirled around him . . .

The next day I bought myself some workman's overalls.

'So, monsieur's leaving . . .' said the janitor at my lodgings, to whom I gave my old clothes.

'Yes, my friend.'

'And where is monsieur going?'

'I don't know . . .'

In the street I saw men as crazy apparitions, as very old and rickety skeletons, whose bones, being badly tied together with bits of string, fell on the pavement with strange clattering sounds. I saw skulls wobbling on top of broken spinal columns, dangling over disjointed clavicles; I saw arms come away from their frames, and frames lose their rows of ribs. And all these wrecks of human bodies, stripped to the bone by death, still driven by murderous frenzy, still spurred on by pleasure, fell on each other and fought over stinking carcasses . . .